W9-CMG-333

SHALLOW GRAVES

SHALLOW GRAVES

A NOVEL

REV. GOAT CARSON

HUNGRY PROPHETS PRESS
RHINEBECK · NEW YORK

SHALLOW GRAVES © 2007 by Rev. Goat Carson. All rights reserved. No part of this book may be used or reproduced in any manner without written permission from the author except in critical articles and reviews. Contact the publisher for information.

Printed in The United States of America.
First Edition

Library of Congress Control Number: 2007925028

ISBN 978-0-9789427-2-4

This is a work of fiction. Names, characters, places and incidents either are the product of the author's imagination or are used fictitiously, and any resemblance to any actual persons, living or dead, events or locales is entirely coincidental.

Bulk purchase discounts for educational or promotional purposes are available.

First Edition

10 9 8 7 6 5 4 3 2 1

Hungry Prophets Press
A division of Epigraph Publishing Service
27 Lamoree Road
Rhinebeck, N.Y. 12572
www.epigraphps.com

CHAPTER ONE

BABYSITTER TO THE STARS

I WAS TRYING TO SLEEP it off when the smog crept through my window and started choking me. It was hot, much too hot to sleep. I tried to remember why I'd been drinking till 3 a.m. and whose funeral I had to attend today. I didn't like waking up, ever; it made me tired, real tired. I was tired of losing sleep, tired of losing friends, tired of waking up. I rolled over and pulled the pillow on top of my head. It was Paps; Paps had died and he'd be much happier if I didn't go to the funeral. I was almost back to sleep when the phone rang. It was B.B., offering me condolences and a ride to the funeral. I had almost married B.B. once, but as I got to know her better, well let's just say there are a couple of shades of jaded that just aren't on my palette. I accepted both the ride and the condolences because I was still asleep. At least that's what I told myself as I struggled out of bed and limped to the shower. I also had a hangover, which always made me feel a little more vulnerable, a little more sentimental. I hoped it had not figured into my decision making process when I accepted the ride from B.B. The thought of her breast implant scars rustled through my mind as I relieved myself of the past night's indulgence. It was a big help in de-sentimentalizing the situation.

Once inside the shower the steam clouds blurred my vision and I drifted back in time to the moment B.B. and I had parted. I was standing on the lawn of her Beverly Hills home. I had just told her it was over between us. She was holding my right arm and swinging her handbag at my head while her six-year-old son was taking pot shots at my nuts. Hell of a way to end a relationship, I thought. But the mind plays tricks on a man when he showers for his best friend's funeral. I began to go through a whole series of what-ifs in my head. I had been close to marrying the wealthy daughter of a wealthy, established show business family. What if I had tied the knot and was waking up in a Beverly Hills mansion instead of a storefront loft on Pico? Would it make a big difference? Not to Paps, that's for sure, he was dead, but how different would my life be?

Steaks interrupted my thoughts. She was the girl who lived in the loft next to mine. We shared the shower, a long concrete room that joined our lofts. I had forgotten to lock the door that lead to her side. Steaks gave out with a rude wolf whistle to announce her presence. I gave her the ol' bump and grind as an answer.

"What's up Steaks? You want the shower or what's in it?"

Steaks was big, for a girl, with lots of curly brown hair and a face not unlike a wishnik doll. She was cute. She wore a pink terrycloth robe and a silly wishnik smile as she leaned against her door.

"Naw I just came to watch," she laughed, "Christ you're skinny!"

"You get that way when you don't eat regular."

Steaks softened at my reply. "You want some breakfast?"

"Can't," I said, turning off the water, "gotta' go to Paps' funeral."

I wrapped a towel around myself.

"The shower's yours Steaks...you can leave the door to my side open if you want."

"Naw it's sexier when you peek in the windows."

She walked me to the door and I heard her lock it behind me.

I liked Steaks; we were almost friends now after three months of living next to each other. We both had the same landlord, Pauley, an art director I'd worked for at M.G.M. during the good times. We were both artists, so we were both broke all the time, but Steaks was a New Yorker and naturally felt superior, I was from Texas and naturally couldn't take that attitude. After annoying one another for two months we finally called a truce and had been talking with reasonable courtesy for almost a month now. She only dated hotshots and I rarely "dated."

I straightened my tie and slipped into my bronze sharkskin suit. Paps and I had come out to L.A. a few years back with the idea that we could shake the grief of a close friend's death by taking Hollywood by storm in his honor. The storm had rained on us and we spent a lot of time scuffling. Paps had noticed early on that people in Hollywood had kids but no time to take care of them. So he'd become babysitter to the stars, making good money, living in mansions and taking care of the children of the busy rich.

His death was a real shock, one of those tragic accidents that have become part of today's big action movies. His latest babysitting client was a producer who offered him a chance to pick up some extra money as an extra in a battle scene. Paps was to sit behind a desk, the camera at his back when the bad guys blasted open the door in front of him. Somebody put a little too much powder in the charge and the door splintered with such force that Paps was blown out of his chair, a thin sliver of wood sticking right through his heart.

I looked at the clock; B.B. would be here in a few minutes. B.B. was the archetypal Hollywood woman. Born into the system, she had rebelled in the sixties and gone to live in an Ashram somewhere. It was there that she had her only son. They had a theory at this Ashram that little boys were just like big boys. When a baby cried it was because either he was hungry, or in pain, or had shit himself, or he wanted a blowjob. In a way I couldn't fault the logic, once I had accepted the premise, it had been after all a staple for the nannies of European royalty where a crying baby might get you a lashing. After she had told me that, I had a hard time French kissing her without thinking about it. It was one of those images that hung in the back of your mind.

I had told Paps about it one night over a couple of beers at Barney's Beanery. Paps assured me that this kinda' thing was relatively common among his wealthy Hollywood clientele.

"Most of these people have some kinda' weird trip going on with their kids," he said, looking thoughtfully into his beer, "Sometimes real weird."

He had called me, not long ago, to ask me about witches and their children. He wanted to know if I'd read or heard anything about any special rituals witches might use to initiate or train their children in the dark arts. I told him there were all kinds of stories and legends about witches and other people's kids.

"Why," I asked, "what's on your mind?"

"Maybe nothing," he said, "I mean, I've seen all kinds but these kids I got now... I dunno'... something's real strange."

He wouldn't say anything else, except that we'd get together real soon and talk about it. Two weeks later Paps was dead.

I hadn't thought about that conversation and now the thought gave me cold shivers.

I walked over to the stack of cardboard boxes. Paps' things. His final client's driver dropped them off yesterday. The production company was paying for his funeral and cremation. He had no living kin; I was to receive his ashes. Paps didn't trust banks or the economy; he spent his money as fast as he made it, most of it on the girls at the Oriental Health Spa down the street from my loft. I had considered scattering his ashes in the Jacuzzi there in compliance with his last request but I knew I'd never get away with it. Even if I did, the thought of Paps winding up in the scum filter of a whorehouse bubble tub didn't sit well with me.

I stared at the boxes. Somehow, there was a strange malevolence buzzing around inside of them like a trapped fly. There was a knock at the door and a familiar voice calling my name. It was B.B.

"Hurry up, we're running late," she said, grabbing my hand and pulling me out into the bright afternoon. B.B. was a "take charge" kinda' girl. I barely had time to close the door. Within seconds we were locked in air-conditioned comfort, speeding down Sunset Boulevard in her brown B.M.W. "Before I forget, here's something Paps asked me to give you. "She handed me a small envelope with a birthday card and a small key inside. "When did you see Paps?"

"About two days before the accident. I was on the set visiting Ed, the producer, when Paps came up to me." She sighed. "We started talking about old times." She smiled. "He gave me this envelope as an excuse for me to see you again. He was gonna' mail it to you but, I guess he read my mind." She sighed again. "He always thought there was something special between us. I told him I'd picked you up hitch-hiking not long ago but that you didn't give me your new address and phone number so he did..."

I sighed. "If I remember correctly, you didn't ask."

She turned to me and sniffed at little at my interruption. She was almost lovely in the afternoon light, her long, black, wavy hair blowing in the air-conditioning, those large, doe-dark eyes, that thin surgically sculpted face: she coulda' been an ad for some sports car with a name like LeMans. Sexy-high-tech-city-night: you've seen the commercial, meet the girl.

"Anyway, I'd decided to mail it to you when this happened. It's such a tragedy. I feel so sorry for Ed; it seems like somebody dies on every movie he makes. He was just getting over the guilt from that last accident where that clumsy gaffer electrocuted himself when this had to happen."

I was trying to get a headache from her conversation just to relieve the heartache of hearing it.

"Right,' I said, "poor Ed."

B.B. wheeled her car into the parking lot of the funeral home and hurried me inside. The services had already started so everyone had to turn and stare when we entered. B.B. loved it. She waved at her friends and winked at the usher who escorted us down the aisle to one of the front pews. I sat uncomfortably through the strange eulogy being delivered by this bearded guy in a leisure suit with the compulsory dark shirt unbuttoned to the chest.

I was glad this was a closed coffin service and that Paps was not looking up at this guy who must have considered himself God's press agent. A diamond encrusted dollar sign hung against his hairy, tan chest, a chilling reminder of the growing belief that somehow there was an equation between God's love and money. It said basically the same thing as a jewel studded cross or a gold Star of David, it just said it a little louder.

After the service I was taken to a small side room by the usher and stood with Ed, the producer, while Paps' ashes were turned to ashes. The setting sun coming through the cheap stained glass window flashed off of Ed's expensive sunglasses as he talked patronizingly about "dear Paps." Just when I thought I would throw up, a man in a dark suit appeared with the urn, which he ceremoniously handed to Ed. Ed, in turn, handed it to me with the words,

"You don't know how sorry I am."

"I understand," I said, "but I wanted to ask you something."

He was trying to make a quick exit when I'd caught him with that question. He turned back to me with a paranoid smile.

"Of course, what is it?"

"Well, it's not really important, but Paps and I were from Texas..."

"I see, and..." He stepped closer.

"And I was wondering, did he die with his boots on?"

That question caught Ed off guard for a moment; he relaxed, and then said with an edge to his voice, "No, actually the blast was so powerful it blew him right out of his boots."

I sensed a veiled threat here but B.B. came tearing right through that veil. She gushed sympathy all over Ed, then took my arm and led me back to her car and into the sunset on Sunset Boulevard.

Two days and two long nights later I opened the safe deposit box at the Lloyds Bank on Sunset with the key Paps had left me. Inside the box were a small amount of money and a letter concerning what he believed to be signs of the demonic rituals the children of producer Ed had undergone. The letter read like the circle of hell in the movie Salo. At the bottom was a cryptic note warning me about another Texas friend of ours, Burns Sawyer. Burns might be in the same coven as Ed and he might have a grudge against me. On the whole, the letter was unpleasant reading.

I took Paps' ashes up to Moonfire Mountain, in Topango Canyon, and scattered them to the evening breeze, blowing out to the barely visible Catalina Islands. It had been a long, dark summer. The Santa Anna Winds were blowing the Fall in. I could see the stars up here, big ones, little ones, scattered like sparks in the dark sky. I wondered if Paps was up there now, babysitting one of those tiny baby stars tucked way off by itself in that blue-black California night.

CHAPTER TWO

WHOLESALE HORROR

I T WAS A DARK DRIVE into the Hollywood Hills and the late October night was already playing trick or treat with my mind. I was on my way to see Burns Sawyer, the legendary horror film director, at his request, which made me uneasy. The combination of Paps' note and Sawyer's habit of having only one friend at a time was a bad omen. I had been that one friend for several years when, as he put it, his "butt hole was snapping just inches above the pavement." Sawyer had just about invented the "splatter flick" back in the early sixties. He rode the wave of notoriety from Texas to Hollywood then lost it all in the shallows of low-budget independents with producers who were determined to explode the myth of his genius. He had also lost a lot of money trying to make a starlet out of his girlfriend. "The rubber tits and pug nose were just the tip of the iceberg," he would lament during those pre-dawn talk sessions that he called "story conferences." Sawyer, you see, did not trust the night and could never relax until the sun came up. This town is full of witches just waiting for me to close my eyes so they can, varuuuup, suck my soul straight to hell!" Old Dad, as I called him, was a big believer in evil forces. He was known as a horror film director; movie society took for granted that he was a dedicated Satanist. At parties the darker element of this society gravitated to him, offering him admittance to their covens, hinting how much he'd enjoy their rituals. All of this scared the shit out of Old Dad. He fancied himself a great comedic talent who had only done that famous horror flick as a way to get quick bucks and instant recognition. It had worked; he had gotten both, but was still paying for it.

My headlights lit up the eyes of the Sawyer family cat as I pulled into the driveway. At first the cat didn't move then suddenly he hissed and ran crazily toward the house. The cat looked like it was on acid as it zig- zagged its way to the front door, dodging the night phantoms. It missed the door and went scratching off the porch, down into the bushes below. I rang the bell. Old Dad's son, Stony, answered the door.

"Have you seen my cat?" He asked, as we walked into the living room. Stony was about fifteen now, tall for his age, with long brown hair and a freckled face that hadn't changed much in the five years I'd known him.

"Yeah I saw your cat; he looked freaked out to me. You haven't been experimenting on that poor cat again, have you?"

Stony blushed. "Naw," he grinned, "he's been in 'Nam; Captain Cat's just having flashbacks of the Tet Offensive. You should see the great war movie I made with him on my 8mm."

Walking into Old Dad's house was like stepping into somebody's nightmare. Props from his movies lined the walls, dismembered ugly things mounted like trophies.

"I'll tell Dad you're here."

Stony bolted up the stairs to Sawyer's bedroom, which we'd always called "the sanctuary."

"Dad says come on up."

Stony passed me on the stairs as I headed up.

"See if you can talk him into watching a movie with me later."

The sanctuary had always had a unique odor. It was fainter now that he could afford a maid, but it was still there: the smell of decay.

"Come on in here, man."

Dad was sitting on his bed, as usual, surrounded by used tissues and empty pop bottles. He was a dark heavy man, black eyes, thick beard, but with a strange air of jolliness about him: Satan's Santa Claus.

"Come over here and have a seat, man, I was just filling up the pipe. Listen, Katey," he turned to the thin young "actress" seated at his feet, "give the Professor and I a little slack time here, would ya?"

Katey rubbed her nose a little then stood up and stalked out of the room, leaving a trail of expensive perfume to do battle with the smell of death. Burns called me the Professor because during our working partnership I had always done such detailed research on all the grisly topics covered in the screenplays. From Jim Jones and John Wayne Gacy to Voodoo and Vampires, I had a talent for digging up unusual tidbits. Sawyer's nickname, "Old Dad" had come from my Jim Jones research: it had been one of Jim's favorite handles.

"What'd you want to see me about?"

"Oh, nothing in particular, I just wanted to see how you were getting along. Say, did you know I was starting another movie real soon?"

"Yeah?"

"Righto man, big, big budget too. Biggest yet."

"So, now you can pay me that thirty-five grand you owe me!"

"Heh-heh, well not just yet man, I inked the deal today but I won't see any real money till we start production—next year. I could give ya' maybe fifty, sixty bucks here if you're running tight."

He rolled over a little on one hip to give his hand enough room to reach into his pocket and pulled out a small wad of crumpled bills. He twisted his stocky frame to hide the amount of his pocket money from me and selected a bill from the wad. He tugged hard at the bill, wrestling it from the others in his hand. It was a gesture I had seen many times before, one hand wanted to keep the money so badly that the other hand had to actually struggle to pry it loose.

"Here go, man."

He handed me a fifty and quickly shoved the wad back in his pocket. The money returned to his pocket a lot easier than it had come out.

"Listen man, you remember that witchcraft thing you were looking into for me a few years back?"

"The one about that actress with that coven up here in the hills that you still owe me for?"

"Heh-heh. Righto, well, it's a lot bigger than we discovered and it ain't just candles and chanting."

Old Dad's eyes narrowed; there was a taste of fear in them—just behind the twinkle.

"And by big I mean big names, powerful people, dark, dark goings-on."

He paused, nodding his head. He put a pinch of grass into his small brass pipe and lifted it to his lips.

"Dark things," he repeated, then fired up the bowl and took a long deep pull. He handed me the pipe which now contained nothing but pale gray ashes.

"Here take a hit," he muttered, holding in his toke.

You didn't get high smoking with Old Dad, but that was okay because usually you didn't want to be high and hear what he had to say and tonight was definitely no exception.

"Hollywood is a decadent, old whore," he philosophized, "and there's only one way to make it in this town and that's you gotta kiss the old whore's ass! Yep, kiss it right, dead square in the middle. I told you that years ago but you didn't listen. Now I'm directing my third feature and you're still waiting to get paid. Do you know why? 'Cause you ain't got down on your knees and puckered up."

This was Old Dad's version of a pep talk. If I let him, he would drag on for hours.

"I hate to interrupt you but I've heard this speech before and unless you got something you're building up to ..."

"Damn right I'm building up to something! Witchcraft! The Oracula Malefactorum! Right here in the Hollywood Hills!"

The Oracula Malefactorum was the ancient ceremony that sealed the witch's pact with the devil. It involved kissing the devil's asshole. The significance of the ritual came from the medieval concept that man was the image of God. Satan, therefore, was God's excrement, hell was God's bowels, so the gate of hell – God's asshole. Hence, the witch's fascination with the excretory system and its products. Aleister Crowley lived for many months in Mexico on the dung of diseased prostitutes in order to gain the Serpent's Kiss—a bite so toxic he could cause sickness just by breaking the skin with his sharpened canines. In his letter, Paps had mentioned the children's peculiar attitude towards feces.

I was adding these things up in my mind while Old Dad, who had stood for his declaration of witchcraft, settled back down to his bed and his pipe. He took another deep pull and handed me the burned out bowl.

"Do you know what evil is?"

He spoke to himself more than to me.

"Evil is a wind, it's like the jet stream in the atmosphere, the at-most-fear. The human spirit is like a wing set in that stream of power and the tilt of the wing determines its physical manifestation, do you follow me?"

He didn't wait for an answer.

"You remember that fat kid down in Miama, now that's a good example, you see, his wing was tipped up, like this,"

Old Dad held his hand at a forty-five degree angle.

" ...into the stream causing the power to swirl around and around and create this big, fat ball of greed at the lowest possible level of eating and shitting."

"This IS leading somewhere, right?"

Old Dad chuckled to himself then slowly turned and stared that dead stare of his right into my eyes, as if he were looking for the back of my head.

"I'm about to enter a very powerful part of that jet stream of evil, man, I've been invited by people I cannot refuse.

His lips trembled as he spoke now.

"I want you to go with me. Your wing is set straight, like this.

He held his hand level.

"Evil flows over and past you, for some reason, like it doesn't know you're there. I need you with me, to hold me level." He turned back to his pipe, "The stream is powerful enough, where we're going, to flip me over and suck me right down."

"And where are WE going?"

Old Dad smiled to himself, took another pull and passed me the empty bowl.

"There's a coven up here in the hills—big time, heavy names, people who run this town—and I've been invited to a landmark meeting: THE

FEAST OF THE BEAST. Only happens every twenty-eight years. I can't imagine what it's gonna be like but I do know that at their regular weekly meetings they have a human sacrifice."

I knew I didn't want to be stoned when I heard what he had to say.

"Wait a minute, you're telling me wealthy, intelligent, highly-placed people, in the show business community, are involved in some crazy Mansonesque rituals up here in the hills?"

"Manson was small potatoes. I told you, this ain't candles and chanting. This is not a test. I been INVITED." Old Dad looked at me, slowly smiling that demented Santa Claus smile of his. "Well, can I count on you?"

"What'd they invite you to do—bring the victim?"

Old Dad laughed like a bowl full of jelly, "Nooooo...No...man... They get drifters for that—pretty little teenage runaways, milk carton kids, unwanted babies, nameless, faceless." He scooted over on the bed and put his arm around my shoulders. "You hurt me by saying that; why you're family, you damn near raised Stony." His touch was not comforting. "No—I need an anchor here, that's all. Here, let me fill that bowl up for ya' with some of this good-good Highwayman, four-hundred smackers an ounce smoke." He is planning to kill me, I thought.

"You want a little tootski?"

I wanted a little outski. I began planning a graceful exit as Old Dad produced a mirror, from under the bed, with rows of white powder on it. He did a couple of quick snorts and offered me the mirror.

"Listen man, research Satanic rituals for me and give me some background on this stuff; I can't afford to look stupid here. Watta' ya' say?"

"Not for love or money."

Old Dad solemnly withdrew the mirror; my answer had offended him. I stood up just as Katey returned—rubbing the radar in her nose that had told her the lines were out again.

"Am I interrupting something?" She purred as she settled down at Old Dad's feet.

"No, I was just leaving."

"Do that research for me, man, I'll pay ya' good money."

"Right."

I kept moving toward the door.

"That party's coming up real soon." I turned back to Old Dad, Katey had her nose buried in the white stuff; Old Dad was patting her head gently. He looked up at me and smiled, "Call me."

The ride back down the hill seemed darker than the ride up. Maybe it should have. I kept hearing moans and wails coming from the black hills, sounds that told me it was time to get out of Dodge. I felt like a magi leaving Herod's palace with the screams of the slaughtered innocents ringing in his psychic ears, hoping to find another way home.

CHAPTER THREE

IN SEARCH OF ASYLUM

THE SUNRISE WAS GRAY, chilly—almost, almost Fall. I didn't go home after I left Old Dad's; something told me not to. Some ancient, genetic program bubbling in my blood had me sitting like Mr. Primitive Man staring through the mists before my cave, waiting for the pale pink light of dawn to give form to the creatures that haunted my night.

I needed a place of refuge, a place of asylum. I was sitting at a small metal table in the Farmer's Market having a Hot-el of coffee. Life was becoming a nightmare. I was starting to see demons everywhere I looked and hear the moans of their victims drifting up like smoke from my cigarette. I had seen the beast—dear God, he was huge. He was as big as business, he was as bad as government and he was after me.

I watched the sparrows pick at the scraps of pizza on the ground as I tried to put these new feelings into the context of what I'd known before last night. Things began making a strange kind of sense. If I was right, Paps had not been murdered because he knew something about the coven but because they thought he didn't know anything. It was important that the victim be ignorant, innocent, a "virgin" sacrifice.

If Old Dad's offer was genuine, they did not want to kill me; they wanted me to join them. They didn't want my life; it was my soul they were after. They were not afraid of being exposed; they were not afraid of being caught. They had the power to make my life miserable and my misery would increase their power.

I decided on a cinnamon roll to go with my breakfast of coffee and depression. I loved cinnamon rolls. When I was in high school I would go to the cafeteria early in the morning and get a cinnamon roll and a carton of milk. I could only afford to do this on Fridays by saving up my milk money all week. Just asking for one made me smile. I came back to my table with the knowledge that maybe they couldn't make my life as miserable as I had thought.

I reached into my pocket and pulled out a faded scrap of paper. On it was written the only poem I'd been able to save from the Common Poets book I had been working on when I'd met Paps all those many years ago in Texas.

I had dropped out of college because of the appalling hypocrisy of the institution. It was the sixties. I had taken a job in a metal workshop in the Oak Cliff section of Dallas. The honesty and good nature of the men that worked there inspired me to do a book about them and their way of life. It was to be a collection of the stories and jokes they told, a reflection of a passing generation's way of looking at things. I called it Common Poets, with the phrase, "Poetry is a common occurrence," underneath the title. For months I taped and photographed these men with the eye of an anthropologist saving for posterity the last glimpses of a soon-to-be-extinct tribe. It was there I met Paps and his friend Goat, also college dropouts.

Goat Boone had a brother named Chris. The Boone brothers were notorious Dallas artists. Chris had actually gone to New York City and established himself as a writer, of sorts, for magazines. Chris said he would take my book to the Big Apple and try to get it published for me. He was right about one thing—he took my book. He got an advance from a publisher and took that, too. I had saved this one poem as a reminder of those men and a warning never to trust Chris Boone again.

I unfolded the page and read the poem:

Trout
By Claude Evans

One Saturday I was fishin
the Trinity River bottom and hooked
A fish the size of my leg.

But
When I pulled it in,
It had long hair all over and big teeth.
I grabbed up my knife, but it jumped off my line
And ran up a tree. I picked up my shotgun,
But as I drew down on it
The damn thing hollered: "Gotta go!"
And flew away.
I turned to my dog, Miss King,
Who was sittin there watchin it all: "Miss King,
What was that?"
She say: "Trout."
Don't you know I kicked that dog's ass for lyin!
Tellin me: "Trout."

I felt I had hooked something like the creature in Claude's poem. The unknown was pulling at my line and I had better be ready for more than trout when I reeled it in.

It was dark again when the phone rang, waking me out of a dead sleep. It was Chris Boone, wanting a favor. Normally Paps was Chris's errand boy but, with Paps dead, he decided to call me and offer his cab fee.

"I just need you to take me over to Kathy's accountant's house, wait for me, then drive me back home. You can do that for me, right?"

I thought for a minute, Chris was tied into this thing from some angle. I didn't know how but maybe I could learn something by hanging out with him for a while tonight.

"Sure, why not, what time?"

"In about an hour, I'll leave your name at the gate."

Chris had married the superstar actress, Kathy White, a few years back and moved into her mansion in the Hancock Park area of L.A. off Wilshire Boulevard. Paps and Goat, after supporting Chris for many years, paying his huge phone bills, giving him projects like mine to steal, and in general seeing to it that Chris had the wherewithal to continue his struggle to the top, thought that this marriage would be a great step into the spotlight. Nothing, of course, could have been further from the truth. In his first major interview after the wedding, Chris described himself as an orphan Indian who had been raised by the Jesuits and struggled to the top alone. Chris had an explanation for this, of course, and Paps bought it. Chris's brother Goat, however, went off on his own after that and was turning heads in the Hollywood scene with his Last Prophet to L.A. act. He seemed on the verge of establishing himself when he mysteriously disappeared. Chris seemed to grow a bit in the eyes of certain powers after the disappearance of his brother. Paps became the babysitter of Chris and Kathy's first-born son, Orn. Paps and I remained friends but I had always suspected cahoots between he and Chris and some sort of foul play involved in Goat's disappearance. Chris' star seemed to fall as fast as it rose, and, after only a few months, he was back to being the spouse of a famous actress. For Chris, who was literally addicted to feelings of superiority, the shuffle was more than painful. He picked up a Hollywood nose candy habit and normally these little evening jaunts with Paps were to the candy store. Paps would drive and score while Chris would sit in the car and snort. The funny thing was, Paps was getting the reputation as a heavy coker and Chris was playing himself up as a concerned friend. Hollywood was strange; the only way to avoid being the target of gossip was to start your own and make it more interesting than anything that was going around about you. In Hollywood the story was more important than the truth. The town was built on stories.

I approached the guardhouse; a guard with a terrifying acne problem asked me my name and called the White mansion for clearance. I was cleared. As I drove down the small private street, I listed in my mind the names of the rich and famous neighbors who had moved in since Kathy had discovered the area. Halfway down the first block I turned into the large, circular driveway with the stone lions out front—the White house. As I made my way through the gardens I wondered what this was all about. Was this some code for a coke score? Did he have to get money from her accountant first? I entered through the garden door with an uneasy mind.

Chris was sitting in the kitchen of his wife's house, listening to classical music on his wife's antique radio. He looked troubled, more troubled than I'd ever seen him. It was obvious he hadn't slept well in a long time. My footsteps startled him as I entered the room. I also startled four of the maybe forty cats and kittens which inhabited the White house and gave it the distinct aroma of the world's most lavish kitty litter box. The cats went scrambling for the nearest window or door, Chris jumped up so fast he knocked his chair over and the large grandfather clock, in the empty dining room off the kitchen, toned ten o'clock. It was an eerie moment. I stood there waiting for the intense expression on Chris' face to soften into hospitality as the gongs from the clock echoed through the house. Suddenly it was quiet, except for the clickity-click sound of tiny claws still scoring the polished hardwood floors in the rooms beyond the kitchen. Chris smiled. His face seemed to creak.

"You're right on time. Pull up a chair."

He lifted his chair back up and sat in it. I moved around to the other side of the large table and sat down. His kitchen was as big as an average two-bedroom apartment, complete with a fireplace. When he'd hired Goat and Paps to re-do it, they had spent months taking the cabinets back to the bare wood to give it the look and feel of the old Boone family place in Texas. It had worked. In spite of its overbearing size the room felt warm and cozy. Tonight, however, with the October mists drifting in the open windows, the stale smell of cat piss and the forlorn figure of Chris Boone sitting across from me, the place felt like a favorite aunt dying of cancer. In Texas, Chris Boone had been the kind of man who would stop his car to help a turtle across the street. Now, looking at his worn face, I had to wonder what kind of a man he had become.

"So, how's the wife and kid?"

"Just fine, they're in Florida right now. Kathy's doing some in-depth training out there at a special school. I talked to them just a little bit ago and they sound like they're doing great."

There was nervousness in his optimism that told me not to ask any more questions about the family.

"So, what are we doing tonight?"

He smiled a little and lit up a cigarette.

"I'm on this new health program, Kathy's idea, special diet, special exercises and these special vitamin shots...."

"Vitamin shots?"

"Yeah, I get them from her accountant."

"Pete? You get these shots from Pete? But he's not a doctor."

"Sure he is, I mean, in their church he is."

"Oh, so were going to Pete's and he's gonna' give you a shot?"

"Yeah."

"So what do you need me for?"

"Well the shots are pretty strong and sometimes I get a little dizzy so I would just feel safer if you took me there and back."

"Sure, fine with me. When do you have to be there?"

"Actually we should be leaving right now."

"Let's go."

"I'm gonna' lock the garden door; we'll leave by the back."

Chris went to lock the garden door then led me out the back door, which was behind the kitchen. As we walked out I caught the strong smell of a dead animal.

"Christ! What died?!"

"Oh, a couple of the kittens. Orn was playing with them and he accidentally choked them. He was pretty upset about it. But you know kids, they don't realize how fragile those little kittens are, they think they're like stuffed animals."

It was a quiet drive over to Pete's and back. Chris had stayed in Pete's over an hour while I sat in the car. When he came out he was puffy and his skin was bright orange, an effect of the niacin he told me. On the way back to my place I puzzled over two big questions that had come out of the evening drive. One, as far as I knew Pete had no other client, just Kathy—so how come he drives a Rolls Royce and Kathy drives a Honda? Two, how can a pseudo-religion give you a license to practice medicine and purchase the syringes and injectable vitamins necessary for such a venture? The answers were not on the tip of my tongue but perhaps I knew a man on whose tongue-tip the answers stood, just waiting for me to ask the questions. I'd call Mank in the morning but for tonight I'd crawl into bed, pull the covers up over my head and pretend I was safe, that I had found asylum.

CHAPTER FOUR

A GENTILE PROBLEM

"WITCHCRAFT IS BASICALLY A GENTILE PROBLEM; Jews stopped believing in the devil a long time ago. Freud put the nail in the devil's coffin by saying the devil was just your cock telling you what you wanted to hear. 'I am the magic wand. I make fantasy into reality. I am the seed of life.'"

I was having coffee with Mank at his house off Beverly Boulevard. Mank was from an old Hollywood family; his people had practically invented movies. Mank, himself, was a gossip columnist for the L.A. Times. He was still in his early twenties and somewhat of a black sheep. It was taken for granted that by the time he was in his early thirties he'd have a nice Jewish wife and a couple of T.V. shows to produce before going on to make a name for himself in the movies like the rest of his family.

His apartment was a study in chaos financed by a grant from his parents to the University of Soft Knocks in an attempt to discover which would run out first, his trust fund or his parents' patience. Piles of clothes, newspapers, records and bedding were scattered around the apartment with an intentional, almost comic, disregard for order. A lot of small change and even a few low-denomination bills were sprinkled on the floor, adding to that touch of disdain for money only the truly wealthy can afford. Mank was a study in casual. He had the face of a child and the body of a fifty-year-old card shark. He dressed in wrinkled chic, a style he originated by wearing his expensive, unearned clothes un-ironed. However, there was a royalty about him, something in his being, that if he told you he was a Gypsy Prince you'd look at those dark eyes piercing through that shock of black hair hanging in his face and think, Yeah.

"Most witches, historically speaking, started out as Catholics, although in this country, with its great religious freedom, you had Puritan witches, Church of England, Baptists, the whole smear. Like everything else, people get into it for the money. And show business, Gentiles definitely do not understand show business. They have always believed it was the devil's work. The major Gentile contribution to the field of entertainment is the rodeo. That's it."

"Mank, you're not helping me."

He smiled then looked down at his coffee cup.

"Sure I am. You have to understand the essence of your problem then you can deal with the particulars."

"Mank, I do not need a beginner's course in this, I have been researching the occult for the past five years here. I need definite information about definite covens and the people that belong to them."

"Okay, I'll quit doing George Burns. What do you want to know?"

"Is there a coven that specializes in initiating children into the black arts?"

"Well, not exactly. There's the Molochians, who do things to their own kids, but for them it's like they didn't get enough money or power by selling their own souls so they sell the souls of their children. They're more likely the ones you're after. In the movie community, these guys usually produce splatter flicks aimed at giving teenage boys fear erections to enforce the equation of sex with violence. Violence then becomes a socially acceptable form of sex and that gives these guys the feeling that they've harvested a few more souls for Satan.

"Like I say they use their own kids but it's not like a concert violinist teaching his three-year-old to play Bach. Basically the kids don't know what's going on and their parents really don't want them to. Is any of this helping you?"

"Maybe – I've been told about human sacrifices...."

"Murder is the ultimate status symbol. It goes all the way back to prehistory. Scalps on a belt, notches on a gun, stars on a general's collar, they all mean the same thing: this man got away with murder more times than you did. But it took religion to elevate murder to the highest status, that of a holy act. Now you're generally dealing with bourgeois, social-climbing, status-seeking assholes when you talk about your modern-day witches and warlocks. So, to answer your question, I would say there is a good chance the stories you heard about that stuff are true. But really, killing any helpless creature gives them a similar rush, a dog, a cat..."

"A kitten?"

"A kitten, a goldfish, a cockroach—none of us are immune to this sensation, but these people get addicted to it. They turn their back on any real talent they might have and, like a junkie, spend all their time looking for a bigger rush. They become dangerous and the rich ones become real dangerous."

"And the poor ones become sad headlines."

"So, what else you want to know?"

"What have you heard about Chris Boone and Burns Sawyer?"

Mank didn't know much about my friends but he said he'd look into it for me. It was good to talk to Mank. What he had told me was like a ray of sunlight hitting last night's dragon and turning it into a tree stump. It made the drive down to the beach spellbinding. The orange autumn afternoon light played through the palm trees like a senorita's smile through a lace fan. I drove my battered M.G. with the top down; the air felt silky. I parked by the pier in Santa Monica and walked out on the sand as the red sun kissed its reflection on the darkening sea. They were turning on the lights that outlined the roofs of the arcades on the pier above me. Night was coming back again with its fog dragons, looking for me, waiting for me to close my eyes.

CHAPTER FIVE

THE NIGHTMARE BEGINS

H IS CORPSE WAS COLD, gray, split open down the middle from the sternum to the pelvis. Jimmy didn't like the way he looked. He examined the empty flaps of skin left by the coroner's incision, the hollow cave where his intestines, heart, lungs, stomach, liver, kidneys – in short, his guts, had been. Jimmy's spirit hand touched the lifeless hand of Jimmy's corpse. Spirit tears, like tiny jewels, fell from his spirit cheeks onto the tattered flesh. The corpse was covered with wounds. He had been shot twice, stabbed over one hundred and fifty times but he still would not die. At last, they held his fighting body to the ground and drove a rat-tail file through his skull. The sound of that terrible hammer and the pain of that ugly file, creeping blow by blow through his sputtering brain, began ringing in his spirit ears. He touched the hole in the center of his body's forehead and screamed a silent spirit scream until the corpse rattled and shook the metal table it lay upon. It sat blot upright, jaw open, all its wounds spitting cold, black blood. It was time for the spirit to move on, to leave its shaking corpse to the elements of corruption and spin howling into the night in search of revenge.

Chris Boone would wake up, perhaps in a few moments. He would be clammy wet with sweat and fear. Jimmy's ghost would sit beside his bed and send cold chills up his barely conscious spine.

I had just come back from a Halloween party up in the Hollywood Hills, all done up in my special wolfman make-up. Steaks, in her Betty Boop outfit, had actually dumped her chic date at the party and was sprawled out on my couch chugging down the last of my tequila. It looked like I was finally gonna' find out if New York stayed open all night. We had just decided to leave our costumes on when the phone rang. It had to be bad news. It was. Chris Boone had just seen a ghost.

"You've just seen a what?"

"I've just seen the Rabbit."

"You mean Jimmy, from Texas—He's been dead over five years."

"Can you come over? I can still feel his presence. The cats are going crazy."

Steaks was actually turned on by the prospect of seeing a real ghost on Halloween. We jumped in my ragged M.G. and headed up Wilshire to see Chris Boone. I was glad to have her company even though I didn't share her frisky mood. Jimmy was the last chapter of my book. He had died a grisly death only a few weeks after Chris had married Kathy in the hot Texas summer of '73. It was in his memory I'd made the trek to L.A. Maybe he was angry that I had not done his memory justice, but what did he have against Chris.

The pimply-faced guard looked askance at the wolfman and Betty Boop driving up to his guard box at four in the morning. Usually just the sight of my battered car was enough to send him into a stuttering fit. Tonight it took him a full five minutes to get our names out of his mouth and into the telephone. As we pulled into the driveway of the White house I noticed the flickering of candlelight coming from the kitchen of the otherwise dark house. Considering how we were dressed and Chris' current state of mind I led Steaks up the long brick path to the front door and rang the bell. Chris was still freaked a bit when he answered the door, candle in hand.

"What's the matter, you blow a fuse?"

He motioned for silence, his finger to his lips.

"Can you feel him?" He whispered as he ushered us into the great entrance hall of the mansion.

Our footsteps echoed through the empty house as Chris led us past the dark dining room towards the kitchen. The cats yowled and hissed unseen from the corners and under the chairs, moving like shadows in the candlelight. It must be my outfit.

In the kitchen Chris had arranged thirteen candles in a circle on the kitchen table. In the center of the circle was a large manila envelope with the words Common Poets written on it with black magic marker— my book.

We sat down at the table. I felt a chill as I picked up the envelope and opened it. Rabbit's picture was on top of the stack of photos and poems. I looked at Chris across the table; he seemed to shiver. Steaks leaned over and looked at the picture.

"That's him isn't it? That's the ghost."

"Yeah, that's the ghost."

I handed Steaks the picture of Jimmy. Chris just kept staring at me. I shook my head and shifted through the stack of photos and poems, words and images I thought I would never see again. Steaks held the picture against her breast and closed her eyes.

"I'm gonna' see if I can feel his presence. You guys be quiet."

I stuffed the pictures and pages back into the envelope and lay it solemnly back in the center of the circle. Chris shoved the envelope back towards me.

"Take it, it's yours."

"What's the angle?"

"Sssssh! I'm getting a vibration."

I looked at Steaks; she was trembling.

"He's here, in this room."

Chris paled and turned his head from side to side, cautiously inspecting the room. I don't know, maybe it was the booze or my book suddenly appearing, wrapped in the bloody hands of a dead friend, but the whole scene—Chris Boone and the wolfman sitting around a circle of candles waiting for Betty Boop to trance channel the Rabbit—it was starting to piss me off.

"Is this what you wanted to do, give me my book back? Is that it?"

Steaks eyes popped open.

"I can't do this if you guys don't shut up!"

Chris slumped back in his chair, frazzled, nervous.

"Yeah, that's it. Take it and go."

I grabbed the envelope and stood up. Steaks looked at Chris then back at me.

"Well, you ruined it. I was just starting to pick up on him."

"Yeah, what'd you pick up?"

"Rage."

CHAPTER SIX

COMMON POETS REVISITED

I T WAS DAWN when Steaks and I pulled into the small gravel parking lot behind our storefront loft. Her chic date from the party was sitting on the trunk of his red B.M.W. convertible with a cheap bouquet of flowers in his hand. She ignored him and headed straight for the back gate, which was the entrance to our lofts. He groveled a bit and offered her breakfast at her favorite little sidewalk café in Beverly Hills. She asked me to join them. Although the thought of wolfman scarffing up Eggs Bennie on Rodeo drive was tres amussant, I turned them down. Her date gave me a discrete "I owe you one" look and they disappeared in a cloud of dust. I unlocked the gate, walked down the back steps, past Steaks' cactus garden and into my empty room. Halloween, at last, was over.

I stretched out on the couch and opened the envelope. I felt old as I turned the pages and looked at the photos. Texas came running back to me, hot and full of pain. I felt the burns from the sparks of the welding torch and the loneliness born of sorrow, for welding was a solitary task. Once the hood swung down over your face it was just you and the darkness staring through that small window of black glass at a ball of light twenty thousand times brighter than the sun. Sometimes it would get unbearable for Jimmy. He said all that high voltage electricity made his brain run faster and faster; things he'd done, things he'd said, fights with his wife, all spun and blurred together in the darkness under the hood until he felt his soul burning and melting like the metal at the tip of his welding rod. He'd stand up shaking, lift his hood and stare at nothing, his face dripping wet and black from the greasy smoke, then he'd sit his hood down and walk slowly to the shop office to ask the foreman to let him do something else for a while. After the summer he stopped welding all together.

We had worked together that summer welding huge sections of steel pipe big enough for a man to stand up inside. We stood up inside those pipes and welded. In July. In Texas. All day. It wasn't so much the hundred and thirty degree heat or the thick smoke from the burning steel, but the sparks had no place else to go but through your clothes and into your skin and all you could do was cuss and bear it—you didn't come out until you'd finished your seam. It was a government job, air vents for a copper mine, and welders could have all the overtime they wanted. Jimmy and his wife had just had a baby; he needed money to get out of debt. I had promised my girl a trip to Mexico. Two good reasons for two good Texans to stay in that living hell three good hours after closing time. We got to know each other during those long nights. I heard about Nam; he heard about college. I learned how to spit tobacco; he learned to split fractions. God, that was a long time ago.

I sat there for a moment, lost in time, then slowly it came to me Chris Boone had something to do with Rabbit's death. Trouble had been brewing between Rabbit and his wife for a long time but it didn't get violent until Chris became involved in the book I was writing. What power did this man have? How long had he been practicing the dark arts? Hypocrisy was the mainstay of evil, this I had learned from my research. Satan appears as an angel of light, the Bible says. All the pieces were there but how did they fit together? Why, after all this time, did he decide to return my book to me? I searched through the papers for the last chapter, the one about Jimmy's death. If Jimmy's ghost was haunting him maybe there was a clue in the last chapter that would tell me how Chris was accountable for Jimmy's death. Something I had written down, without knowing, all those years ago could be the key I was looking for. I found the chapter and began to read.

CHAPTER 31
ASKING FOR IT

T HE PLANT WAS HOT that July morning, and it stayed hot all day. Late in the afternoon a flatcar loaded with stacks of sheet metal pulled into the East Bay of the plant. The car creaked down the ancient railroad tracks that ran the length of the plant. Rabs loved the railroad, and every time a car like this came into the plant he'd tag it with his old hobo handle, Pecos Star.

"That way my buddies still think I'm riding the rails."

"Ever think about going back on the bum?"

"Goaty, every night when I hear the train pass down in the bottoms, son. I slept better on the rails then I ever slept in my life; them old cars just rock you to sleep."

Goat and Rabs had lunch together as usual with Frank, Rusty, Hunchy, Paps and myself. I taped a few more of Hunchy's stories and took a few shots of the guys. (Chris Boone had put selling my book on indefinite hold for several months but I continued to work on it for my own satisfaction.) Goat told us all about last weekend's big wedding, between his brother Chris and movie star Kathy White. Nobody seemed very impressed, which hurt Goat's feelings. Goat idolized his brother and wanted to share what he thought was a big step up for everybody because, at last, the book would be published. Hunchy just laughed.

"Goat, your brother ain't gonna' do nothing but sit up there in that big house with his feet up and his dick hard. I know that's what I'd do if I had fucked up on a fortune like he did."

"You mean you wouldn't help Frank a little?" Goat chided.

"Fuck Frank! He got a dick, too. Let him fuck his own self a fortune."

"Bullshit!"

"No, you right I probably would help Frankie but I'm a fool; your brother ain't a fool, you hear me. I been knowing all you Boones ever since you was kids and your daddy first came to work here. Don't expect too much from your brother Chris, you hear me? If you had money I know what you'd do, you'd act like Sir Walter Raleigh an' go broke helping folks. But your brother ain't like you, you better listen to me 'cause I don't wanna' see you get hurt."

"He's my brother."

Things got quiet. One by one the men got up and left. I sat there with Goat, staring at the tape turning in my cassette recorder.

"He's my brother."

The buzzer sounded: end of lunch.

Rabs and Goat walked back to the welding shop together.

"I want that for my tombstone." Rabbit pointed at the giant metal horse Goat Boone had been working on for the past many months.

"You ain't gonna' die anytime soon Rabs, this horse is for my kids."

"You never know, son. Promise me you'll put my name on it."

"I'll put your name on it."

Goat had created the monster horse out of scrap pieces of metal rod he had found on the floor of the shop. It was seven feet tall and weighed three quarters of a ton. The horse was rearing up, its front legs pawing the air. The back legs were attached to a thick metal plate, about four feet long, in such a way that the weight of the horse balanced perfectly against the length and thickness of the base. So perfect was the balance that a small child could sit on the horse's back and push his neck and the horse would rock. Because it was made of many small pieces welded together, the horse had the look of a Van Gogh worked in steel, yet, the musculature and shape were perfect enough to make the real horses in the field next to the plant, neigh and paw the ground. It was indeed a masterpiece.

"I need your help this weekend, Goat. I'm going over to Sylvia's to get my car off the blocks."

Jimmy and Sylvia had broken up a few months back. She had taken their child and car and gone to live with a Mexican Pimp. Since then Jimmy had been dating a legless woman, Sweet Marie, whose gentle nature seemed to soothe his pain but lately he'd taken up with an Indian woman he called Helen Highwater. She was wild. She had the word kiss tattooed to her upper lip. She ran guns and drugs for a motorcycle gang and, according to Jim, made love like a tiger in heat.

"I ain't going over there. And I'll tell you something else; you don't need to be going over there either."

"Gotta' get my car, son."

"Drive that Indian's car like you been doing."

"A man oughta' have his own car."

"You ain't going over there for the car, Rabs."

Jimmy just smiled and walked off.

By quittin' time Rabs had Goat talked into helping him go get his car over the weekend. The next day was Friday. Rabbit came in early and sawed the barrel and stock down on his single shot shotgun. Goat came in late and never heard a thing about that.

As Rusty tells it, on Saturday morning Jimmy woke up and took his shotgun and blasted the walls out of the shack he was renting in the Trinity River Bottoms. He called Goat, but the line was busy. He called Helen and borrowed her truck. He went across the river and bought a case of beer and headed to Leroy's house.

Leroy was another welder from down at the shop. He had a child's heart, a good wife, two kids, and a strong desire to drink beer and watch Mighty Mouse on Saturday mornings.

This morning, he was broke and had resigned himself to just watching Mighty Mouse, when in walked Jim with a case of beer. Late in the afternoon they picked up another case of beer, and Rusty, and headed over to Sylvia's to get Jim's car.

Sylvia stood on the front porch of the duplex, next to the outside stairs that led to the apartment on the second floor. She held two year old "Little Jimmy" in her arms; it was as if she were waiting for Rabbit. As if she knew, beyond all doubt, that he'd be there before dark. When Jimmy pulled up she didn't move. She just stood there, her red hair glowing even redder in the red rays of the setting sun. She looked hot and nervous in her white shorts and red tube top. Jimmy got out and stood beside the truck; Leroy and Rusty were already moving toward the house.

"Your car's out back." She said, and then turned to go back into the house.

Jimmy watched her a moment then turned his head slowly to his left, as if he'd seen something out of the corner of his eye. A dark man was leaning against a tree about ten feet away, smoking a cigarette. Jimmy turned back to his wife; she was about half way through the screen door. He shouted.

"Hey is that the son-of-a-bitch you're with now?"

In a flash, Jimmy had reached under the front seat and pulled out his sawed-off. The dark man ran toward the house. Bam!

Jimmy fired but the dark man was out of range and galloping up the stairs. Jimmy reloaded and slowly closed in. The dark man reappeared at the top of the stairs firing a .38. Jimmy took a shot in the neck, then one in the stomach; he doubled over and fell at the foot of the stairs. Leroy took a shot in the back of the head as he ran toward the truck and fell dead on the dry, yellow lawn. Rusty got hit in the arm as he ducked behind a tree. The tree took two shots and the dark man had to reload. Rusty ran to the truck, jumped in and peeled rubber for three solid blocks, but couldn't leave Rabs behind. When he returned the dark man was stepping slowly down the stairs smiling at Sylvia as he blew the smoke from the barrel of his revolver. As the pimp stepped to the porch Jimmy jumped up and cut him in two with a blast point-blank from his sawed-off. Sylvia screamed, hysterical. Rabbit spun and held out the shotgun for her to see the .38 slug embedded in the stock. He slammed another shell in the chamber and shouted.

"Where's the rest of these motherfuckers?!"

Sylvia knelt down and cradled the head of her fallen lover. She looked up at Jimmy, half crying, half sneering.

"Don't go out back, Jimmy, just leave. Get out of here."

Jimmy just smiled and walked slowly to the rickety wooden gate that led to the backyard.

I couldn't finish reading the last of the chapter; the grim details of Jimmy's death had been seared into my memory at the time it happened. Besides, at this point my eyes were burning and I hurt all over. I had to sleep.

I went into the bathroom and removed my wolfman make-up as best I could, considering my condition, and crawled into my unmade bed. There was a moment, right before I fell into a deep dead sleep, when I thought I felt a presence in the room with me. That's all, just a moment, then silence, then black.

CHAPTER SEVEN

A HOLE IN THE VOID

I BLEW A HOLE in the afternoon with a .38 caliber dream. Its blood soaked my pillow purple and bits of my brain went swimming in the vision-wine, while sunset wrote with shades of brown and electric pink on the wall beside my bed.

I woke up shivering, terrified by things I'd seen with my eyes closed. My tongue was clicking like a cricket in my mouth as my now open eyes danced from what I was sure was blood on my pillow to the dark ghosts jumping out of the sundown shadows. It took a bit to pull myself together. That's not blood, that's wolfman make-up; my mind was working again. There is a strange voodoo in pain, present or remembered, and I was still coming out of its spell.

When the phone rang I ducked. It took a minute or two for me to realize the sound I was hearing was not necessarily life threatening. I crawled out from behind the bed, still shaken, and slowly lifted the receiver to my ear.

"Ah, Professaur you're home at last."

It was Speedster. He always pronounced "Professor" as if it were "dinosaur" because he felt both species had died out a long time ago.

"Speedster, my old friend."

I called him "my old friend" because of his age not the length of our friendship, though I felt, in an odd way, that it was true in both senses.

"You sound like shit! Whatta' you been doing, going to A.A. meetings?"

"Worse, I think a coven of witches are after my ass—I just woke up from a nightmare that left bloodstains in my underwear—and then you call—Things couldn't get much shittier."

"You know better than that, things can always get much shittier."

"What's that? Speedster's Law."

"Right. What's this about witches?"

"I dunno, I think I've uncovered a coven of witches who sell their children's souls to the devil to get even more of the things they sold their own souls to get. Am I making sense?"

"That's an old joke professor."

"What joke?"

"You mean you've never heard the one about the agent who's sitting in the Polo Lounge and the devil walks up to him and buys him a drink?"

"No."

"Well, the devil buys the agent a drink and tells him, 'I can get you Cher, Meryl Streep, Robert DeNiro and Jack Nicholson, all on exclusive contract but I want your soul, your wife's soul and your children's souls.' The agent looks around the bar then turns back to the devil and says, 'Okay, but what's the catch?'"

For some reason the joke seemed hysterical to me. When I'd stopped laughing I told Speedster that I really needed a shower and a cup of coffee before I would be in any kind of shape to discuss the events that had my life so uncharacteristically morbid. He agreed to call back in an hour.

I spent half that time in the shower trying to get Halloween off my body. Images from my dream kept buzzing in and out of my head. First the blackness that was pierced by this strange pinhole of light and the sound of voices chanting—Then a severed arm with a knife in its hand floating down a tunnel of dark clouds toward a candle—Then a circle of naked people wearing strange masks gathered around that candle passing a photograph from my book of Rabbit, Goat and the iron horse, from one to the other, taking turns stabbing the picture with a ceremonial blade. Then Jimmy, in the hot Texas night, with the file through his head, staggering around in his death rage as his attackers laughed and shouted, "Toro, Toro!" and slashed him again and again with their knives. Then the photograph again, being held over the candle and burned. Then Jimmy again, but this time all clean and glowing and smiling with his wounds turned to jewels. He's sitting in the blackness with the pinhole of light behind him. He raises a finger to his lips then touches the pinhole sealing it over and leaving me alone in that silent night.

I was having my third cup of coffee when the Speedster called back. I told him about Paps and Burns Sawyer, Big Ed and Chris Boone, and about my Halloween dream. He listened patiently and made only five or six wisecracks during my whole spiel, which must have been a real record for the Speedster, who usually has a field day with other people's problems. He did let me know right away when I'd finished that he thought everything I'd told him was a crock of shit.

"You've been in Hollywood too long. Your imagination is dying of starvation. Is this the best you can do? This is B movie stuff."

"Yeah, well believe me, I'd love to get out of this town. Are you inviting me to Sag Harbor?"

"Speedster's Law number two: no house guests, sorry. But there is a young actress who's wintering in the neighborhood—all I can do is introduce you, and she won't be back in town here for a month."

"I could be dead in a month."

"Bullshit. You want my advice?"

"I'd rather have the young actress."

"Listen, stay in L.A. Face these fantasies you're having. If you need help there's a friend of mine who teaches at U.C.L.A. who's got a Doctor's degree in this occult stuff. I could turn you on to him; he's a great character, face like an elephant and the mind of a poet. He'll straighten your young ass out. Then, in a month, if you still want to come up, you can rent a room at that motel on the backside of town and I'll introduce you to Sharon. That's the best I can do. But seriously, what are you gonna' do in Sag Harbor, the place is dead in the winter and a tourist trap in the summer."

"Well, I thought I'd sell my car, buy a boat, then sit in that boat with a rod in my hand and a line in the water till my pecker hair turned gray."

Well, Professor, I can tell you from experience, that's a long time to fish without getting a bite."

"Well, sometimes fishing ain't about catching anything."

"True enough, Professor."

I took the name and number of Speedster's friend and hung up. It was already dark outside. Dark. The word was starting to have too many meanings for me. I knew a Mexican restaurant down in Venice where a few dollars still went a long way and where the booths were dimly lit and quiet. I could feel the puzzle coming together in my head, growling like the emptiness in my stomach, demanding to be satisfied.

CHAPTER EIGHT

BACKFIRE

THE DRIVE TO VENICE is easy—just straight down Pico. It was, however, an ugly drive and tonight the fog started getting thick about halfway to Culver City. We called the fog "the fat woman" because in L.A. the air is bad and when it mixes with the sea mist it has that distinct aroma you smell when a fat woman sits down next to you on a bus in the dog days of August. So the fat woman was sitting heavy on the town of Venice, blurring the streetlights and slicking the streets.

Don Pedro's was loud and crowded when I walked in, carrying the armload of papers and photos I had gathered for the night's work. I convinced the waitress to give me a booth in the back and I set my paperwork up on one side and sat down on the other. I ordered the combination plate with extra corn tortilla on the side and a Corona. I also ordered a little cobweb burner shot of tequila to burn out the last of the cobwebs still hanging from the corners of my head, which it did with admirable precision. I was clear as a bell when the food arrived. Good Mexican food was my favorite fuel for thought. Something about the sticky piles of refried beans and yellow rice that brought out the wily Yaqui Indian in my mongrel blood. It was peasant food and peasants endure.

From what I knew of my family tree, the Irish side had been pirates, the Hoodoo Italian side had been magic artists and the Indian side had been Indians. There is a definite strength and grace here, I thought; Indians need no occupational title to establish their identity. I had always felt my lack of occupation was more a part of my sacred heritage than a social stigma. I also realized that the expression "the only good

Indian is a dead Indian" was part of this sacred heritage. I ordered another cobweb burner and moved around to the other side of the table where the pieces of my puzzle lay stacked and ready. I started with the Boone family album I had found among Paps' things.

   —To Nathan, our beloved son, on Christmas 1970.
   From Mommy and Daddy—

I studied the inscription on the opening page. It was curious to me that Paps had somehow wound up with Goat's family album. I took out my pad and pencil and began making notes. As I opened the first pages and looked at the pictures of little Chris Boone in his first sailor suit, I wondered why someone with such obviously loving parents would have a fantasy about being an orphan. I had been a "love child" and had grown up in a series of relatives' homes, so I understood a little of the pain that an orphan suffers. Why such pain would become a fantasy for someone who had such a stable background bothered me, somehow it had to be a big piece of this puzzle. As I turned the page I noticed a change in Chris Boone's face after the arrival of baby Nathan. Chris must have been about five when Nathan was born. He still smiled the same but his eyes were always narrowed and staring at Nathan instead of the camera. Nathan was about one when Nick arrived. The family was now complete and the year was 1946. I ordered another Corona and made a few more notes on my pad.

It was during the middle '50s that Nathan developed his characteristic stoop. He walked as if he were carrying a weight on his shoulders. Chris was fat during this period and was always striking bullyboy poses for the camera. Nick was small and cute with a '50s pompadour that gave him the look of a miniature Ricky Ricardo. Some pictures were missing from the '60s section and the book ended with a shot of Nathan's wedding in 1962. I studied the picture. Here was Goat, skinny, stooped-shouldered, with braces on his teeth holding the hand of his obviously pregnant bride, running down the steps of someone's suburban home under a hail of rice.

It had started to rain. I stared out the window next to my booth at the wet parking lot outside. It took a minute or two for it to dawn on me that I'd driven to Venice with my top down. I jumped up and made a mad dash for the parking lot with the waitress yelling at me in Spanish. A burly man stopped me at the door; he insisted I pay my bill before going to rescue my car. It was poring when I got outside and struggled to put my top up. I looked like a wet mutt by the time I returned to my booth and found it occupied by a young couple munching chips and dip. I asked them if they had the books and papers I'd left on the table. They told me the booth was clean when they sat down. I grabbed my waitress and demanded my stuff. She pretended she didn't know what I was talking about. I freaked out and started shaking her and screaming about how valuable my papers were. That was a big mistake.

The rain had stopped; leaving "the fat woman" with a few extra pounds, when I came to—sprawled across the hood of my car in the empty parking lot. I was sore all over. I sat up and felt for broken bones. Thank God I was a regular customer here; the damage was minimal. I slid off the hood and into the driver's seat before remembering my top had been down during the worst part of the rain. The cold shock of sitting in a puddle about an inch deep caused me to jump and smack my already throbbing head against the metal rod that held my top up. The Speedster was right; things can always get much worse. Maybe it was time to go home.

As I drove through the empty, fog-bound streets, I tried to collect my thoughts, which had been scattered around inside my head by the fists of the bouncers at Don Pedro's. There were things I knew, things I thought I knew, and things I knew I didn't want to think about. Topping the list in the third category—the disappearance of my books and notes, which meant that someone was following me. I knew I didn't want to think about that so I went to category two. I thought I knew the reason for Chris Boone's fantasy about being an orphan. For the first five years of his life he had been an only child. It was my bet that he never forgave his parents for having Nathan and he never forgave Nathan for being born. When he married a famous movie star and moved up the ranks of the rich and powerful, he fulfilled his childhood fantasy by symbolically killing his parents and becoming an orphan. I wondered if Goat had gotten off with a symbolic execution or if perhaps in his case it had taken something more permanent to set the matter straight in Chris Boone's mind.

Paps had been a close friend of the Boone family for a long time and often referred to himself as a 'half-brother." There was a chance that Chris had offered Paps a way to become a "full-brother" at Nathan's expense. The album gave Paps membership in the family.

In the dream I'd had about Rabbit, a photo had been used in the ritual and there were photos missing from the family album. Maybe there was some truth in the old Indian belief that photographs captured the soul of a person. At least there was a possibility that the witches believed this and used photos in their acts of sympathetic magic. If they did believe this, then stealing the photos from me would have been a necessary act. This meant that someone from the coven was following me. I did not want to think about that.

Paps' death may not have been a virgin sacrifice. It could have been Chris Boone tying up a loose end. Paps may have felt it coming and decided to tell me the whole ugly story. He may have even been a member of the coven himself. If this were true, these people were toying with me, letting me discover just enough about them to make me paranoid.

Old Dad had asked me to research the Feast of the Beast. I no longer believed that this was an offer to join their coven. It was an old tradition in the dark arts to fill your victim with fear before executing him. Fear was a dead weight hanging on the soul, which could pull it down into despair and hopelessness and make it impossible to escape the hands of Satan as it departed this world. He wanted me to know what they were planning for me. He wanted to torture me with that knowledge. The puzzle was coming together.

The "fat woman" had wandered up Pico and was sitting on my loft when I got home. I was stiff from the evening's altercation and stumbled as I went down the steps to my door. It did not take me long to pour a double shot of tequila and toss it down. I undressed slowly and bathed my wounds in the kitchen sink. I felt I knew their plan now. I also felt that with that knowledge I could come up with a way to make their plan backfire. I had an ally in this that perhaps they were a little afraid of: the Rabbit's ghost. This ghost had scared the shit out of Chris Boone and had shown me details of the coven's rituals. Perhaps tonight as I slept he would lead me once again through that hold in the void and show me a way out of this trap that was being so carefully laid for me. I no longer feared the dark.

CHAPTER NINE

RICOCHET

R ABBIT WAS NOT COOPERATING, or if he was, I was not aware of it. Sleep that night fell over me like a black blanket—no sights, no sounds, no visions. Right before I woke up though, a tiny quiet dream tiptoed into my head. I was sitting with Ben Franklin in a small antique room while a group of naked women with bags over their heads paraded in front of us. It was a pleasant way to wake up. I was still plenty sore from my bout with the bouncers as I stretched and looked at the clock. Four in the afternoon, down at the beach another day was drowning in the gray Pacific. I decided to gather a little more information about my enemies before the night crawled over the mountains and came after me. I called the Speedster's friend, Doctor Zachary MacDonald, at U.C.L.A. He invited me over after his last class. He had a place off Sunset down below the campus. I agreed on 5:30, even though it meant I'd barely have time for the big three S's before heading down to his place to continue my occult three R's.

I always enjoyed the ride down Sunset during rush hour traffic. There is a wide, tree-lined median strip that divides the two directions of traffic. From the outskirts of Beverly Hills down to the inskirts of Santa Monica, this strip becomes a stage for some sort of jogger's Gong Show. Since the health advantages of an hour of extreme physical exertion while deeply breathing exhaust fumes, was the equivalent of smoking three packs of Turkish donkey dung cigarettes, I concluded that the true motivation for this pageant was the thrill of parading half-naked past the lines of creeping cars. It was the thirst this town has for more and more insipid forms of exhibitionism that kept the wheezing old queens, in their satin shorts, chasing their pretty boy days through the smog and haze up to Beverly Hills and down to Santa Monica. The same was true for the office bimbos out tightening their tummy tucks and fanny lifts in outfits that exposed a flirtatious peek of bosom and cheek. Today's show was a real three star extravaganza. I counted at least four confirmed sightings of real prostitutes; the wigs and flashy make-up are a dead give away but I only confirm the sightings when they actually approached a car. And I saw, God bless America, seven out of town students in string bikinis who thought they had finally discovered the really "in" place to jog.

As I sat in my car and admired the passing parade, the smoggy, hot-orange light of the late afternoon began to burn my tired eyes. I massaged them gently from the apple to the edge. When I opened them I saw my dream girls jogging naked with bags on their heads through the sweet streams of sunset light. I heard sounds now, like singing, but not like singing, human voices just holding a single note. Suddenly the chorus of voices became a chorus of car horns, the spirits vanished and I was left holding up traffic.

I was still a little shaky when I pulled into the good doctor's drive way. I double checked the address then walked up the winding brick path that led to a house which would have been more at home in New England. It was that English manor style with broad wooden beams exposed in the brickwork. I rang the bell, a small man, with the face of an elephant, opened the door and bid me enter.

I followed him to the library where a steaming pot of tea and two cups sat ready on a small table between two Queen Anne chairs. The walls of the room were lined with books packed into dark wood shelves. In the rear of the room was a small marble fireplace, and in the front, a huge dormer window of leaded glass. The floors were a darkened hardwood covered with oriental carpets. It all looked somehow familiar, maybe a scene from an old movie or a painting I'd seen somewhere. The light pouring in from the window made little diamond patterns on the floor, the chairs and the table.

"How can I help you?" The good doctor asked as he poured my tea.

"I need some information about witchcraft."

"I see, what country and time period?"

"Here. Now."

He leaned back in his chair and sipped his tea thoughtfully.

"Are you in trouble?"

"I think there is a coven after me, the Molochians, but I have no proof and I don't know why they'd want to harm me—I don't even know, for sure, that they really exist."

"Oh, they exist alright, and if they are after you, well, then you are in trouble."

I sat there for a moment, fumbling for words as the light outside paled to a tender lavender. The doctor stood up and walked over near the fireplace to a small bookcase with a glass door. He unlocked the door and selected a book. He stood there for a moment, reading to himself then returned to his chair. As he sat down, he handed me the open book.

"The Feast of the Beast," he said, "that's what you've come to see me about, isn't it?"

"Speedster told you?"

"No, he said you were having paranoid delusions and asked me to dispel your fantasies."

"Great introduction."

"It was your mention of the Molochians that gave me the idea. How much do you know about them?"

"Only what I've heard, that they use their own children in their rituals and place a great value on corrupting youth."

"The name is biblical, from the god Moloch, to whom the children of Israel sacrificed their children. They made a great iron statue of the god, which they would heat until red-hot then they placed their infants onto his upturned hands. King Solomon instituted the practice during the last years of his reign to appease his pagan wives. As you know, Solomon is considered the greatest magician that ever lived and is believed to have written down conjurations by which the infernal hosts can be controlled..."

As I sat there listening to him I began to feel dizzy. Then I saw a circle of medicine men from different nations, different time periods. They were standing around a fire chanting, "What is his name?" They all point at me. "Nine Wives is his name." They laugh. Naked women with bags on their heads came sailing through the dormer window on the last beams of twilight. The good doctor turned into Ben Franklin and the room went spinning into darkness.

Out of the darkness came the eerie chant of witches. I saw two tiny hands wrapped around a kitten's neck, squeezing, squeezing, until the fuzzy little creature went limp. Then came the sound of applause. I saw a small boy, naked, smeared with dirt, wearing a Halloween devil mask, triumphantly swinging the dead kitten before a group of naked, masked adults. Now a small and thin, crying baby was placed at the boy's feet and he was handed a dagger. The chanting began again. The boy looked at the baby then suddenly dropped the knife and ran crying to a female member of the group. The chanting stopped. The woman slapped the boy, then turned him back to face the pitiful infant, but the boy refused to pick up the knife.

A young girl, about nine, also masked and naked, stood up from behind the group and shouted, "I'll do it!" She walked around in front, picked up the dagger and turned to the boy. "I want to be a star," she told him defiantly. She then tossed her head, raised the blade and knelt down over the baby. The chant began again. There was a slight moment of hesitation then she plunged the dagger into that tiny heart.

I came to, screaming, in the good doctor's bed. Doctor Zak held my shoulders and calmed me down.

"Relax my friend, you've had an out-of-body experience but it's over now, you're safe."

It took me several minutes to get my bearings, I felt like my soul had been slam dunked back into my body.

"I am quite experienced in these matters, so please relax and when you are ready I want you to tell me everything that you saw."

I took a deep breath and looked around the room. It was small and bare compared to what I'd seen of the rest of the house. It had the look and feel of a monk's cell. Something in his manner made me feel secure enough to talk about the vision. I started babbling about witches and baby killings, sounding a little crazy even to my own trained ears. But the doctor just took it all in. He had me go over certain sections, searching for details. What kind of knife was it? What did the handle look like? Was there an inscription on the blade? Did I recognize any of the participants? Did I recognize the room? I went over and over the vision for over an hour with him. It was strange, I had never had an experience like this before and reliving it over and over was not making it any easier to take. I definitely was not having fun yet.

"Tell me, was there anything strange that happened right before you blacked out?"

"Yeah, right before I passed out I saw a group of medicine men and they called me Nine Wives. Then group of naked women with bags on their heads walked through your dormer window and turned you into Ben Franklin."

"I beg your pardon."

It was time to bring the good doctor up to date on all the bizarre happenings of the past months. I knew this would take some time so I suggested we do it over dinner. The doctor was delighted. In no time we were back down in the library enjoying a lovely dinner of homemade chicken soup, fresh baked bread, apples and cheese. Once again the doctor had me go over certain sections of my story until he was sure he had all the pertinent details. When I had satisfied him completely I waited a beat then asked:

"What's the Rabbit up to?"

"Your dead friend has become your spirit guide and protector. Though I'm not sure why, you are being allowed to view these evil rituals through his intercession. The case of Rudolph Steiner comes to mind. He was allowed to view the black magic rituals of high-ranking Nazis during World War II, in much the same way. He was protected from both the evil energy being generated and the psychic view of the adepts he was observing."

"You think I'm observing actual events?"

"Yes, I also believe you are observing them in different time zones: past, present and future. I think that is the meaning of the medicine men, but Nine Wives I will have to ponder."

"This is all real great but what are the naked women with bags on their heads?"

"Your friend is telling you to fall in love."

"What?"

"Ben Franklin's advice on how to choose a mistress—you put a bag over her head and make love to her. You must have mentioned this to your friend at some time, am I right?"

"I may have...Oh! Wait a minute I did tell him that. After he broke up with his wife and was looking for a new girl. But I still don't get it; shouldn't I be learning some sort of white magic, some sort of counter spell?"

"In my opinion there is no such thing as white magic. All magic is tainted by deception. Evil can only be defeated by good. Love, compassion, kindness, these are the forces that destroy evil. One Mother Teresa is worth a million Merlins."

"Yeah, but Doc, I'm not exactly the Mother Teresa type."

"On the contrary, you have many character traits in common. You have an obvious disdain for money..."

"That's lack of money, Doc, LACK not disdain..."

"Don't quibble. You have an honest mind..."

"Not with girls or government officials—I lie to them al the time; I can't help myself."

"Nonsense...but most of all you have compassion, otherwise your friend would not have returned from the grave to protect you."

"But Doc, this is Hollywood, you can't expect me to fall in love in Hollywood. Can't you just give me a magic charm or incantation or something?"

"Absolutely not; it would be far too dangerous. These are Molochians we are dealing with. As I was about to explain to you before you had your experience, Solomon himself, the greatest magician, was lead astray into this abhorrent practice, deceived by the power of his own magic. We might be able to get away with it once, twice at the most, but in the end the astral disturbances created by the counter-spell could be a grave disadvantage. Your friend is leading you on the correct path. Fall in love and base your attraction on feeling and not on appearance; that is the meaning of the bags. Search for a pure heart, not a pretty face."

I was more confused then ever as I drove back up Sunset. I was uneasy with the prospect of being yanked out of my body at any given moment and shuttled off to view some horrible evil incident. Being compared to Mother Teresa did not sit well with me either; I had too much respect for the woman to be comfortable with the comparison. But the real kicker was this task I'd been given to fall in love with a pure-hearted girl. It was a little too much like Dorothy being asked to steal the wicked witch's broomstick. This was the "Me Generation" after all and I was living in the dark underbelly of "Me Town" and without seducing a nun, I didn't see much hope for this scenario. Driving through Beverly Hills only served to reinforce my conviction that I had been given an insurmountable task. I decided to pay a surprise visit on the Mank, perhaps he had gathered some information by now that would lead me out of this ever-encircling labyrinth. I had bounced like a speeding bullet off the solid wall of the unknown and was spinning out in a direction far away from my intended course.

CHAPTER TEN

ENTER THE TEA BAGS

"DOOR'S OPEN, come on in!'
Mank's voice called out from behind the ornate, dark
wood door of his Hollywood Spanish style apartment. Mank was
on the phone, standing in the kitchen by the stove, boiling water in a
dirty pot. He motioned me to sit down at the kitchen table and kept
on talking.

"Yeah, well cancel that last remark, I have, repeat, have, a date for
your friend...Yeah...No...he just walked in, I've been trying to reach
him all afternoon...Yeah...he's really a cool guy..."

Mank looked straight at me and made a silly face.

"Right, well, we will meet you girls there...in an hour—hour and a
half...No, it's not Solesy, it's somebody you've never met...Okay...Fine.
Bye."

Mank hung up the phone and busted out laughing.

"Boy, are you in luck tonight."

Funny, I don't feel lucky."

He picked up the pot of boiling water up off of the stove and began
pouring it into a waiting drip down coffee pot: the kind with the plastic
funnel on top and the filters shaped like little dunce caps.

"The tea bags are in town."

He waited for the first dose of hot water to settle the black grounds
around the sides of the little dunce cap, which at this point I felt matched
the one on my head.

"Who are the Tea Bags?"

"Those English girls Solesy and I are always talking about, you
know. Remember a couple of months back I was telling you about

them, Tiffany and T.Z., decadent English aristocrats. They are in town for a couple of weeks starting tonight."

He poured the rest of the hot water into the little funnel then went to the cupboard and dug out a couple of almost fresh cups.

"We're meeting them tonight at the roller rink for an evening of fun and excitement."

"We are?"

"Come on, you heard me on the phone. What's the matter? -- If it's money, I got fifty to start you with."

"No thanks, I'm—I'm—this witchcraft thing I've been into has got me totally freaked out. I haven't slept right since it started. I think somebody's following me—Really I just came over to see if you'd been able to dig up some information that might put my mind at ease or at least give me a handle on this situation."

Mank poured us both a cup of coffee and sat down at the table.

"Here, drink this...No, Wait!"

He reached under a pile of clothes beside his chair and produced a half empty pint of decent brandy. In one elegant move, he spun the cap off, sending it rattling across the table and splashed a bracer in both our cups.

"To the Tea Bags!"

I wearily clinked his cup and took a sip; it was tasty.

"No real gossip lately, the town's too quiet, hasn't been this quiet since Sal Mineo died. Nothing but 'Poor Dear' gossip, you know, 'Poor Dear so-and-so', that kind of stuff. But if you asked me, you're barking up the wrong tree with Sawyer and Boone. Sawyer's got no real black magic clout, in fact, he's known as a neophyte in the devil business. He probably really does need your information to keep from looking stupid if he's really been invited into a heavy coven, which I doubt. Chris Boone's old lady's been putting the screws into him. They've separated and he won't be allowed to see his kid until he is a member in good standing of her pseudo-church. There is a lot of Poor Dear Chris gossip going around. Poor dear Catholic boy holding tin cans hooked up to a lie detector, telling his story to some brainwashed bozo. Did you know he spent a year in a Jesuit seminary outside New Orleans?"

"Really? My grandfather used to run a shrimp boat out of New Orleans. I used to go back there during the summer when I was a kid."

"I thought you were from Texas."

"Well, I grew up in Texas. See my mom fell in love with this young French-Indian swamp boy. His family had an Italian last name and folks said they was Gris-Gris people. Anyway they was just teenagers. They'd been going together about six months when the boy disappeared. His dad shows up and gives my mom this strange Creole style painting of Mary Magdalene. He says it's for protection of the child. Some how he knew she was knocked up before she did. Anyhow folks started talking, saying I was gonna' be a Hoodoo baby. So my Irish grandpa sent her up to Dallas to be with my Mexican grandma's family to birth me."

"Hoodoo child, huh?"

" Well folks is funny about that shit back in the swamps."

"Sad story, man."

"Right, I feel like I ought to be holding a pair of tin cans hooked up to a lie detector."

"So you've never met your Dad?"

"No, just the painting of Mary Magdalene his father had done. I used to stare at the signature—Hugues Plantard de Rocca—and try to imagine what my granddad looked like with a name like Hugues."

"Sounds more French than Italian."

"I think he was both."

"Anyway, Boone's got his balls in a vise, so I don't think he's got time to voodoo anybody."

"What about Big Ed the producer?"

"He's out of town, so that's the news, one bid blank."

"I can't believe it, I mean, all of these strange things have been happening to me lately..."

"Hey. You're a really strange guy—Oh! I did find these two little things for you."

He stirred the pile of papers and record albums on the table and came up with two odd-looking envelopes. He opened the first one and handed me a cheaply printed, ten page list of personal ads under the bold print title, "SCAT'N CATS A. I. NEWSLETTER."

"You mentioned the excrement fetish: this is the excrement fetish Bible; got it from a friend in the hardcore business down town. He tells me it's got a mailing list of about half a million in L.A. alone and it runs over a thousand ads a month."

"Ads for what?"

"For people with excrement fetishes. Look, see it's all in code. Cigar smoking—that means turd-sucking...Ah, here—a raunch pig. That's somebody that likes to roll around in the stuff."

"I think I'm getting sick. I ask for occult information and you give me this stuff."

"Hey, look at the numbers: 500,000 in L.A. hardcore enough to subscribe. So how many occasional "cigar smokers" do you think are out there? What I'm trying to say is maybe the things Paps described in that letter have more to do with bad toilet training than devils and demons. Here, put it in your pocket; maybe it'll lighten your perspective on this whole thing."

"What's in the other envelope, something just as nice?"

"Right again, Professor.'

He handed me a couple of Xerox pages with photos of some Incan figurines. In one photo was a statue of a man with eyes as wide as saucers stroking a prick that came damn near to his chin. In the others two saucer-eyed guys were frozen in the act of anal intercourse.

"Looks like Santa Monica Boulevard at four in the morning."

"Actually, these are depictions of royal coca religious ceremonies. Going to church, for the Lord High Inca and his court was slapping a wad of chewed coca leaf on your cock or poking it up your buddies butt."

"Mank, my life is in danger and you're giving me scat cats and coke pokers."

"Only trying to help. Drink up; it's almost time to go. Oh, by the way, the first country to exceed Peru in coca consumption was Nazi Germany."

"I'm going home. I feel depressed."

"How long has it been since you got laid?"

"What?"

"How long?"

"I don't know, two months maybe."

"No wonder you're depressed."

"But I'm telling you, things have been happening to me…"

"Tell me tomorrow, after you've had a night with T.Z. Look it's 10:35 B.T.Z., before T.Z. Talk to me tomorrow at 10:35 A.T.Z. All right? I gotta pee then we are outta here. Deal?"

I didn't say any thing, Mank just grinned and disappeared into the bathroom. I stood up and stretched. The good doctor had told me to fall in love. Maybe Mank was right; maybe this was my chance. As I pulled my arms up straight over my head, I felt a warm glow run down my spine, like I'd just dropped a fifty-pound backpack. It was strange. For the first time in a long time I felt good.

CHAPTER ELEVEN

LITTLE WHEELS

THE ROLLER RINK WAS ON HIGHLAND about a block down from the Strip. It had been a sleazy bowling alley before disco roller-skating became the thing to do. Tonight a small line waited under the neon awning, totally at the mercy of the doorman. Mank just nodded to the guy as we brushed past the line and entered.

Inside, the place was all decked out like an extra in an old Xaiver Cugat movie—all plastic fruits and paper palms, so 1930's, soooo Rio. It was a weeknight so the crowd was light, hardcore, no big stars, just people dressed like stars. The rink was as large as the ten bowling lanes it had replaced. The music was ungodly loud but not loud enough to drown out the roar of the thousands of little wheels whirling in endless circles over the hardwood. Mank and I walked over to the railing at the edge of the rink and eyed the skaters, searching for the Tea Bags. It amazed me that this form of recreation and become fashionable again.

In the Fifties, I'd gotten my first sight of a teenage girl in nothing but her panties at a roller rink. It was one of those bizarre accidents that seem to tilt one's sexual tastes for life. I was there for an altar boy outing; I must have been all of eight years old. We'd been skating for hours. There was a young girl there, hired by the management I guess, who wore a little red skating skirt and a little white blouse tied up under her bosom. All at once, there was a terrible collision, and the little skating girl was in the middle of it. The hands that tried to catch her as she fell only succeeded in tearing her top off, and when she hit the ground, another skater actually rolled right over her bottom, tearing her skirt off. Everyone in the place came to a dead stop and watched the little skating girl, red-faced and teary-eyed, struggle to her feet and skate, arms folded across her bare breasts, to the girl's bathroom. Mank nudged me out of my reverie and pointed out to the rink.

"The Tea Bags."

Two girls were skating towards us waving their arms. One was a blond hardbody, flashy, decked out in black spandex and silver chains, but the other was something I hadn't expected. She was a soft looking brunette in a long full denim dress and a yellow flannel cowboy shirt with cute little cowboys riding rocking horses printed all over it. Her hair was long and curly; she had the face and full body of a big kid and skated with her arms and legs kina stiff, like a little girl. She skated right up to me. As her freckles and smile disarmed me, her cool-gray eyes held a shotgun on my heart.

"Professor, this is T.Z."

She held her hand out to me and I took it.

"My pleasure."

"Do you skate?"

I do not skate: I find it makes my butt sore. No one seemed to mind that I held the table because the waitresses here were a little over-conscientious and had a nasty habit of removing your half finished drink and giving your table to someone else the moment you left to skate. So, I sat at our table near the rail and toasted my companions as they whizzed past. T.Z. had the cutest way of waving, as she'd roll by, lifting her arm slightly and going a little off balance. Christ, the only thing worse that falling in love with a girl was getting a schoolboy crush on one. Perhaps it was psychological baggage of that alter boy picnic but I felt so clumsy, so silly, so overwhelmed. I had been expecting some rich bitch, who would look down her prefabricated nose at me, not this lovely, awkward creature who giggled and blushed. If it were all just an act I was definitely falling for it. From time to time she would scoot off the rink, skate over to the table and sit with me, her sweat sparkling on her cheeks like dew on a flower. We'd try and shout a conversation out above the din of the music and skaters but would always end up laughing at our inability to communicate. Then, one of her favorite songs would come on and off she'd go again. It may sound boring but it wasn't.

I'd spent most of my dating time in L.A. being not "the right career move" for the girls I'd meet. It seems nobody just comes to L.A.; they're all here for a purpose. With so much to do and so little time, dating must also serve that purpose. So, aside from a few girls, who informed me later that they were "just slumming," my social life consisted of getting drunk at parties I had not been invited to attend. I was able, from time to time, to walk off with the waitress from a large catered affair or seduce a Polish journalist at a small literary function, but as for seeing the same girl every week on a regular basis, that was way out of the question once I answered the question—"What do you do for a living?"

I had discovered a strange pattern in all this, a definite sexual cycle for singles in career towns. I also felt it was only a matter of time before the Russians discovered this cycle and leaked it to the tabloids. It seemed I could go for about two months without attracting the attention of a single female then suddenly I'd get hit on by five or six girls, one right after the other. That would last about a month then boom—another dry spell. I tried to correlate this pattern with astrological movements, weather reports, air quality, and seasonal changes. Nothing worked. Finally, I noticed that after two months without sex I was so horny I couldn't see straight. I concluded there was a distinct possibility the same was true for members of the, currently, "almost opposite" sex. Long periods of self-denial left both sexes so blind they would actually bump into each other and couple without considering the financial advantages of the action. I'd also determined that the sex organs themselves had developed radar-like devices that homed in on other organs pulsing at the same rate; this kept those that still had their eyes on standard business procedures from committing indiscretions with those that just wanted to get laid.

I was about to drown in my own reflections when Mank skated up with T.Z., Tiffany, and two Valley Girls in tow. I was introduced to Candy and Donna, Tiffany's friends. We were invited to "this great party at this wild party house up in the hills not far from here." The story was this: the house was owned by this guy with the odd handle of ByeCharlie. He was a Viet Nam vet who'd gotten shot up in the war then sewn back together wrong. He'd sued the government and won a half a mil' cash settlement plus twenty-five hundred a month for the rest of his life, which unfortunately was not going to be a long time because, like I say, he'd been sewn back together wrong. So, ByeCharlie bought a nice house with a pool in the hills and he had a constant party going for the past six months.

"He's like kinda' messed up and can't really do much himself, but watching other people have fun really gets him off."

For some reason this sounded like fun to Tiffany, which obligated the rest of us to go along. Candy and Donna wanted to skate "for at least another hour" and "work up a good sweat" before diving naked into ByeCharlie's pool.

The Vals skated off and Mank took Tiffany to the bar, which left T.Z. and I alone smiling at each other. She moved close so we could scream in each other's ears. We were still unable to communicate. I suggested we move to another table as far away from the rink as possible; she suggested we sit outside on the steps while we waited. That sounded even better. T.Z. went to turn her skates in and I went to the bar to tell Mank where we'd be.

"The steps are filthy, man, why don't you guys wait in your car. We won't forget you."

It was quiet and cool as we walked out into the night. We held hands on our way to the car, which was parked in the lot behind the roller rink. We got in and, it was funny, just sitting there with her was enough. I couldn't think of any thing to say. She just kept smiling, looking at me.

I could hear the bass line of the disco song playing in the roller rink and the muffled roar of all those little wheels when she leaned over and kissed me.

CHAPTER TWELVE

BYE CHARLIE'S AND BEYOND

W E HAD ALMOST SETTLED into a longing embrace when Mank and the other girls pulled up and honked.
"Follow us."

"Do we have to?"

Tiffany hung her head out the window and gave me a dirty look.

"Come on, it'll be fun!"

I was already having plenty of fun but I started my car anyway and wheeled out into the street after Mank and the gang.

ByeCharlie was defiantly not sewn back together properly. He made a sad sight in his Hawaiian print baggies welcoming us into his party with his good hand. T.Z. and I only stayed long enough to smoke a couple of shots of tequila and watch Candy and Donna put on a nude synchronized swimming display.

"Watch this—our impression of baby porpoises!"

Candy counted to three then she and Donna did a shallow surface dive together. As their round little bottoms broke the surface of the water they spread their legs slightly and squirted a short stream of water into the air out of their pussies. They continued bobbing and spurting in near perfect synch the entire length of the pool looking indeed like baby porpoises wearing toupees on their blowholes. I figured the party could only go downhill from there so I asked T.Z. if she was ready to go. Anxious to go was closer to how she felt. I called my answering machine on the way out. Two calls had come in: one, from Doctor Zak asking me to call him in the morning, the other from Burns Sawyer offering me five hundred dollars cash for information. Somehow Burns' call had screwed up my machine, which just kept repeating the five hundred dollar offer over and over. I took that as a sign.

T.Z. was staying at a friend's house on a dark side street off Laurel Canyon Boulevard, up from the Canyon Country Store. We pulled up under a large avocado tree near the curb at the base of the steps that led up to the house. There were still lights on. The ivy hanging from the tree and the other dense foliage that surrounded the house and spilled down the little hillside to the street gave it a cozy sequestered look. I started to get out of the car but T.Z. held me back. She took my face in her tiny aristocratic hands and slowly, passionately kissed me. She then one by one unbuttoned the buttons of her adorable little cowboy shirt and revealed her adorable little breasts. My mind turned to putty. All I could think of were those hot letters in the soft porn mags that begin, "you're not going to believe this." I leaned over to touch her and jabbed the gearshift into my lower abdomen. I fell back into my seat. T.Z. giggled.

"You need a bigger car," she said in her delightful English accent as she leaned over, unzipped my jeans and exposed my biblical nakedness to the pale blue moonlight.

"Oh my, you don't need a bigger one of these."

Before I could think over a clever retort she took my prize deep into her mouth. I caressed her hair, gently moving those lovely curls away from her cheek. The sight of her child-like face doing what she was doing almost brought me to tears. I'd really wanted my schoolboy crush to last but it was too late, we'd graduated. This was adult.

Later that night, upstairs in her room, I kissed her naked body again and again. Her breasts and nipples, belly and thighs, her lips, her lips, her hair, her eyes, her fingertips, her feet and toes; she had become a treasured gift. A creature to be reverenced with light kisses. A reliquary, which held the magic shard of a saint with the power to heal those who believed. She was this to me that night and more, pretty as laughter, dear as pain. I pried open my heart and emptied into those touches every feeling I could find there. We did not stop for hours. She knew me that night, yes, she knew all about me in the way only a woman can know a man. Even though at times my eyes were closed,

I could see her watching me, recognizing all the meanings in those small expressions that cross a man's face as his seed pours out. I felt she'd peeled the flesh away, bored right through the bone and handled with her hands the very stuff of me. What a fuckin' night.

The next morning she got up before I did. I caught her drinking coffee and going through my pockets.

"What's this?"

Her voice was music.

"What's what?"

"This Scat n' Cats Newsletter."

"Oh, nothing, just some research Mank dug up for me."

"Really—what's a raunch pig?"

"That's a guy that makes horror films. You got a phone I can use?"

I called Old Dad and told him I had some valuable information for him. I also made him crinkle the five $100 bills into the phone to make sure he had the money. I told him to put it in an envelope and I'd be right over to pick it up. He asked what I had for him and I told him I had procured, at great expense, a copy of a secret newsletter that only high-ranking Satanic cult members knew how to get a hold of. I also warned him it was all in code but that I'd explain a few of the terms. I told him it listed various practices a activities of cults across the country and that just having it around his house would make him very hip to his witch friends. He got excited and told me to hurry right over. I told him I was bringing someone with me who shouldn't know anything about this; so, we'd have to do the exchange as quickly and secretly as possible. I also told him I was getting a detailed description or the Feast itself from a very heavy source and would be in touch soon.

I was in and out of Old Dad's in a flash. I explained that Scat n' Cats A I was an anagram for Satanic Acts and that cigar smoking referred to a witch's concoction of pot, coca leaves, belladonna and other drugs rolled in a tobacco leaf and sealed with human blood.

"It's a big part of their rituals, if you want to look hip just flash the newsletter and say you're really into cigar smoking."

He happily gave me the money and took the newsletter up to the sanctuary. I could hear him practicing the cigar smoking line on his way up the stairs.

I took T.Z. out to breakfast at the Tropicana on Santa Monica. Every now and then the thought of Old Dad at some fancy dinner party, leaning over to his Satanic host, opening his jacket just a bit to reveal the newsletter in his inside coat pocket and saying with practiced dignity, "I'm really into cigar smoking," would send me into spasms of laughter.

When we got back to her place I put a call into Doctor Zak. He seemed very serious and concerned.

"I must see you right away."

"I'll come over."

"No, not here. Meet me in Santa Monica on the promenade that overlooks the pier. And come alone."

I felt cold as I hung up the phone. T.Z. noticed my change of mood and came over to me. She put her arms around me and hugged me so close. I told her I had to go out for a while but that I'd come back and take her out for dinner.

"Don't be silly, we'll have dinner here. What'd you think I can't cook?"

We kissed goodbye like lovers being separated by a war. A scared, desperate kiss full of both longing and foreboding, the kind you have to tear yourself away from, the kind that doesn't want to end.

CHAPTER THIRTEEN

NAMES

I COULDN'T FIND HIM. I walked the promenade from the pier to the far end without a trace of the good doctor. The promenade was quiet today, flower- pretty in the afternoon. It bordered the tall cliffs that looked out over the Pacific Coast Highway, the beach and the great sea beyond. It's winding paths circle ancient poinsettias and grand eucalyptus trees. Stone gazebos edged with flowers and shrubs, wide stretches of cool green grass, shaded by tall palms and evergreens, beckoned the elderly and mommies with kids out in the afternoon, still warm enough in November for light sweaters and shirt sleeves. For some reason, very few teenagers and swingles found the park attractive and only the most brazen bums and winos lounged on its benches or begged from its steps. The centerpiece of the park was a stone grotto with a statue of Saint Monica in it. She faces the condos and expensive hotels across the street, her back to the sea. I was looking into her tired stone eyes when I felt a hand on my shoulder.

"I hope that I haven't kept you waiting."

The ease with which he'd been able to sneak up on me made me feel particularly vulnerable. We walked over to a quiet bench with an ocean view and sat down to talk.

"I'm afraid I've done something that may have put us both in danger."

He looked away from me and off into the empty sky.

"After you left last night, I performed a conjuration to counter the forces being directed at you."

"But you said...."

"I know what I said, and I was right, but I felt your desperation so strongly—I had to do something. Tell me, did you feel any spiritual relief around 10:30 last night?"

"Around 10:35 B.T.Z. I felt enormous relief, like a huge burden had been lifted."

"B.T.Z.?"

"Before T.Z. T.Z.'s a girl I met last night."

He arched his eyebrows just slightly and cocked his head toward me then looked back at the sky.

"I see. Then it worked—good. You are safe for the time being, but do not go home for the next few days. The spell has cloaked you from the powers that are pursuing you but they will be buzzing around your house trying to locate you again. Yes, you are protected, at least until I complete the second part of the ritual, then they may come after me."

"And if you complete this second part undetected?"

"Then we're both safe for quite awhile provided we live with compassion and charity. As for them, they will be thrown into utter confusion."

"And who are they?"

"That's what disturbs me. You said the Molochians were after you and yet I didn't sense them at all. I sensed another force, more ancient, more powerful. Something absolutely dedicated to your destruction— a force coming across centuries of time. Tell me, do you have any knowledge of your family heritage?"

"My mother was half-Mexican half-Irish. I never knew my father, he left before I was born."

"What are your parents names?"

"Hugues Plantard de Rocca was my grandfather's name and my mother was Maria O'Malley."

He wrote the names down in a little leather bound notebook.

"You say you never met your father; how do you know his father's name?"

"From a painting of Mary Magdalene he did for my mother. He said it was for my protection."

"Mary Magdalene, interesting. Why is it you don't use either of your family names?"

"To avoid embarrassing my mother I was given my uncle's name and we pretended I was her cousin. She was only fifteen when she had me; she died by the time I was four. They didn't tell me the true story of my life 'til I was twenty-one. So I dropped out of college I started using nicknames. Since I've been out here I haven't had a job that requires a real name; I work on a cash only basis for 'geniuses' too lazy or too 'busy' to find out what they're supposed to already know. The Professor title was hung on me out here, it stuck, so I don't use anything else."

My voice trailed off at the end. Talking about my past made me feel stupid and alone. I stared out over the rail at the sky and sea. On the beach below, a bum was trying to panhandle a couple of joggers. Another nameless Joe with his hand out trying to stall oblivion. The good doctor respected my silence but when he saw I was sinking too deep he cleared his throat a bit and spoke.

"Did you know Ben Franklin had a friend who was only known as 'The Professor'? An interesting bit of history—it seems that this man helped Washington, Franklin and five others, design the flag for the new nation. He also predicted that the flag, once accepted, would need little or no alteration when America achieved her independence. History records no other name for this man than 'the Professor.'"

I turned from the sea to face him. He smiled at me as if he had told me a deep secret about myself. I smiled back, as if I understood.

"You know a lot about history, huh, Doc?"

"I know a lot about Masonic history and the great part metaphysical knowledge has played in the discovery and formation of this wonderful country that we live in."

"Well, Doc, the way I see it, this country stopped being wonderful a long time ago."

"Nonsense, you're just being cynical, a pose which, by the way, does not suit the great golden light you carry around in that tired soul of yours. You must fight to hang onto that light. Washington had a vision at Valley Forge of the three great conflicts that this nation would endure. The first was the revolution, the second was the Civil War and the third is the conflict we are going through right now, and you are dead set in the middle of it. It is an attempt of the forces of darkness to take control of the very spirit of this country. The Satanic powers which seek your destruction are chasing down every free soul in this nation and somehow, I don't know how or why, you are very important in this battle. It's as if once they have done away with you the rest will be easy."

"Thanks Doc, that's just what I needed to hear—the fate of the country hangs on my shoulders. Christ, I can't even make a living."

"Perhaps I have said too much. But, soon I will have the answers to these questions. When the pieces of this puzzle snap together the knowledge will flip a switch in you. It will be your Excalibur. You'll see."

He patted my knee in a grandfatherly gesture of encouragement.

"For the time being, just lay low and I will work all of this out. Call me in three days time. Have no fear, the forces that protect you are much stronger than those that attack you."

He patted my knee again, then hopped up and strolled off without so much as a backward glance.

CHAPTER FOURTEEN

THE HIDEOUT

THE GOOD DOCTOR'S ADVICE was a lot easier to follow than his train of thought. I really needed no encouragement to spend the next three days at T.Z.'s place—fortunately neither did T.Z. She had her special spaghetti dinner waiting for me by the time I got back. She told me we were having dinner in bed, so we clattered up the stairs with trays of salad, antipasto, sauce, noodles, and a bottle of rich Chianti.

Her room was a sixties time capsule, an attic room that the owners hadn't really used for the past ten years. Its last occupants were actual hippies; despite the time elapsed, it looked as if they had just moved out. There was the mattress on the floor, the Indian paisley hanging from the pitched ceiling, the little crystal rainbow makers hanging in the room's one large window, and even a couple of psychedelic posters on the backs of the room's two doors. The bookshelves, which ran around the window, were stuffed with books on magic, astrology, and the Tarot as well as a few spaced-out comics and a couple of old Earth Mother News. "Today is the first day of the rest of your life!" was written with the scent of patchouli on the air of this room. Beneath the window was a small desk of white painted wood with drawers down one side. We sat the trays on the desk and opened the wine.

"Why doesn't the guy who owns this place fix up this room?"

"Oh, this room is very special to Charles, he's gone to a lot of trouble to keep it just as it is. I'm one of the few people he'll even let stay up here."

She undressed as she spoke.

He comes up here once in awhile to meditate. He found a couple ounces of weed in the rafters up there after he bought the house in the early Seventies, so he sat down at that desk there and rolled a joint. He told me that he felt so peaceful sitting here smoking real ten-dollar-an-ounce weed that he decided never to change this room. He spent a lot of money buying those original Sixties posters and books and stuff."

She was completely naked now as she set our dinner plates, silverware and napkins on the floor.

"Get undressed while I light the candles."

We ate in the nude then licked the dribbled sauce from each other's face and body. We made slow love that night, talking between caresses about things we'd done and places like New Mexico and Ireland. We did not pry but rather we floated through each other's pasts, snatching moments of emerald and magic turquoise from the stream of time: still, clear moments to be held in the palm of the hand and shared with a touch, and with a touch returned and tucked away, between the kisses and candlelight.

The next three days melted together like butter on hot pancakes. Without realizing it I was falling back into the whole routine of cohabitation. I was shopping again for things that didn't come in a can. I watched sitcoms and laughed when I was supposed to. I caught myself having brunch and actually calling it that. The steady and seemingly endless supply of sex, food and affection had lullabied all sense of danger, put the warning lights out and tucked my brain in for a long sleep. I'd almost forgotten to call Doctor Zak until I felt this tingling sensation in my head. It was the same kind of funny tingling you get when your foot falls asleep. I was watching the local six o'clock news—a full half hour of human misery, narrated by dead brain cells dressed in corpse clothes with cartoon perfect hairdos. Sports and weather coming up next; don't go away. Tingle-tingle. I was watching the news! Tingle-tingle. My brain was waking up. I never watch the news! If it's not in the tabloids, it didn't really happen. Suddenly, all of the madness of the past six months came rushing back into my consciousness. It was time to call the doctor.

Doctor Zak was in a cheerful mood, which surprised me. I hadn't seen this side of him before.

"I've found the answer. It was so simple really, staring me right in the face the whole time."

"What was?"

"Your name."

"You mean 'the Professor?'"

"No, no. Plantard and the Magdalene, it all makes perfect sense—Ormus, Godfroi de Bouillon, the Sangrael—What do you know of the Magdalene."

"Lotta legends, little history."

"The story of the Magdalene, like everything related to the Christ is to be found in prophecy. The story of the Magdalene is the Psalm of Psalms and Chapter Twelve of Revelations. They think you're Sangrael but you are Nine Wives Tecumseh. Perfect sense you understand."

"Sorry Doc, your perfect sense means nothing to my imperfect mind."

"Oh, yes, yes, of course not yet, but it will. Can you come to my house on Saturday? I'll explain everything."

"What time?"

"Early evening, about seven, and please don't go anywhere until then; it's very important."

The good doctor had started me thinking again. Unfortunately there is something about the sight of a man sitting in his chair and staring off into the recesses of his mind that women find intensely irritating. By dinner time I had been accused of "spacing out", "ignoring her", "being wrapped up in myself" and, as a direct shot to the heart, "being boring." I tried to explain, which of course started an argument. She stormed out, leaving me alone with the dishes and my thoughts.

Doc had tantalized me with a few strange names. At the moment, I was able to place only two—Tecumseh and Sangrael. Tecumseh was a Native American mystic leader. His brother, known as The Prophet, put a curse on the U.S. government after the Battle of Tippecanoe. Every President elected in a year ending in zero dies in office. I had learned this during the aftermath of the J.F.K. murder. The Sangrael or San Grael was the Holy Grail. How it was tied to the other names I couldn't figure out and what he meant by Plantard being the key was equally mystifying. One of the odd pieces of information I had about the Grail was that Hitler had spent more money trying to locate the Holy Grail that he spent on rocket research. Perhaps it was being sought again for the great Feast of the Beast. But what did I know about the Grail that could possibly be worth my life? I needed to clear up a few things in my head first to make room for this new puzzle.

Number One: Where was the Rabbit?

It was odd, but from the moment I had counted him as my major ally in this situation, his messages had become more vague, terrifying and sporadic. Since the experience at Doctor Zak's place, which was almost five days ago, he hadn't come at all. In a way I was glad he had not made my love affair with T.Z. a ménage-a-trois, however, most of the information he had given me had now been contradicted by my other sources. It just didn't add up. He had pointed me toward Chris Boone; Mank had pointed me away from Chris. He had shown me the Molochians, but the good doctor now insisted they were not the ones who were after me. If he had come back from the grave to become my guide why would he lead me around in circles and then disappear?

Number Two: Chris Boone.

Going by Mank's story, the events of Halloween night were brought about by a combination of the stress he was under, the guilt dredged up by those brainwashing sessions and whatever was really in those "vitamin shots" his wife's accountant was giving him. Logically it made sense and if the Rabbit had not illogically visited me the following night I would have been inclined to accept this version. What the whole truth was about Chris, at this point in time, I didn't know.

Number Three: Burns Sawyer handed me money

Number Four: Was someone still following me?

Number Five: When was T.Z. coming back?

I had just about put myself to sleep blowing up this brain bubble in my mind when T.Z. returned. We had the necessary fight and reconciliation, the violent stealing pleasure from pain. We made deep, angry love and I forgot the puzzle, its pieces scattered like soldiers on a battleground. Until, while falling asleep in sheets our tangled fury had twisted like wires around us, I saw a light flicker in the window against the new dark night.

A cold hand grabbed my hair in the middle of the night and yanked me right out of my body. It was the Rabbit, with fire flesh and jewel wounds. He slammed my soul against the wall and pointed to the window, which opened like the mouth of a great beast and roared. Inside the mouth a vision played. A hooded figure stood before a wall of flame, his dagger raised above an unseen victim, and shouted in a strange slow-motion roar that echoed the roar of the window-mouth and pierced the ears of my soul. He slashed the heart from his victim, tore off a hunk of it with his teeth and spit it back into the victim's face. He roared again and held aloft his bloody blade and the torn heart. I turned my eyes from the vision to the Rabbit's face, his eyebrows arched as if to say, "are you ready for this guy?" He stared into my face then slowly shook his head no, his mouth curling slightly. He pointed to the mattress on the floor where my body lay, tangled no longer with sheets and a lover, but now with a nest of serpents. He struck the back of my head and sent my soul falling toward my body, falling toward the snakes. It seemed I could feel them before I touched them, feel the cold scales sliding over my back and embracing my neck.

CHAPTER FIFTEEN

IN ARCADIA EGO

I SNAPPED AWAKE, clawing at the dream coils around my neck only to find myself holding the eyeball end of a long peacock plume instead of a snake. At the other end of the plume was a strange, thin man, with a balding crown and a trimmed mustache, dressed in a gold and black Chinese dragon gown and Turkish, red velvet slippers. He sat on a small chair next to the bed, smiling down at me.

"You can let go of my feather now."

I released the plume and tried to shake the confusion from my still spinning head. T.Z. opened one eye at the sound of his voice then smiled to herself as she closed it again.

"Good morning, Chuck."

She purred and stretched as she rolled over, sliding her back against my chest, concealing me as she exposed herself.

"Chuck, this is my lover...."

"His position is clear; I'm the one that need explaining."

"She giggled as if embarrassed by forgetting to follow some aristocratic protocol.

"Of course, Chuck's the guy I was telling you about, the one who owns this place, the one who wasn't supposed to be back in town for another week."

"I'm sorry to have startled you but I came up to wake T.Z. for breakfast not knowing she was..." He swayed his peacock plume like a scepter as he searched for a dignified word then dipped it to tickle the nipple of her exposed breast. "...occupied. Yes, that's the word."

Her nipple stiffened to the teasing of the feather. She purred again and cuddled back into me, playfully batting the feather away.

"Occupied. Right. For Christ's sake Chuck, do I need to put a sign on the door?!"

The feather returned, this time tickling its way down her belly.

"Oh you're cross with me, and I thought I'd devised such a quiet way of awakening you."

I grabbed the intruding feather but missed. He had been expecting my reaction.

"Leave her alone."

"Ooooh, Macho-Macho...." The plume became his scepter again. "I have this theory that macho men make love to women as if they were making love to another man. The characteristics of dominance display, lack of finesse, and speed of completion have their social back up systems only in jail, mortal combat or athletic contests. It's a wrestling technique, seizing a physical advantage, pinning the opponent for a three count then jumping up with a hand raised in victory."

He gestured at me dramatically with his feather. T.Z., who'd been giggling through his little speech, suddenly sprang like a cat and snatched his feather away. She sat up now, adopting a regal attitude of her own, swaying the feather in front of his nose.

"You've been a naughty boy again Chuckie, fantasizing about men making love to other men."

"Touche. Well, if there's nothing more I can do for you."

He stood up to leave, a slightly hurt expression on his face.

"Breakfast will be served in one hour."

He turned and walked slowly toward the door.

"Oh, just a minute."

T.Z. hopped up and skipped to his side. With her hand on his arm, she leaned to his ear and whispered.

"Books?"

He turned back to face me.

"There's a copy of Eschenbach's Parzival in the bookshelf there and I believe I have some other books downstairs on the subject of the Sangrael."

T.Z. kissed him lightly on the cheek and handed him back his feather. He flourished his plume in my direction.

"Be careful Sir Knight, me thinks your lady has a checkered past. And when Romance flies in the window, Caution often exits by the door."

I had to admire his stagecraft but after last night's vision the thought of anything flying in that window was deeply disturbing. T.Z. returned to my side on the bed.

"How did you know I wanted books?"

"Men can't think without reading," she said, pushing me flat on my back and straddling my stomach. She leaned over me all smiles, soft curls and warm breasts. "You're an absolutely delicious fighter but as you can see I'm on top, I've won."

She leaned down and kissed me, her hands gently pinning my arms to the bed.

We missed breakfast—we were occupied. When the house was empty she got up and fixed us coffee and cantaloupe. T.Z. amazed me. By three in the afternoon, she had me tucked away in a quiet room with a snifter of brandy, reading Parsival. I only pretended to read. The vision of the bed snakes coupled with T.Z.'s uncanny prescience about the books I needed had me wondering what else she'd done in finishing school besides getting her bottom spanked for gossiping. Her story was she'd heard me talking on the phone about the Sangrael. Actually I had never mentioned the word; the good doctor had said it to me, not vice-versa. This meant she was either lying all together or she'd been listening in on my phone conversation. Both possibilities begged the question, "Why". The book was also strange. It was one of the most famous tellings of the Grail legend and it was not on the bookshelf when I'd looked at it yesterday. I waited till T.Z. had left to go shopping before calling the doctor again. I told him the vision. After his usual habit of having me retell the story a hundred times while he searched for details, a dead silence pounded my ears from the other side of the phone.

"Well?" I said at last.

"You have seen your pursuer. He is a Molochian prince and he wishes to be made grand prince over all of the Satanic cults and orders in this country at the great Feast of the Beast. He thinks he needs you to secure his claim."

"Me! What claim?"

The doctor explained that the last Grand Prince was of a warrior cult and that he'd been crowned twenty-eight years ago at the last feast. Warfare was then made a top priority for all the cults. They had created the Viet Nam War, established the hopelessness of it's strategy, and the savagery of it's execution, by using cult members who were high-placed in the armed forces and government. The warrior chief died about five years ago and the Molochian Prince attempted to assert his claim to power with a dazzling display of cruelty and violence. The elders were impressed but decided to wait for the feast before making the final decision. He, in turn, promised to celebrate a black mass at the feast using the Holy Grail. This was the same feat Hitler had spent so much money trying to accomplish. The doctor was in the middle of telling about my part in all this when I heard T.Z. pull up in my car. My car had a very distinctive sound. I told the doctor I'd call him back and hung up.

I was pretending to read Parsival again when T.Z. came in and proudly displayed the trophies of today's shopping. After the compulsory oohs and aahs and a few sweet kisses, T.Z. disappeared and I began leafing through the other books Charles had gathered for me. In one I came across an old engraving of the First Masonic Lodge in America. They were all wearing some sort of little miniskirt over their tight pantaloons. Washington stood in the middle with Franklin and Jefferson behind him. Which one was the Professor, I wondered. Another book held the paintings of Poussin, a red velvet bookmark on the page "Les Bergers d' Arcadie" rested. It was a beautiful painting of Arcadia; serene and still, the pastoral paradise of classical mythology. In the painting, amid the lush vernal landscape, three shepherds are showing one of the muses a tomb with the inscription ET IN ARCADIA EGO. I was taught in high school that this painting was a somber reflection on the universality of death. The inscription is normally translated "In Arcadia also I am", meaning, that death haunts even paradise. Yet, in Latin the phrase really has no verb, making the literal translation simply "And in Arcadia I". I felt a strange chill as I reread the inscription, as if someone were standing on my grave.

Though I didn't know it at that same moment, somewhere real close, someone was staring at that same inscription and turning the letters around in his mind to read "I TEGO ARCANA DEI"—"Begone I conceal the secrets of God."

CHAPTER SIXTEEN

CHOSEN RESPONSE

I ALWAYS IDENTIFIED WITH THE CHARACTERS in the books I'd read. I did the same thing with T.V. shows and sometimes even with the commercials. In Texas, I'd sit around with my girlfriend and her two kids and we'd all be watching T.V. saying things like, "Uh-oh, what's Mommy gonna' do on this show?" or "I knew you were gonna' lose that money." We'd even make pet names for common things out of T.V. characters' names. My favorite was the name we had for those small, white, powdered donuts that come in the little cellophane packages. These we called Snoopy Buttholes.

This morning I was having a couple of Snoopy Buttholes with my coffee and actually reading Parsival. Most authorities considered this book to be an occult initiation document with mystical and metaphysical symbolism throughout the plot.

In the beginning of the book, the author maintains that his story is the real story of the Holy Grail. He also makes a curious statement about this guy, Kyot, who supposedly wrote down the first source of the adventure. He says that in order to write it down Kyot had to "learn the ABC's but without the art of black magic." Makes you kinda' wonder about the grade schools they had in the middle ages. I also wondered if T.Z. had gone to one of these schools.

The book is about this young kid, Parsival, who lives with his widowed mother at the edge of a large forest. One day the kid sees these knights ride by and he gets totally enthralled with them. They look like gods to this kid with their armor and warhorses. So he follows them and they take him on as a squire. He goes with them to this magic castle where he meets this guy known as the Fisher King. Now the King's got a wound in his genitals that won't heal—I'm not making this up—because of it he can neither procreate nor die. The knights tell Parsival he's supposed to ask the king this magic question at dinner that night: "Whom does the Grail serve?" But, the kid is so floored by this wild dinner that he forgets to ask the question. See, the way they have dinner is they all sit around the round table and this beautiful girl, named Repanse de Schoye, which means Chosen Response, brings down the Holy Grail and the Grail gives the knights whatever they want to eat by magic. So the kid forgets to ask the question and he wakes up the next day to find everything has disappeared—no castle, no knights, and the land is suddenly barren. Well, to make a long story a little shorter, the kid is given this impossible task to perform, which will make everything right again, like Dorothy in the Wizard of Oz. Parsival must steal the magic spear from the warlock Kingslor. It takes the kid years and years to finally get to the wicked warlock's castle and many of his fellow knights die along the way. Finally he enters the castle and Kingslor is so pissed that he throws the spear at Parsival. Parsival catches the spear and guts Kingslor with it. When he does this the whole evil castle crumbles and disappears. He brings the spear back to the Grail Castle and touches the Grail with it and everything becomes beautiful again. The Fisher King can finally die, and when he does, he leaves his castle, the Grail and everything else to Parsival, who turns out to be the king's nephew. It was kinda' like a Conan adventure.

Naturally, in this story, I identified with Parsival. T.Z. became Repanse de Schoye and Charles became the Fisher King with the wounded genitals. If everything went like in the book, I'd get T.Z. and this beautiful house all done up in tasteful Art Deco with a hippie room in the attic. Not a bad plot. The funny thing was that in the book the Grail wasn't a cup at all. In fact, it was never really described except as this a nebulous thing covered with gold and jewels. It was more like a magic stone with names written on it. If you were looking for a cup to have a black mass in this book was not much help. In the translator's notes, however, two other legends about the Grail were listed. In both the Grail was the cup Jesus used to celebrate the last supper and in which Joseph of Arimethea had collected the last blood of the Savior before burying Him. In one legend, Joseph had taken the Grail to England; in the other Mary Magdalene had brought it with her into France. Something was clicking in my head. The Magdalene holding a cup was the picture my father had painted for my mother. Plantard was a French name. Maybe—naw, that would be ridiculous—even if somewhere back in time my ancestors had gotten the cup from Magdalene, they definitely had not passed it down to me. But, if someone thought they had, it would explain why these devil worshippers were trying to use my ass for a dartboard. Maybe I could sell them Paps' urn and tell 'em it was the Grail. I'd have to take the cactus out of it first—naw—I liked the other plot better, where I got the girl and the fancy house, even though it meant that Charles was my uncle.

I was getting bored and I was out of Snoopy Buttholes. Downstairs, the Saturday afternoon football game was on. I poured another cup of coffee and walked out into the living room where T.Z. and Chuck were curled up on the lavender sectional, watching the game.

"Who's playing?"

"Dallas and L.A."

"I'll be Dallas."

T.Z. patted a spot on the couch next to her invitingly.

"Sit by me, love. Move over, Chuckie."

Chuck scooted over a bit, keeping his eyes fixed on the game.

"There's Bloody Mary in the pitcher."

Sure enough, there was a crystal pitcher of V.8. and vodka on the blue mirror-top table in front of the couch. Coffee came in a slow second to vodka, so I put my cup down and poured myself a tall one.

"Who's winning?"

"Nobody. It's still the first quarter."

As I settled back against T.Z., Chuck turned to us and deadpanned.

"Is it just me or is football getting faggier as time goes on?"

"It's you, Chuckie; the older you get the queerer you become. You're gonna' be a real flamer when you get old."

T.Z. was in good form today.

"My dear girl, just look at those outfits they're wearing now; those pants are so tight you can see their panty lines. You can't tell me all that butt slapping they do doesn't feel more intimate in those tights than it did in the old uniforms."

"Relax Charles, you're starting to sound like a senator's wife discussing rock lyrics."

Fortunately, the Cowboys completed a forty-yard pass and we were out of the fashion scene and back into the ball game.

Football games were one of the few ways to tell the passing of the seasons in L.A. Most of the trees didn't turn colors in the fall and the weather didn't change much either. Without sports and the holidays, time would almost stand still out there. As it was, time on the coast moved a lot like Stepinfetchit. I'd always felt that was the reason it took so long to get thing done in Hollywood. Movies stayed mired in development for years, shooting schedules consistently sloshed months past their deadlines. A simple idea could wade around in the molasses of a studio executive's mind for damn near ever before that little cartoon light bulb over his head would light up and the words, "I get it," would come out of his mouth convincingly. The football game ate up my dead time like a vulture leaving me late for my appointment with the good doctor.

On my way down Sunset I thought again about being Parsival and about Chosen Response. What a lovely name for a girl—girl who carried the magic Grail and became the beloved of the knight with the magic spear. There was a certain sexuality in the symbolism here of the cup and the spear, but then I had always believed in magic, even before I believed in sex.

Magic had been a fascination of mine ever since I was a child. I remember talking to the older men at Atlas about it. It seems country people are great believers in supernatural powers. Away from the cities the forces of nature take on a majestic power and mystery. To a man, these old country people all had known someone back home who seemed to be able to join forces with the great power of the elements. They talked about an old fella' who could stop blood from flowing from a wound. Why, even if the injured horse or cow was over in the next county, you'd just have to call this old boy and he'd say some kinda' words and you'd go back out to your barn and the bleeding would have stopped. "Them old folks knew things about life you kids would never even guess at." I was told many times. "And they didn't pass that knowledge down neither, no sir; they could see what was happening to the world." At this point they'd nod knowingly and I'd nod back. There was a lot more knowing in the nod I nodded this afternoon. I was beginning to see what was happening to the world. It was no longer a good place to pass on words of great power.

CHAPTER SEVENTEEN

LOVE DEATH AND SORROW

T HE EARLY EVENING AIR was sweet and showers of twilight fell through the trees onto the lawn and the winding brick path that led to the home of the good doctor. His door was ajar and opened quietly when I knocked.

"Doctor Zak—I'm here.

I walked in. I could smell the blackberry tea steeping in the library and hear the low crackle of the fire in the small marble fireplace. The house seemed quiet and undisturbed. Everything seemed the same, as it had been our last meeting. On the table, in the library, next to the hot pot of tea, was a small stack of books and rolled parchments.

"Doctor Zak, you in here?"

I went over to the table and poured myself a cup of tea. On top of the stack of books was an opened copy of Parsival. I picked it up and sat down, content to read and sip tea till the good doctor got out of the bathroom or where ever he was.

"Thus the maids are sent out openly from the Grail and the men in secret that they may have children who will one day enter the service of the Grail, and, serving, enhance its company. God can teach them how to do this...."

As I was reading these lines I thought I heard a noise coming from the kitchen. I paused. No, now it was quiet. I almost continued reading but decided just to look at the pictures instead. The engravings were old, very detailed, and yet primitive; they looked like the alchemical illustrations I'd seen, definitely Middle Ages. I thumbed through the book, looking for a picture of Repanse de Schoye. There it was again, that noise in the kitchen. I put down the tea and closed the book. I set the book on the mantle above the fireplace and headed towards the kitchen —it was time to check out the noise.

"Doctor Zak, it's me, is that you?"

Turning the corner into the kitchen—did something whisk past, just outside my peripheral vision? I moved cautiously in the direction of the specter. I heard a slight creak sound. I went through the kitchen and found a utility porch off to the left with a door that led out into the backyard. The door was closed, but next to it was a small window. I could see the backyard. It was a simple lawn of cool, green grass with a giant weeping willow. A small bed of red and purple flowers ringed the willow and around the whole yard, dark ivy-covered walls. In the very back, an old wrought iron gate creaked in the failing light. I returned to the library and my tea. I finished the cup and was pouring myself another when I heard another sound, a low sound, barely there, so faint—a whisper calling my name. At first I thought I was hearing things but then it came again, more distinct, from the direction of the front stairs. When I reached the stairs it came again, beckoning me upstairs.

"Doc, is that you? Are you alright?"

I started up the stairs slowly, one step at a time. When I reached the landing I saw the door to his bedroom was slightly opened. In the light that spilled out of his room onto the dark carpet I could see his shadow move in slow circles as if he were pacing, waiting for me. I felt relieved.

"Hey Doc, I'm here."

I opened the door. Doc wasn't pacing, he was hanging by his neck from the small black iron chandelier, turning slowly around and around. I stood still and frozen. His face was swollen, blue, the tongue thick and parting the lips. His eyes, bulged and glazed over with milky pus, stared at me then slowly turned away. Suddenly the air was thick, stifling. I fell backwards out into the hall and staggered, vomiting, toward the stairs. I reached the landing, then I saw them coming up the steps. Imps. Hideous-looking creatures the size and shape of babies but their skin, gray, wrinkled like a shaved rat's, snake-eyed and claw-fingered. They stood up and hissed when they saw me, raising their obscene little arms in the air. There were so many of them. I turned back to the hall just in time to catch a vicious slap from a dark hooded figure. I fell and rolled down the stairs into the Imps. Their baby claws tore at my flesh as I tumbled past them down onto the cold marble floor of the entrance hall. They came after me and I totally lost it, pissing and shitting all over myself. I remember screaming, trying to pull myself to the door but every time I'd reach for the doorknob, tiny paws with needle claws would shred my hands, my arms. They were all over me. I felt like I was being torn apart. Suddenly the door opened with such force that when it hit my forehead I went out with the sight of shiny black round-toed shoes stinging my mind in the darkness.

The world was cold and white when I came to; the stench started my throwing up again. Soldiers called it "the blue funk," a combination of bodily eliminations and morbid sweat. It happens right before a battle; it's caused by the knowledge of sure death. I was covered with it. The pain in my head was burning. I could hear voices and many people moving around, flashbulbs going off. I tried to sit up but slipped quickly back against the slick white world that held my shaking body. I heard a voice say, "Look he's coming around." Then another voice said, "Get him cleaned up; the lieutenant wants to see him." Suddenly a forceful stream of cold water hit me. I was in a bathtub, wallowing in the blue funk fear had left; a shower was running on me. A hand caught my arm and started pulling me up.

"Come on kid, you're all right. Get out of those shitty clothes and get cleaned up."

As I stood up, I could see into the next room. Doctor Zak was still hanging there while police photographers took a few more pictures. I stripped out of my clothes and let them fall in a pile at my feet. The water was warmer now, as I soaped and scrubbed, trying to wash the nightmare away. Wrapped in a towel, I was led past the doctor's body, just as they lowered him onto a stretcher. I was taken downstairs to the library where a detective named Jacobson was standing by the fire, smoking a cigarette. The fingerprint boys were dusting the room. I stood next to him, in front of the fire, shivering.

"Okay, spill it. What happened here?"

I stared at the fire.

"I really don't know, I was supposed to meet him here tonight."

"Were you his boyfriend?"

"No."

The cop narrowed his eyes at me.

"I want the truth, kid. Old man like that, never married, living alone like a hermit. Maybe he gets lonesome, picks up a young hustler...."

"You're barking up the wrong tree, Lieutenant. I barely knew the guy. He was helping me with some research, that's all. No fairy godfather stuff."

He rubbed the back of his neck and looked down into the fire.

"Maybe. How long you known this guy?"

"Couple of weeks, that's all, he was a friend of a friend—I needed help."

Suddenly he wheeled around and stepped right up into my face.

"Listen kid, a couple uniforms found you stoned out of your mind, rolling around in your own puke, piss and shit. So don't bullshit me. You and that old guy upstairs were having some kind of weird sex but you got so stupid stoned that you freaked out and killed him. I know all about that strangulation thing—supposed to give you a super cum. I've had to cut down more than one creep who thought he'd found the ultimate orgasm. Now I want the truth and you better tell me."

He stared ice into my eyes. Just then a young cop came up.

"Telephone for you, Lieutenant. You can take it in the kitchen."

"Who is it?"

"It's the lab. They've got a preliminary analysis on the tea."

The Lieutenant had not stopped staring at me during the entire exchange.

"I'm not through with you, punk. Keep an eye on him."

As he walked away, he caught sight of the body being wheeled out with the medical examiner in tow.

"Hey Doc! Check out the punk over there, see if you can tell me what he's flying on."

The doctor came over to me and looked at the huge bump that had formed in the middle of my forehead.

"Bring me a chair...make that two chairs."

He looked at me with a slight smile. "I'll bet you'd like to sit down."

The young cop brought over the two Queen Anne chairs and we sat down. I was still shivering from my own nakedness and fear as the doctor got out his little flashlight and peered into my eyes.

"Mild concussion...."

His manner was calm and sympathetic. He took my pulse then settled back in his chair and smiled.

"You've had quite a fright, haven't you?"

"How'd you know?"

"I was in 'Nam. I ran a M.A.S.H. station; I know the smell of 'lovedeath'."

"The blue funk."

"We called it that too; lovedeath was my name for it. After a man would go through that experience enough times he'd start to love it, actually get an erection over it. It starts out as the blue funk but if they live long enough it turns into lovedeath."

Jacobson returned at this point with a real shit-eating grin on his face.

"That tea was a real witch's brew of hallucinogens, stimulants and opiates. You and your playmate really like to get out there. Come clean, kid, the drugs will reduce the charge to manslaughter. I can't promise you anything but I'd say you got a good chance at doing short time and a long probation if you start cooperating."

"You're not suggesting this young man was involved in the death of that man upstairs."

"Let me handle this, okay Doc."

"All right, but you have to prove that he was here yesterday around five o'clock."

"What!?"

"That's when the guy died, give or take a few hours."

"Why didn't you tell me this?"

"I just did."

"What about the spiked tea?"

"Obviously it was intended by the murderer for this young man."

"But why would he do that?"

"You're the detective, I'm just the doctor. By the way, I'm taking this young man down to the hospital, he's got a mild concussion, I'll need to put him under twenty four hour observation. You can question him tomorrow."

With that the doctor helped me up and into a borrowed trench coat. I was still unsteady on my feet and my brain was burning and humming like an over-amped motor. He put me in the back of the ambulance with the good doctor's body and handed me a plastic bag with my wet, foul clothes inside.

"I'll have them laundered for you at the hospital."

They turned on the flashing lights and siren and we went screaming off into night. I hoped I would not become addicted to this feeling; the relief that comes after surviving terror is a powerful euphoria, what the Greeks called "catharsis"—the emotion that purges the soul. I felt that and sorrow, as I looked at the black body bag on the stretcher and mourned the loss of a dear friend, who had given his life for me.

CHAPTER EIGHTEEN

LOVE DEATH AND DIE

I WAS GIVEN A BED in the emergency ward with one of those little shower curtain-like separators around it. I was also given a nurse to wake me up every three hours. The doctor told me he'd look in on me later. I still didn't know his name. Before he left he gave me a shot of something to put me in what he called a "twilight state." It seems the danger in cases of mild concussion was the possibility of falling asleep and slipping into a coma. So the shot was something like a John Belushi Cocktail, part upper/ part downer—the nurse coming in was my back up. Obviously the doctor had never tried to sleep in an emergency ward. The screams of the other victims on the opposite sides of my paper-thin curtain were more than ample to ensure a sleepless night. I had thrown up everything I'd eaten or drank for the past forty-eight hours, so they really didn't have to pump my stomach again for the spiked tea, but they did it anyway. I was also put on an I.V. of glucose. They called it "just a precaution"—I called it excess. I did not want to be in this hellhole, surrounded by battered bodies fresh from car wrecks, drug shootings and domestic violence, with my blood system hooked into a plastic bag of sugar water. Then the drug hit me and I couldn't complain, in fact I couldn't move. I lay there with my mind awake and my body sound asleep—the twilight state.

At first, the burden of consciousness was overwhelming. The moans, the rattle of hospital business, all the sounds around me pulled at the pain sleeping in my head. I tried to think, to clear my mind. Someone had been in the house. Someone had drugged the tea and since the pot was still hot, that someone had to have been there just before me. But, the good doctor had been murdered the day before, how did the killer know I was coming? How did he know the doctor and I had tea at our last visit? Why drug the tea? Also, there was no sign of a struggle anywhere, or a forced entry—I had seen both the front and back doors. More importantly, how was the murder committed? The good doctor was a large man and not an easy one to hang from a chandelier. There were too many pieces to this puzzle.

I replayed the night a hundred times, as Doctor Zak had taught me, searching for details. What had whisked past me in the kitchen? I forced my mind to slow down the event. Slower, slower, until at last—a shadow, a face, a profile. A man's face, thin, aristocratic, a pure Roman nose, smooth and fine as a statue. It was working. The hospital was gone; I was back in the house, this time in complete control. I followed the shadow out to the utility room. I watched myself step to the window and peer out. I saw the back yard again, clearer than I'd seen it before. The shadow was passing through the wrought iron gate.

"Wake up. Wake up, sir"

A large black woman in a little white outfit was pulling my mind back into the noise of the hospital. My head was pounding; I could barely slit my eyes open.

"Good boy, now go back to sleep."

Again I ran my mind back to the house by repeating the same scene over and over: I am sipping my tea. I watch myself carefully. I hear the whisper. I know what I'm searching for. The dark, hooded figure. He is not there when I go up the stairs. He is not there when I open the door to the good doctor's room. I stumble back to the stairs. The Imps, good God, the Imps are real. There, the dark hood stands and strikes, too fast. Slow. There, his face: a kaleidoscope, thousands of mouths, eyes, cheeks, chins all swirling around into each other. He is Legion. He strikes and is gone. Now I'm falling again into the claws. I can feel the terror building again, my heart racing.

"There, there now, it's just a dream."

I feel the needle slide out of my vein. I am aware of the hospital. It's not the nurse—it's the doctor. He's draining the glucose from the tube. He knows I am watching him. He smiles and inserts the empty tube back into my vein.

"You know what this bubble of air in your vein will do when it reaches your heart?"

Dear God, he was killing me. He squeezed the plastic bag to force the trapped air up into my vein; with his other hand, he held the needle tight in my arm. I could feel the bubble travel up my arm. Death was coming. It was hot, making my body sweat, sucking my life till I felt like an empty pocket. It hits my heart. My heart implodes, collapsing in on itself. In a burning white moment I shudder, gag and blackout.

CHAPTER NINETEEN

IN AND OUT

"WAKE UP. WAKE UP."
The voice was nervous, pleading. I cracked one eye open. It was the nurse; she was shaking me.

"Thank God, I thought you were gone. Been trying to get you to open those pretty brown eyes for almost five minutes; another few minutes and I'd a gone for the doctor."

She unhooked the glucose and rolled it away. I was still dazed from the drugs and the doctor's late night visit.

"I didn't look in on you at 1:00 or 4:00, the doctor did himself, you must be somebody special."

She checked my pulse.

"It's a good thing he put you in the hospital last night, boy—you just about went comatose on me. Why, if that had happened to you and you'd been sleeping by yourself, Bye-bye...how's your head?"

"What head?"

"Humph, still feeling that shot, huh?"

"What shot?"

"You got your sense of humor back, I see. I had your clothes washed; they're in the bag there, over in the corner. They were sure a mess. Oooowee, you get drunk and fall down or something? Is that what happened to you?"

She was fussing with my covers and pillow, forcing me to sit up a bit.

"Yeah, great party."

"I'll bet. Sit up a little more, child, now that's better isn't it?"

It was not better. The room was fuzzy and trying to spin out from under me.

"Get yourself together, I'll be back in a minute with some papers for you to sign. Then Doctor Samuels will be around to take a look at you."

"Doctor Samuels?"

"He's on duty now, your doctor; Doctor Mayer's not with the hospital, he's with the city."

I thought I would be prepared for a near death experience. I had read all about it in the tabloids. I'd waited for the tunnel with all the light at the end with Auntie M waving hell-o. It didn't happen. All that happened was I felt absolute terror and then ceased to exist. Not a very uplifting experience—Real hard to build a religion on that one—The Church of the Terrified Nothing. I pulled myself up, straightened my back, and held on to the bed for dear life. The room was slowing down a bit. It was time to make a mental list of things to do this morning.

1.) Get the fuck out of here pronto.

Of course, that involved doing things like getting out of bed, standing up, getting dressed.

2.) Get my car.

Another tall order as the police had more than likely impounded it. I had parked it a few blocks away from the good doctor's house, just in case I was being followed. But my car was the kind of car that didn't really look at home in a quiet neighborhood.

3.) Call T.Z. and establish my alibi.

There was plenty of time for that.

4.) Figure out what the fuck was going on.

This was harder than standing up. The medical examiner was either another coven member or just a creep that got off on sending people into lovedeath. I opted for the latter. I remembered the sort of warm glow he got when he talked about 'Nam. There was also a strange gleam in his eye last night at my bedside. It was not hard to imagine him lusting at the sight of young men going through the experience for which he'd developed that pet name. God knows what he did with all those corpses that fell into his hands on the job.

96

The euphoria of survival was setting in again. I figured the delay was due to the drugs. Again I prayed that I would not get addicted to this. It was more intense than the last time. The adrenalin caused by the urgency of my need to escape was kicking my euphoria in the ass. I was unsteady but exhilarated as I stepped down from the bed and wobbled to the corner to get my bag of clothes. I dressed quickly. The trench coat and towels were with my belongings. I remembered the parchments and books the good doctor had left me. I grew sad at the thought of what helping me had cost him. I was going back for my car; maybe I could sneak into his house and retrieve the books for which he had paid so dear a price. I put on the trench and shoved my hands in the pockets for the first time. In one pocket was a badge, in the other, about ten bucks and a pack of gum. I looked at the badge. I had sergeant Murphy's coat. I didn't look much like Murphy but flashing his badge might get me in. If I did get in there was a slight chance I could uncover something that would help me answer the questions I had pondered before being death-raped by Dr. Mayer.

Just then the wail of an ambulance shook me back to the emergency ward. There was a lot of noise and commotion. Another O.D.? Another car wreck? No matter. I stepped out from behind the veil of my bed space and walked, very business-like, through the running maze of nurses, interns and stretchers, out into the morning light and hailed a cab.

CHAPTER TWENTY

HANGING ON

THE CAB WAS STUCK in the morning rush going down Sunset. Outside my window passed the parade of exhibitionist joggers. They're very existence, though depressing, was also comforting—like the handlebar on a roller coaster. Sometimes you just hang on; you hang on to anything that doesn't change. My life was moving so fast that I could easily fall right out of the roller coaster.

I couldn't think about last night, the confusion was actually becoming painful. Then it hit me, I didn't have to—I'd been replaying the wrong scene. Instead of last night, I should have been replaying my last conversation with the good doctor. Replay that last moment of clarity, not the miles of confusion. When I did, a few pieces fell into place. The good doctor had told me there were two covens involved in this affair, the warrior cult and the Molochians. The warriors would be into things like lovedeath. Doctor Mayer may not be just a creep; he could be a warrior creep. Lieutenant Jacobson had described the tea as a "witch's brew"—I believe now in was exactly that. Someone had put me into a vulnerable mental state, under a spell, on a bad trip, there were a lot of ways to say it but they all boiled down to the fact that my mind had been tampered with. The Imp claws had left no marks. I must have been followed to the good doctor's on my first trip there, followed and observed. But then, maybe not. One thing I was sure of was that the warriors did not want me arrested, they wanted me addicted, addicted to lovedeath, the supreme warrior drug.

Doctor Zak could have been murdered at anytime, with the medical examiner on their side, nobody would be any the wiser. My feeling was they had murdered him someplace else then carried him upstairs and strung him up. That would account for the absence of any sign of struggle; there was no forced entry because they used his keys. The books and parchment had been arranged on the table which led me to believe that the murder had been committed earlier the same day, maybe even hours before my arrival. I wished I had known the man better, known his habits. Maybe he took a walk after dinner, or went to visit a neighbor. I did know that his backyard and the back gate to that yard were very private, surrounded by high walls. It would have been easy to carry him in that way completely unnoticed. He had said that there was a danger the astral disturbances created by his spell could lead the dark forces right to him. There was a lot I didn't understand about the world of magic and I had no time to learn. The good doctor had told me that there was something in his books that, once I learned, would spark a power in my soul that could conquer all of the forces leveled against me. My "Excalibur" he called it. That was what I had to find. That was what he had prepared for me. That was what was waiting for me at his house.

"Sergeant Murphy, Homicide."

Thank God for chain of command. The uniform out in front was younger than I was.

"You're a little early, but go right on in. By the way, what happened to your head?"

"I bumped it saluting a superior officer."

The kid saluted and opened the door for me.

I must have arrived in between shifts. There was nobody around but there was also no guarantee this privacy would last long. I went into the library and the books and parchments were gone but they'd missed the Parsival I'd left on the mantle. I grabbed it. No time to snoop around, I needed to find my Excalibur first. I decided to leave by the back door and find out where that old wrought iron gate led. As I walked out into the yard I could feel the hair on the back of my neck stand up and cold chills rippled down my spine. Something evil had happened out here, I was sure of it. The gate led out into a gravel alleyway, bordered on both sides by the high back walls of the neighboring houses. There were also small garages for each neighbor, back gates and racks with trash cans. The good doctor's garage was to the left of his gate and his trash cans to the right. One of his trash cans was upset, just a bit, and some trash had been scattered on the ground below. Damn dogs, I thought. In his garage was an old VW Carmen Ghia with a U.C.L.A. bumper sticker. I walked down the alley to the side street then up a few blocks to where I'd parked my car. No one had bothered it; my car must have a guardian angel somewhere watching over it. I wished he would talk God into giving me one. I got in and drove down to the beach. I needed some time alone to examine the treasure the good doctor had left me.

The Parsival had been marked in several places, all having to do either with the Grail Family of the location of their castle. The places had been marked with small cards, handwritten family trees of an earlier group of French kings; the only name I recognized was Clovis, the first Christian king of the Franks. History lessons.

I braced myself for school. I opened the book and started scanning the pages. Then I just let go. I broke down crying. My life was totally out of control. I was in deep, deep shit. I had no idea how or why these things were happening to me. I stared at the churning sea and screamed with all my might. It did not make me feel any better. Suddenly I was hit by wave after wave of exhaustion. I felt hot and flushed, then dizzy and so damn tired. I was flying off the roller coaster into a black and terrible void. I went limp and fell forward, smacking my sore head on the steering wheel. The pain was like a jolt of electricity, fired right through my brain. I was awake again and real glad to be alive. Suddenly I realized I was in the well-patrolled beach parking lot at Santa Monica, wearing a cop's trench coat, more than likely wanted for murder, unlawful flight to avoid arrest and impersonating an officer. This was a real dumb place to sit and try to study. I took off the trench, rolled it into a tight ball and dumped it into a nearby trash can. I needed to get out of here quick, but where to go? Mank's. I should go to Mank's. Mank was with the press, a member of the fourth estate. He'd know how to help me. He might even know a sympathetic lawyer. If I could make it to Mank's I might stand a chance. I could sleep, maybe sort this mess out or read my books. I pulled myself together and headed back into Hollywood. I used the freeway even though Sunset would have been faster. Passing the good doctor's house again would have been tempting fate at this point and I did not want to press my luck. I was hanging on again but I could feel my hands slipping.

CHAPTER TWENTY-ONE

FALLING

O N MY WAY OVER to Mank's, my brain began to cool down a bit. If I were caught, the bump on my head could explain everything. Temporary insanity, loss of identity. Yeah. Doctor Mayer, for his own perverse reasons, had gotten me out of the murder rap. The jolly, black nurse would testify I was a little off this morning, after all, I couldn't even find my own head when she asked me. I could have found the badge in the trench and actually thought I was Murphy. No, that wouldn't wash. Picking up the books had put me back on the number one suspect list. Before I was feeling good, I was depressed again.

I pulled into the ally behind Mank's apartment building and parked in his garage. I gathered up my books and headed into the back of the building. The hallway leading to Mank's was cool and dark with a red Persian carpet running down the middle to quiet the footsteps. His door was partly open, the keys hanging ominously in the door. I thought of the good doctor's door and shivered a bit as I creaked it open. What if they'd beaten me here, and Mank was hanging by a wrinkled necktie form his shower head? I made no sound as I took the keys from the door and entered. The room was its usual mess. Hard to tell if a struggle had occurred; Mank's place always looked like the tail end of a bad brawl. I heard a low moan coming from his bedroom. I could almost see his twisted remains. I burst through the bedroom door. What I saw broke my heart. There was Mank stretched out on his bed, his pants around his ankles, and between his legs, T.Z., doing what T.Z. did better than anything. Mank lifted his head a bit at my loud intrusion.

"Hey Professor, can't you see I'm busy."

T.Z. turned her head slightly and smiled at me without interrupting her activity.

"I...I...I I'm sorry but your keys were in the door."

"Right. Well, we were in a hurry. You want to call me later, like in a couple of hours."

"Look Mank I'm in a lot of trouble."

"Great. I'm proud of you. Call me."

I dropped the keys on the floor and walked away. I was shaking before I made it to the door. My alibi was blow-jobbing my last hope. This was not a good start. I had no place left to go. I had no one left to trust. In spite of the risk, I went home, back to my loft on Pico. The game of hide and seek with the powers of darkness was over with any way. They'd found the good doctor—they might as well find me. It was a spirit of absolute fatalism that steered me back to my loft. I wanted very badly to run over the black cat that had crossed my path and left me with this unending stream of bad luck.

As I pulled up to Pico and signaled to turn up the side street that led to the gravel lot behind my loft, I noticed a group of young black men stacking my possessions on the sidewalk out front. I yelled at them, as I squealed past the corner and into the parking lot behind my place.

Inside, the owner, a swarthy Saudi whom Pauley had nicknamed Mohamed Ill Façade, was ordering the last of my belongings out into the street.

"What the hell is going on!"

"That's easy, I throw you out."

"But I have a lease."

"You have a sublet, Pauley have lease."

"So!"

"Pauley dead over a week now. I try to call you. You never home. I post eviction notice on your door five days ago."

"Whoa, wait a minute, you say Pauley's dead?"

"What, you don't speak English?"

He laughed at this and turned to his foreman, who, of course, laughed too.

"But I have rights."

"You out. New tenant coming tomorrow. Commercial. Big Money."

I was being erased. A big, rubber, pencil top was going back and forth over my life and I was disappearing. I went out front. A line of curious neighbors was already forming around my stuff. There was nothing left to do. I took a pad and felt-tip marker out of my briefcase, which was lying on top of Paps' boxes and began making price tags for everything I owned. I gathered the book out of my car and a Bible and a couple of books from my possessions. For the rest of the afternoon, I lay on my couch, looking through my books for Excalibur, and selling what was left of my past.

Inside Parsival, Doc Zak had placed a picture of a cave painting from 25,000 B.C. In the painting, nine moon-phased women dance in a crescent around a Shaman who stands where the star stands in the Crescent Star symbol. On the back of the picture was a note that said: Order of Melchizedek. The Nine Wives. The Psalm of Psalms. Sarah the Egyptian. The Blessings of Israel. Where is Joseph? I looked at the picture, then back to the note. I'd read the Psalm of Psalms—if this was a prophecy of the Magdalene then she was dark but lovely. Dark skinned like the Indian maid in my grandfather's painting. At the end of the Psalm she speaks of her little sister who has no breasts and says she will become a silver palace. Could this be Sarah the Egyptian?

In the legends of Magdalene's arrival in France, it is said there was a young black girl with her, known only as Sarah the Egyptian. There is still a church dedicated to her there in France. Could this be Magdalene's little sister who became the progenitor of a royal bloodline? The only thing that made me suspicious of the legend was that the Magdalene here is that saucy redhead that you see in them stained-glass windows. The Black Madonnas also disappeared around this time. And from the Blessings of Israel—"Benjamin is called The Wolf." I remembered the wolf face in the halo of my grandfather's Magdalene. Magdalene was of Benjamin and of the Royal House of Saul. If the bloodline of these kings comes from Magdalene's little sister, they are of the House of Saul not the House of David. The bloodline of Magdalene not the bloodline of Christ.

Joseph is the most blessed of all of Israel's children; he is called the Stone of Israel and The Shepherd. Indeed, where is Joseph? He disappeared in the Diaspora of the Kingdom of Israel. Nothing made sense. By the end of the day, I had made about $150. I had a suitcase of clothes, Paps' urn and the stuff I was reading. I sold the couch to a woman who'd been haggling with me all day.

I tossed the stuff I'd kept in my car, pulled out of the parking lot and up the side street hill. I was sick and weak—no food, no sleep—just one damn thing after another. Like a rock shaken loose from a seaside cliff, I was falling toward the surf, hitting everything in my path on the way down.

CHAPTER TWENTY-TWO

SIDESWIPE

I F MY MIND WEREN'T BUBBLING with ideas and betrayal, I'd have gone to sleep at the wheel. I headed up Mulholland Drive to blow the carbon out of my motor and let the wind clear my head. I had studied the books all day and I had no idea what they were trying to tell me. I had uncovered the meaning of a few names the good doctor had dropped while still alive. Godfroi de Bouillon was a French nobleman who had conquered Jerusalem in 1099, bringing a glorious end to the first crusade. Zak's cards indicated he was of the bloodline of Colvis, the Merovingian bloodline to be exact. The Merovingian kings were renowned for their mystical powers. It was said they could heal the sick with the touch of their hand or the tassel of their robe. The same was said of Sarah the Egyptian.

But then there was Mank and T.Z.. Maybe she was pissed because I hadn't come home last night. But I was in the hospital last night, goddamn bitch. I didn't want to think about it.

The downfall of the magical Merovingians was their funny idea of kingship. They "ruled but did not govern." They appointed a guy called "Mayor of the Palace" to do all of the grunt work while the kings just walked around in fancy robes, gazed into crystal balls and let their hair grow long, like hippies. The Mayors eventually got tired of all this and decided that since they were doing all the work, they should rule. So one of them, Pepin d'Heristal, assassinated king Dagobert II and took over. Pepin was Charlemange's great-grandfather—so I guess you could say the Mayors did all right after they took over.

The bitch wouldn't stop blowing him to ask me what happened. Christ, she could see the goddamn bump on my head. Damn women! Damn love! Damn it hurts.

I was wheeling down Mulholland now. It was getting dark in the valley; rows of small lights turned on and twinkled in the green smog. This was a road with a view. I liked it up here. There were patches of gravel along this winding road where you could pull over and park and watch night soak into the valley while the far mountains glowed neon pink in the last rays of the setting sun. I didn't pull over though; I drove faster, whistling around curves like a runaway comet. I needed the speed, the rushing of air. Too many facts had been force fed to my head, the names of kings, Tribes of Israel, Nine Wives Tecumseh, this puzzle was not coming together. I couldn't really see anything but T.Z., my Chosen Response, in "flagrante delecto", caught right in the act, like Mary Magdalene.

It was dumb to feel that way about a girl I'd just met, but then crushing a bud is sometimes more painful than picking a flower. That is to say, a man is apt to be more jealous over a new girlfriend than an old lover. I wasn't convinced of the truth of that statement; in fact, I wasn't convinced of the truth of any statement, at the moment. Just trying to know for sure which end was up had become a major undertaking. Undertaking. I didn't like that word much either, at the moment. It reminded me of these two graves I'd seen once behind an old plantation house in Maryland. The headstones had just one word carved on them—Nigger. No dates, no names, just that one word. I felt I was looking into the future when I'd seen them, like I was looking at my own grave.

Another thing I'd discovered today was the possible root if my father's middle name, Plantard, the name Doctor Zak had made such a fuss over. The son of Dagobert II, Sigisbert IV, was also known as "the Ardent Shoot", in French, Le Plant-Ard: Plantard. He disappeared after his father's murder and vanished into the mists of history. From the old parchments, it would seem he hid out in the Pyrenees, for he was listed as one of Godfroi de Bouillon's ancestors in that region. So I may have been descended from a line of French kings that hadn't ruled anybody since 679 A.D. That was great. I could claim diplomatic immunity. But what did the kings have to do with the Grail, better yet, what did the Grail have to do with me and Tecumseh?

If you keep following Mulholland drive, after you go through all the ritzy sections of Beverly Hills and Bel Aire, it turns into a ragged little road that presses on through some pretty rugged terrain and dead ends near the Ventura Freeway across from the garbage dump. The road was a lot like my paternal bloodline—rolling through the Beverly Hills of kings and queens, down to the garbage dump, me. This desolate area was the haunt of dirt bikers. From where I'd parked, I could see a couple of them burning up the hills to my left. Straight ahead of me was the freeway with the rush hour cars crawling on it. On the opposite side of the freeway was the dump. I could see the big bulldozers churning up the zigzag trails of Refuse Mountain, burying the millions of tons of garbage the city excretes daily. A full moon was rising, orange in the night sky over the dump, giving the whole scene the look of Dante's Inferno. In my current state of mind, it was beautiful, as beautiful as truth.

I was calming down enough to be hungry without getting sick to my stomach. Mexican Food. I could go for some Mexican Food. I was feeling safe again. Why? I don't know. Some powerful urge had pulled me down here to the end of Mulholland and that power felt real good about me being here. I turned the car around and headed slowly back to town.

In the darkness, the road was treacherous, especially down at this end, full of potholes and edged by steep cliffs on both sides. I could still hear the buzz of dirt bikes off in the distance, joined by the howls of coyotes in the dark hills around me. L.A. was a funny town that way. It had grown up so fast; much of the native wildlife got trapped in pockets in hills around this town. Deer and dingos, pheasants and foxes all roamed these hills. The coyotes were the most dangerous and were bold enough to attack. The radio had announced the maiming of a six-year-old girl by a coyote only a month ago. Strange town, half wild, half crazy.

Ahead of me, in the distance, I could see a pair of headlights coming fast. Oh shit, cops, coming to harass the dirt bikers. I really wanted enchiladas at Don Pedro's not baloney sandwich served in a jail cell. I'll just play it cool. I slowed down and pulled as close to the edge as I could, hoping they'd just whiz past me without looking. The headlights were moving fast, jumping up and down from the holes in the road and speed of impact. I was convinced they were cops—nobody would do that to their own car. When they got close, they veered and headed right toward me, their headlights on high beam. It was a van. I tried to pull away fast. Too late. The massive bumper rammed my front fender and sent my car flying backwards over the edge. I was thrown out of the car as it flipped over. I landed upside down in a scrub of chaparral. My car kept going; bouncing end over end till it hit the bottom.

Men in black with flashlights got out of the van and stood by the edge of the road, scanning the ravine with their lights. I rolled over behind the bush I'd landed on and lay still. I couldn't hear what they were saying but I could hear the buzz of the dirt bikes getting closer. The men heard it too. They jumped back in their van and took off. I looked down at my car; small flames were licking around the hood, fanning out into the surrounding brush. I started to climb back up but when I moved my leg, a flash of pain stopped me. Suddenly my car exploded, the gas tank became a roaring column of fire. The smoke that curled up from the flames twisted itself into the shape of a face. It was happening again. I was seeing things.

A demonic face with strange burning eyes seemed to be scanning the underbrush for me. I panicked, clawing my way up the hill, tearing rocks loose, ripping up sagebrush. I looked over my shoulder; the face was after me, hideous, monstrous. The rock I was using to pull myself up crumbled in my hand. I reached desperately for something else and grabbed what I thought were the roots of a bush. I pulled hard, dragging my broken leg. Suddenly the root pulled loose from the earth. It wasn't a root; it was the hand of a corpse and the weight of my body was pulling it out of its shallow grave. Before I could let go I'd brought the rotting flesh and bones down on top of me. Its worm-eaten head slapped into mine, splattering my mouth, nose and eyes with its putrid defecation. I slipped, sliding back down the hillside into the hellmouth of the great demon head. My broken leg twisted and caught on a stump. I'd stopped sliding. I opened my eyes and looked up. The Rabbit stood over me, his hands on his hips. His jewel wound flashing like stars in the night. His face was calm, a slight smile. He just shook his head. I felt his calm and peace, and as the void descended, I felt him touch my cheek.

CHAPTER TWENTY-THREE

WORD OF VISIONS

INTO THE DARKNESS THE RABBIT HAD LED ME. I turned as we went and looked back from above, down at my body and my burning car. The dirt bikers had just reached me as the corpse tumbled down the hill and into the night fire. In a blink it was gone, all of it. The world. The night. I was floating without time or space. I was facing my nightmares. I saw the painting of Magdalene and the cup, the one my grandfather had done. She was alive, before me with wings like an eagle. Before her was a young black girl. She places a crown upon the young girls head and a silver cup in her hands. Before the girl with her were kings and beggars, Knights Templars and minstrels, children naked in rags and in splendor like princes. The cup, in her hands, glowed silver and white. She passed it first to a naked child. She handed it to him and it appeared in his hands yet she retained it. Like the loaves and the fishes, the miraculous cup was passed and retained by all in this company. From the child to a king, from the king to a beggar, each movement was sweetened by sounds like a song whose chorus of harmonies grew with each passing of the cup. I saw a king, dressed like a Templar, a crown of thorns on his head. There were maidens as well, some noble, some poor—all took the cup and, at last, turned to me. From the hands of a poet, the last of his line, I took the sweet chalice and held it as mine in my hands. Its perfume filled my senses, down to my soul, and then the cup overflowed. The red blood ran down my arms and hands.

Then it all vanished and the demons came, walking past me as if I were not there. Behind them, naked and masked, those who worshipped the powers of darkness, their leader carrying a baby whose heart had been torn out. The tiny carcass was placed on an altar and given over to the demons. With vile and obscene mocking of the creation in Genesis, they placed their lips and tongues to the wounds and breathed their own hideous life into the baby's corpse. The skin, wrinkled and grayed, claws tore through the ends of the tiny fingers, the eyes opened—an Imp was born. The worshippers chanted and writhed in its honor. They fell on the floor and soiled each other's bodies with all forms of excretion as the Imp ran among them, beating them with a scourge.

I turned away, sick to the deepest core of my being. It was as if I could feel the great heart of God breaking at the depravity of His children whom He loved so much. I was no longer afraid. I stood alone in the blackness of nowhere and cried burning tears that seared my eyes and my cheeks like streams of hot lead. I had been given heaven and hell, back to back. It was ripping me apart but it left no place for fear to hide.

I could see the white room, my body with a cast on its leg and tubes running out of its arms and nose. The angry Lieutenant Jacobson was pacing around the bedside, wanting a cigarette real bad. He griped to the young uniform who sat in a chair in the corner then he walked back over and stared into my sleeping face. He was ready to leave, to go outside and have a smoke but he wanted to be there when I woke up. It was a conscious decision on my part to wait until he'd given up on me and had just stepped out the door, to return to my body and stir the pain we call flesh back into waking state. I opened my eyes and looked at the cop in the chair. He was still reading his paper. It would take more than opening my eyes to get his attention. I moaned and rolled my head a bit. He jumped as if a ghost had entered the room.

"Christ, he's alive."

He got out of his chair in such a hurry that he slipped on his way to the door. The noise of him banging clumsily into the wall brought the lieutenant back into the room on the double, as well as a nurse and a couple of doctors.

"Can I talk to him yet?"

The doctors didn't answer him, they were too busy snooping and prying into my eyes and mouth and other orifices.

"Just a minute, please...son, can you hear me.?"

I just nodded weakly, not wishing to encourage Jacobson.

"He's still pretty weak, Lieutenant."

"Just give me a minute with him."

"All right, but not long."

The doctors moved away and Jacobson came close, right up to my face.

"Thought you could sneak out on me, huh kid? Well, let me tell you something, you better stick close to me, kid. Somebody's got it out for you. That ravine where they knocked you off the road turned out to be some kind of cult burial ground. We've dug up fifty bodies and counting, all in shallow graves, all with their hearts torn out. You're next, buddy boy, and I want to know why."

I just looked into his hard-boiled eyes and sighed, too weak to respond in any other manner.

"Clam up on me, huh. Okay, no problem, I got plenty of time."

He turned to go, and then as if on a second thought, he turned back to me. He reached into his pocket and produced a cassette tape. He held it up for me to see and smiled.

"Just so you don't get the idea I'm stupid, this is the reason they drugged your tea. I found it in the tape player in the library at your friend's house. You know what's on it? Well at first you might think it's just the sounds of a fire, crackling in a fireplace, but underneath that sound, at a subliminal level, is a soft hypnotic voice, telling you to do things and see things. Somebody was setting you up for a heart attack. You were seeing little goblins clawing you to pieces weren't you? Well, if those cops hadn't come in you'd have watched them eat your heart. So, think about it kid, I'm on your side."

He smiled again as he turned to leave; his smile was sincere. I was not shocked. I had learned from my visions.

"By the way, you've got visitors."

T.Z. and Mank walked in with a tall blond man who looked a little bit like a polar bear. Mank came close, dragging the polar bear.

"Professor, meet your new attorney."

The polar bear extended his hand.

"Mannly P. Tetmire, attorney at law."

T.Z. squeezed past both of them and gave me a kiss on the forehead.

"Hell-o darling, I'm so sorry about all of this, I had no idea you were in this much trouble. We'll get you right out of here and back on your feet just as soon as possible. Right, Mank?"

"You bet. Mannly's already rousted your insurance company for a nice sized check to cover your car.

"Don't tell the hospital," I said softly. "If they think I have money I'll never get out of here."

"Always thinking, huh Professor? That's a good sign. Don't worry we got you covered. Tetmire's also got you out of that impersonating an officer rap. In fact there are no charges against you at all. The cop in the corner is just here to protect you. The Lieutenant seems to think there's a plot to kill you, but don't let that worry you. The paper's agreed to hire you a real bodyguard, in exchange for an exclusive on your story. You're big news, old buddy."

At this point the doctors returned and escorted my friends out.

So now I was news. I really didn't want any more people aware of my name and face. I shifted a bit in my bed; I could feel it would be several days before I would be able to walk out of here. I had to get out of town. I'd call Speedster tomorrow and see about hiding out in Sag Harbor. I'd heard the word of the vision, and the word was "leave."

CHAPTER TWENTY-FOUR

THE DRIFT

JOSE DE JESUS LOPEZ-PINTOS was the name on my driver's license that could not be released to the press, pending the notification of my next of kin. Of course, locating my next of kin was no small task. My mother went by another name entirely and my uncle, whose name I carried, had died about ten years ago. I was safely anonymous unless Mank or my new attorney, Mannly P. Tetmire, opened their big mouths. To insure my status as "unidentified man," I was conveniently too weak or too confused to be much help to the police. I had given San Antonio as my family's place of residence. I told them my family did not use the hyphenated version of the name; try to locate a particular Lopez in San Antonio. Jacobson thought my license was a phony.

"You don't look Mex to me, son."

He was right, I didn't. My genes were so confused by all the different racial strains that I wound up looking more like an Italian-Indian than an Irish-Mexican. It was my second day, first day as a conscious being, and the hospital was already getting nervous about the bill. The police insisted on a private room because they still felt someone would come into my hospital room and try to kill me. The hospital thought I'd be "safer" in a ward. Jacobson enjoyed hanging out in my room, making phone calls and ordering up pizza and Chinese. He was not about to settle for a ward. Toward the end of the day, I was strong enough to get out of bed and go to the bathroom by myself. This spoiled one of the Lieutenant's favorite monotony breakers, watching a cute little candy striper stick an ice-cold bedpan under me. I was questioned and requestioned about what I was doing at Doctor Zak's.

"Looking up my family tree," I said.

"Who's after you kid, some crazy, cult, drug dealers."

"No, just some bill collectors, as far as I know."

I was slowly convincing him that I just stumbled into the wrong place at the wrong time.

"Maybe—there was another name on the doctor's date book. Same day. Same time. Only this name was penciled in, maybe an afterthought. Plantard. Name ring a bell?"

No. Not even a tinkle."

"Un-huh. My theory is the trap, the tea, the tape might have been set for this Plantard."

"Sounds possible."

"And maybe the killers think you're Plantard."

This revelation dropped like a bombshell in the pit of my stomach. I had to control myself; I was talking to a trained detective. The slightest twitch would be enough, in his mind, to reconnect me to this whole horrible chain of events, and if he did, I'd never get out of L.A. I shifted to sit up a bit higher when the muscle in my leg popped and knotted.

"Ooh! OooH! My leg, I've got a Charlie horse...Oh God help...get a nurse!"

Christ those damn things hurt. Jacobson sent for a nurse. While she was rubbing my calve, he commented that I had no prior arrests, no trouble of any kind in my background as far as he could trace. He was still waiting to hear from Texas. I had English nobility, T.Z., as a character witness and alibi. I had a connection to the press and a decent lawyer. If everything checked out and nobody tried to kill me, in a couple of days I'd be free to go.

"So kid, if I let you go, where would you go?"

"Back East, I guess. I have friends back there. I've lost my place here."

"Yeah, I know. Too bad. I heard the guy you had the sub-lease from died."

"Right, Richard Pauley."

"Right. Do you know how he died?"

"No."

"Freak accident, got crushed by his own car. Must have been working on it and the jack slipped, anyhow, they found him under it, his face caved in by the oil pan. No witnesses."

"I'm sorry. I didn't know."

"Death follows you around like a pet rat, don't it kid. If I let you go, you tell me exactly where you're gonna' be. I want to be able to warn the local officials."

Jacobson didn't like me. It didn't bother me. In a way, it was comforting to know the police in Sag Harbor would be keeping an eye on me, all two of them. It wasn't his threat that had me worried; it was the penciled note about Plantard on the good doctor's date book. Doctor Zackary McDonald was a world-famous authority on the occult, with connections in Europe, the Americas, everywhere. Was it possible he had contacted a distant of maybe near relation of mine, or maybe an important member of the Plantard family? If he had, did this man show up? Jacobson sat in the corner and watched me think. I watched him eat. I was getting hungry 'til the nurse brought me my tray. Airplane food.

Mank, T.Z. and Mannly P. arrived after dinner with flowers, ice cream and a bodyguard named Bubba, a three hundred pound black man, who ate most of my ice cream then pulled up a chair next to my bed and went to sleep. Mank had some releases from the paper for me to sign, which I didn't. Mannly P. had some legal papers from the insurance company, guaranteeing me five grand for the loss of my car, which I did sign. T.Z. was all tenderness and light, offering to help me to the bathroom. She dropped discreet hints about how private it would be in there with the door closed but after watching her work on Mank, my appetite for her charms had cooled considerably. I was polite, though, and said nothing she could take as an offense to her talents. I explained how "sore" I was, "all over" since the accident. She smiled so sweet I almost changed my mind.

I had trouble sleeping that night and it wasn't just Bubba's snoring. Several things gnawed at my spirit of ease. I had lost my precious books. If I were to find my Excalibur now I would have to rely on my memory, which wasn't working all that great. Also there was the name Plantard being next to mine in the date book. This was most confusing. Finally, which coven was doing what to me and why? None of this was easy to figure.

Bubba was a great snorer; he could do the Larry, Curly and Moe snore all by himself. Unfortunately, the other end of Bubba was not a quiet sleeper either. From time to time, his stomach would growl then he'd let fly one of those loud, long-winded farts, the kind I'd always believed were created in a recording studio as a special effect for "party" records. I'd have to remember to thank Mank and his newspaper for all this protection. So, I had a choice, I could lay here and play "guess what Bubba had for dinner" or I could limp down to the patient's lounge and sit up all night.

The patient's lounge was depressing enough to make a strong person ill. Actually, it was a fitting place to think, as gloomy as the realities I had to face. The good doctor was gone. Pauley was gone. The books were gone. My loft was gone. My car was gone. My clothes were gone. Everything I owned in this world was gone, even Paps' urn. It was just like a divorce, I even had a lawyer. Like I say, my realities were indeed depressing. This thing about Plantard kept kicking my attention away from my losses and into pure speculation. What if the shadow I'd seen in the house that night was nor a coven member but a member of my family? Why didn't he answer me? Why did he run away? There were no answers just more questions. I felt a terrible isolation creeping into my soul. I was tired of talking to myself but I had no one left to talk to. Mank was ready to exploit me in the press. T.Z. was never really a confidante. The police were not my friends. Everyone else was dead except Speedster. He was couple of thousand miles away and, if I called him, he might be next on their hit list. I was drifting away from the rest of humanity, out into what promised to be a very short and lonely life.

CHAPTER TWENTY-FIVE

THE FLOOD

BUBBA WAS AWAKE when I limped back into the room. He was eating my breakfast.

"Any Good?" I asked.

"Not bad. Say, where you been?"

"Just to the bathroom."

He nodded and washed down a biscuit with a slug of coffee.

"Okay, I'm supposed to stick to you like glue but this glue don't go to the bathroom with nobody."

"You did a great job last night, Bubba."

Bubba smiled and squared his shoulders.

"I'm the best."

"Right."

I crawled into bed and fell dead asleep. Bubba was great. He wouldn't let anybody near me until noon when the lunch tray arrived. He woke me up to tell me lunch was pretty good. Jacobson strolled over to get a good look at me.

"How's the leg, kid?"

"Broken."

He smiled but he still didn't like me.

"Well, come tomorrow morning, if nobody blows your brains out, you can hit the street."

"Orders from the Captain?"

"Orders from the D.A.; you've been scratched right off the 'important to keep alive' list."

"Oh? Big breakthrough in the case?"

"Not really. I still got, what was the last count, oh yeah, sixty-five bodies, no suspects, no evidence, no leads. So what's another body, more or less? It's just simple arithmetic. You're no help to us, so we can't afford to pay your hospital bill anymore. Government cutbacks, you understand; tight budget these days. If you could just shed one ray of light on this case it might be different but, naw, you don't know anything, right?"

"Right."

"So, you can take your know-nothing ass right outta' here."

He smiled again then strolled back over to his chair, picked up his phone and ordered a large pizza with everything on it. Bubba looked at me and spoke with a mouthful of food.

"Fuck him; we'll take care of you."

I appreciated the thought but the idea of Bubba signing the checks at the newspaper was not real enough to make me feel secure. All I could see was me in my hospital gown and leg cast walking down the street with the cold wind kicking my bare ass. I decided I'd better get some sleep while I still had a warm bed.

Bubba didn't wake me until dinner time. He said it was pretty good. Jacobson had gone. I was just sitting up to share the last couple of bites of baked potato when Mank and T.Z. came in, loaded down with presents. Mank carried two suitcases and T.Z. toted a large bag of Chinese take-out.

"Okay Professor, you're all packed, where you want to go?"

"Packed?"

Mank opened the suitcases. They were stuffed with expensive clothes—sweaters, shirts, jackets, pants, and even a couple of nice suits.

"T.Z.'s been shopping all day; she said you and she were the same size."

"But I still had time to get you dinner," T.Z. purred in her adorable English accent.

Out of the bag came all those little square boxes with the wire handles and the red pagoda of the sides. Lemon chicken, Chinese vegetables, shrimp in black bean sauce, the boxes just keep coming. Bubba was grinning from ear to ear. I was undone by all of this; I wanted to break down but before I could Mank produced a piece of paper.

"The newspaper covered everything. I told 'em you wouldn't sign anything until they started taking care of you."

"So, now I got an agent and a lawyer."

"You're in the big time."

The big time. That was just great. If I was going to live a short lonely life, I might as well be comfortable.

"What else can I get?"

"Whatta' you want?"

"I want a ticket to Sag Harbor and a room at the American Hotel there."

"Then you'll tell your story?"

"Hey, it don't cost anymore to go first class, you just can't stay as long."

Mank smiled.

"T.Z., pour the brandy; we're going to have a toast."

"One more thing, Bubba goes with me."

"No problem."

Bubba slapped me five. T.Z. passed out little paper hospital cups and poured the brandy. Mank raised his cup and proposed a toast.

"To an exclusive!"

"An exclusive!"

We ate and drank until Bubba went to sleep again. Mank and T.Z. left around midnight.

I sat up for awhile, trying to be depressed again, just to restore my sense of reality. The picture looked bright and sunny but I didn't buy it. I felt like Noah—I knew it was going to rain.

CHAPTER TWENTY-SIX

THE STORY

THE AMERICAN HOTEL HAD CHANGED a lot since the last time I was here. It used to be a borderline flophouse for seafaring men, the owner slept on a cot in the bar and I slept on the pool table. Now it appeared that the place had changed hands and been done over with a strong desire to remove its distinctive character. They'd cut out the living heart out of the old sailor's bar and replaced it with a Rolex. It had become some yuppie's idea of quaint: uselessly expensive, shamelessly posh, and affordable only on the company's expense account.

It took a moment for me to get over my initial disgust and realize I wasn't paying for this. Great. I decided to enjoy the error of my stay and, in fact, wallow in it. I got room service hopping. I owed myself a celebration, after all. I was alive. I was not having nightmares. I vowed to stay drunk as a politician's wife until the excess itself had purged my soul, cleared my mind, focused my intuition and left me sprawled like a rag across my bed. That took about a week.

A few days before Thanksgiving, just as the bellboy woke me up with a Blood Mary, it happened. I felt the veil fall. I was time to reassess things.

I decided to start with the things I knew the least about. The first was Nine Wives. Using Doctor Zak's technique, I transported myself back to that fateful afternoon I sat on the couch selling my past. I held the card and I stared at the cave painting of the nine women and the Shaman. Being this guy would be a lot more fun than being Parsival. I could just see myself in some ancient, sacred place, dancing with my nine, Neolithic, cowboy cheerleaders and me wearing nothing but a set of antlers and a rocking woody. It also immediately occurred to me I might spend way too much time in this fantasy. Then I decided what the hell! Within moments I was back on holy ground, having a smokin' hot ménage-a-ten. The High Priestess mounts me and man I am shakin' my antlers and curlin' my toes. "My love is like a stag, like a hind on the hill." I was hearing the Psalm of Psalms in my head, drawing me back to the dark Magdalene. The cloud of her enigma was spoiling my wet dream. Reluctantly I turned the card over and stared at the words—Order of Melchizedek.

Melchizedek is mentioned twice in the Old Testament. The first time he is introduced as the Priest King of Salem, who offers the sacrifice of bread and wine and blesses Abram, which is what they called Abraham at the time. Abraham did honor him. The second time Melchizedek is mentioned is Psalm 1:10. Interestingly enough, this is the same Psalm Jesus used to confront the Pharisees on the bloodline of the Messiah. He asked them whose son the Messiah was. "David's," they said. And Jesus answered, "How is it then that David, while in the Spirit says, 'The Lord said to my lord, "Come sit at My right hand until I make thy enemies thy footstool."' If this is David's son how is it that David calls him Lord?"

The Pharisees were all about bloodline; after all, the Bible they studied was basically one man's dysfunctional family album. Jesus, as Messiah, never chose to personify Himself with the totems of Judah, but rather chose the totems of Joseph, the Stone of Israel and the Shepherd. Could the deep, dark secret of Jesus be that he wasn't a Jew (short for Judah), he was a Joe? Further down in the same Psalm David declares, "Thou shalt be a Priest forever, according to the Order of Melchizedek." So, his priesthood was not coming from the Jewish tradition but from a tradition much, much older, which Abraham, the father of a Jewish people, did bow before. Very interesting.

The next point of study was Chapter Twelve of Revelations, in which we see a Sacred Woman giving birth to a Holy Child. Jesus had already been born; this must be a description of His Son. This Child after a very short period is called up into the Heavens to the Throne of God, to avoid being eaten by the Red Dragon, who was awaiting His birth with open jaws. The Sacred Woman is given the wings of an eagle, which carried her to the wilderness, where she was nourished for "One Thousand, Two-Hundred and Three Score days." My reading on this was that Christ and Magdalene did have a child, but that child was taken up to Heaven and the Magdalene was taken to the wilderness. The bloodline of Christ was no longer on the Earth. The Magdalene was taken to the wilderness, but what wilderness? Where? I had asked Mank for some books on Native American spirituality, hoping to discover more about Tecumseh. He had given me a book on the Cherokee, telling me "Read this. All Indians are the same". His gift turned out to be quite serendipitous for my studies. It seems the Cherokee had the first five books of the Bible on seven beaded belts, before the colonists arrived. The Cherokee also had a Sacred Ark, which they carried before them into battle. The oldest Cherokee prayer begins with "Hosannah". Their word for God was Yohweh, Yahweh with an "O". They had the same feasts at the same times of year and they kept the new moons. They valued the dream more than anything, and in fact counted time by saying, "How many dreams ago was that?" not "How many days ago was that?" They also honored the Beloved Woman, who had come to them and taught them to live life as a prayer. Had I found the wilderness of Revelations? Had I found the Tribe of Joseph? And, If I had, what did this have to do with the Holy Grail?

I remembered one more story of the Magdelene. It was said that she appeared before the Emperor to proclaim the innocence of Jesus by saying that He had been wrongfully executed by the Romans and that he had risen from the dead to prove his innocence. At the time it was customary to bring the Emperor a gift when you brought a case before him. Magdalene held an egg in her hand as a gift. The Emperor responded to her request by saying, "It would be easier for someone to rise from the dead that it would be for that egg in your hand to turn red." The egg immediately turned red and the Emperor ruled that Jesus was innocent. It is said that egg was the first Easter egg but I wondered if the red egg referred to the red man. I was getting nowhere fast.

I looked at the word again—SANGRAEL. I had written the word in big, stupid letters on a clean sheet of complimentary hotel stationary.

SANGRAEL. One word. I had sat my drink on the paper as I hopped up to tip the bellboy. I paused from my musings and picked up the Bloody Mary. I noticed it had made a circle around the SANG part of the word.

I'd been dividing the word in the wrong place. The Sangrael was not San Grael, Holy Grail; it was Sang Rael, Royal Blood. It's amazing what a little peace and quiet and a Bloody Mary can do. The Grail family, in the romances of the Middle Ages, was an actual family of kings, the Merovingians. It would be simple now. There was, at last, something to build on. History. More research would be necessary to tie up the loose ends: the connections between the Knights Templar, the Masons, and Mary Magdalene, with the covens, the magic and me. But, I had found something that had eluded the Nazis and maybe even the witches that were chasing me. The Grail of Parsival was not a cup; it was a king or line of kings. I remembered the section of Parsival I'd been reading in the good doctor's house, the part he had marked for me. It said that the men of the Grail leave in secret to spawn children who will someday return to serve the Grail. It was now clear to me that the name Plantard, in the doctor's datebook, was a member of my family who was to meet me there to reveal to me my heritage. But the spell the good doctor had cast had backfired and evil had arrived before good. The shadow had fled, not only to protect his life, but mine as well. It was some family secret that had kept us safe. I also realized it was this Plantard who had called the cops and saved me from a hysterical heart attack. I felt safer knowing that someone besides Bubba was watching over me, maybe even guiding me into a whole new world.

I was ready to leave my room. I called the Speedster.

"Professaur, what's happening, man?"

"I'm in town, down at the American Hotel."

"Very unlike you, I thought you'd be at the Royal Oaks."

"Well, I thought the American was still a flophouse."

"It still is, it just caters to bigger flops, now."

"I'd like to walk over and pay you a visit."

"Sure, come ahead. I'm still in the same place, right behind the Whaler's Church."

"Can I bring any thing?"

"Bring a bottle of whatever you're drinking 'cause I don't keep a drop of spirits in the house."

"How about a bottle of Grand Marnier?"

"Boy you still like to lick the honey off razor's edge."

"Life is short and honey is sweet..."

I paused, not knowing exactly how to say what I had to say next.

"I guess you heard about our friend, Doctor Zak."

"I heard suicide. Bring your bottle and we'll sit upon the ground and tell sad tales of the death of kings."

"Right, Shakespeare. See you soon."

I woke Bubba up to tell him I was going out to visit a friend. Bubba had been spending his nights at the Bay Street Disco on the pier across from the hotel. He needed his rest. I went downstairs and through the bar. It was a sad thing to see. I hadn't left my room for a week and had only glanced at it on my way up when I signed in. Now, I stood still and faced it. It looked like a banker's parlor. The pallid dust that had clung to the hand carved leaves and branches that crawled along the wide edges of the grand old cherry breakfront behind the bar had been swept clean, the wood stripped and refinished. I longed to see that sacred dust, those magic cobwebs where a century of sailors' yarns had nestled sweetly, succored on the smoke of pipes, cigars and cigarettes from turkey, Spain and Cuba. This had once been the kind of dive where poets like John Steinbeck could escape the wife and kids, lose the burden of respectability, toss back a snoot-full and swap tales with the winos. Time is cruel and money is no object but there are treasures swept away by brooms and polish rags that all the shine in the world will never replace.

I walked through the frosted glass doors of the sun porch and out into the late November chill. The town was turning on its Christmas lights. The dark came early here. In the twilight, the whole little Victorian village of Sag Harbor just looked like the liquor store across the street—well stocked and high priced. I took my bottle and walked up the hill of Main Street, past the statue of a Civil War hero, then down a side street to the old Whaler's Church. The church is a wooden replica of Solomon's Temple in Jerusalem. It is an imposing structure, haunting the hill on which it sits. In the heyday of Sag Harbor it had boasted a spire, tall enough to be seen by the whaling ships far out at sea, as they steered home from the gray Atlantic. The whalers were the Saudis of their era. Whale oil was Big Oil; nobody had pulled oil up out of the ground yet. Their wealth built this church. Prophetically, just before their decline, a hurricane came along and blew the spire right off the church. It landed in the neighboring graveyard and the congregation decided to let it rest there. Pieces of it still stick up out of the ground like the bones of a beached whale. I walked past these "bones" on my way down to the Speedster's. Solomon's Temple figured heavily into Masonic lore, in fact, the order claimed its origins from Solomon's chief architect and builder, Hiram, king of Tyre. Hence the name—Masons. I also remembered that the Molochians claimed their descent from the times of King Solomon. The church behind me gave me the shivers. Walking through the graveyard was not doing much for my disposition either. I could not quell the growing sense of impending doom. Was that dull daystar fading faster and were those wind stirred leaves really dancing around the tombstones like witches at a Sabbath? I dragged my bad leg as I hurried my pace, like a mummy in the fifties horror films in hot pursuit of the winsome wench in the satin nightgown. It seemed forever but I crested the low hill of the graveyard and looked down on the street below. I could see Speedster's house from here with its windows of orange light striking the blue-black winter night like a beacon. I was a sailor coming home from the sea with a story to tell that would curl the hair of its hearers.

CHAPTER TWENTY-SEVEN

GRACE AFTER MEALS

"COME IN, PROFESSAUR. WHAT happened to your leg?"

"I broke it."

The Speedster's house was warm and comfortable, a renovated Victorian, naturally, like everything else in Sag Harbor, but then the Speedster himself was a renovated Victorian. Beneath his salty white goatee, the Speedster traditionally sported a handsome scarf tied rakishly to the side, like a playboy from the twenties. "The 1820's," Speedster had noted when I brought it to his attention. The rest of Speedster's wardrobe varied according to occasion but always the scarf. Tonight he wore a faded denim cowboy shirt, boots and jeans.

"You should have told me, I'd 'a picked you up."

"I wanted to walk. I've been cooped up in my room for a solid week. I needed a little air and exercise. The cowboy outfit in my honor?"

He took the coat from my back, the bottle from my hand and led me into his living room.

"In your honor, Tex."

There were two overstuffed chairs pulled up to the fire, waiting for us. I noticed Speedster was unusually spry of step tonight. I had not seen Speedster for quite awhile but something about him seemed younger, leaner. I'd always suspected he might be an alchemist of some sort and maybe two hundred years old.

His legend was that he was hung like John's black mule and had always been a pretty good stick man. His talent and natural gifts endeared him to certain wealthy patrons early in his youth, but Speedster was too wily to rely on women for his means. He once turned down a duchess' offer of apartments in Paris with a generous weekly stipend. Speedster preferred to live by his wits, and though his wits had earned him fame as a man of letters and a comfortable retirement along with this renovated Victorian, he never lost the legend of that prowess that had gained him his early fame. He was like Chaplin in this respect.

"Here, have a seat and warm your cast. LuAnn! Come in here, I want you to meet somebody. And bring three good glasses, snifters."

I sat down in the chair and put my cast up near the hearth.

"How'd you do that to yourself?"

"Car accident."

"Bad break?"

"No break below the knee is that bad. I don't need a crutch or a cane; I just kinda' limp along like an old pirate."

Speedster was busy uncorking the bottle as we spoke. By the time he'd finished, LuAnn arrived with the glasses. She was young and lovely with long straight hair of tawny brown, emerald eyes and freckles. The Speedster legend was definitely not going to die out any time soon.

"LuAnn, this is the Professaur. Professaur, my wife, LuAnn."

I smiled as she handed me a glass. She moved with such grace; I couldn't help watching her. She looked at me quizzically as I sat there, holding my glass out, staring at her and smiling. Speedster clocked my reaction.

"Don't worry darling, the Professaur always smiles like that when someone's about to pour him a drink."

I blushed and looked down at the fireplace. Speedster was almost as good at embarrassing me as I was at making a fool of myself.

"What shall we drink to?"

He laughed as he filled our glasses.

"A warm fire on a cold night."

"Very good, Professaur. To a warm fire then."

Our glasses raised and clinked together. Mine was empty in a flash; Speedster and his wife just sipped theirs. I poured myself another and sat the bottle by the fire to warm.

"So, how was your trip?"

"Like a long night in a very small bar."

"You fly into New York?"

"No, MacArthur, then took a cab."

"Cabs cost a lot of money. How are you managing all this, the cabs, the American Hotel, expensive booze?"

"Someone else is paying for it."

Speedster leaned back in his chair, narrowed his eyes and gave me that Sherlock Holmes look. His mind worked so fast; I knew in a moment he'd have it all figured out. LuAnn excused herself, taking their empty glasses back to the kitchen. She was making some exotic dessert that wouldn't be ready for an hour. She promised to call us when it was done. I poured myself another drink and waited. Suddenly Speedster leaned forward in his chair.

"You're the Herald Examiner's mystery witness."

"So, you've heard about that all the way up here."

"Sixty-five bodies with their hearts ripped out, are you kidding? Made to order for the New York Post, they even ran pictures."

I nodded, then tipped my glass as a salute.

You're the one with the information, supposedly too frightened to talk with the police. The Examiner is hiding you in some secret location."

Speedster winked and started laughing, very "one old con-man to another" style.

"All a bunch of hype bullshit, right. You're too much. How'd you convince the Examiner you had a lead on this?"

"It was easy, they convinced me."

"Ah-hah! Then you're the guy that ran off the road and pulled up the first body."

"No secret remains hidden from an astute mind."

Speedster shook his head and leaned back in his chair; his face grew somber.

"Tell me about Zachary."

Starting with our phone conversation those weeks ago, I proceeded, in detail, to tell him all the bizarre and strange things that had happened to me. I told him about the good doctor, how he'd helped me and how he'd died. About the Imps and the visions and the Grail, and the Order of Melchizedek and the cave paintings—I told him everything. For the first time since I'd known him, he did not interrupt with a single quip or sarcastic remark. He just sat there, taking it all in. When I finished there was nothing but silence. I poured another drink. Finally he spoke.

"Were you followed up here?"

"I don't think so. The paper took elaborate precautions, but that one of the reasons I walked over. I didn't notice anyone watching me. I don't think they know I'm here."

"Do the police know?"

"They think I went 'home'. The paper sent a ringer to San Antonio; I've been told the cops are still following him."

"So, what are you going to do?"

"I'm going fishing."

"Till your pecker hair turns gray, right."

"Well put."

"What can I do for you?"

"Tell me about the Order of Melchizedek."

Speedster smiled. "Well, get comfortable Professor, this is a long story. The Order of Melchizedek was a pet theory of Doctor Zak's. He believed that since there have been shamans for as long as humans have been walking on two legs that there must be a shamanic gene, a storehouse of tens of thousands of years of shamanic knowledge. Zak believed that when man began to walk upright he placed his spine, his psychic antenna, perpendicular to the Earth and its energy fields. The only time his antenna would be back in harmony with these fields was when he laid down to sleep, which brought forth the powers of dream and vision. The shamans were the great dreamers. Seeing the future in their dreams and the hidden meanings in the dreams of others. Everybody has the gene but only a chosen few could access it because the genetic triggering device was not passed down genetically but rather occurred as what he called a spontaneous anomaly. Zak was not sure what forces of nature cause the creation of the trigger but figured it either had to occur at conception or between conception and the fetus attaining gender. The order of Melchizedek was this naturally occurring line of shamans, older than any religion yet active in all religions."

"So everybody's got it but only a few people get it. So the guy in the cave painting points to the beginning of the Order?"

"Well, not exactly. Zak believed this guy was a very specific type of shaman, which he called the Adonia—the Shaman of the Women. Doc found this crescent star shape in women's rituals all around the world. Among the Celts it was called the Clad Circle, the Virgins called it the Crescent Star, the Greeks called it the Dionysian Mysteries. Doc believed the power of this shaman was balance, to balance the male and female energies in himself, and by extension, into society. The Adonia was generally given to the High Priestess, by his mother, right before puberty. Through ceremonies and initiations his energies were balanced until he was given the sign of milk."

"Milk? What do you mean?"

"His breasts would fill with milk. His milk was used as an elixir for the nine women of the circle on a daily basis and in ceremonies for puberty and healing for the pains of menopause. Doctor Zak believed that Christ was an Adonia and just as the Magi of Persia knew of his birth so the Magi of the shamanic cults of the Mediterranean knew when it was time for his initiation. The five cults each sent a Magdalene. From the Druids came the saucy redhead. From India, a daughter versed in the Kama Sutra. This is why the Magdalene has so many faces."

"Are there any books on this subject?"

"Zak only revealed his conclusions not his sources. But, he also believed this story of Christ was intimately tied to the grail. Anything else I can do for you?"

"I was thinking about Thanksgiving dinner."

Speedster laughed and agreed, he also said he would help me with my research. It seems the Grail legend had always been a fascination of his. He informed me that another Sag Harborite, of recent memory and literary reputation, had spent a good portion of his life translating the Morte d'Arthur of Mallory into modern English. Speedster, of course, knew the man's wife, a dear friend, who might be persuaded to open up her library.

"Outside of the Bible, few other stories have had such an impact on the creators of literature."

He said this with such pontifical authority I almost dared not to make light of it, almost.

"Except for perhaps the legend of your massive..."

"Books on the subject will be no problem."

He also offered to fix me up with Sharon, the young actress he'd told me about. I told him this whole mess had already "fixed' me in such a way that he need not bother. He assured me my condition was temporary.

I didn't stay for dessert; the fire and the liquor had put me in a walking mood. Outside, it was the first waning of the full moon, still bright enough to return the way I'd come. I walked through the graveyard; the leaves were still and blue in the moonlight. I'd released those fears that had twirled them round the tombstones with the telling of the tale. The memory of Doctor Zak I'd shared with Speedster spread around me like a golden cloak of harmony and well-being. Perhaps I had only seen one face of the Magdalene. If I were good maybe she would show me more of her faces. I walked past the ghostly church with out a shiver and down the side street. I felt peaceful. Life was regaining a bit of its charm. For the first time in a long while I wanted to say thanks. Thanks for the stars and the cold salt air, for the fragrance of dry leaves and home cooking coming from the old houses on Main Street. Thanks for the small town, the white picket fences, the dreams of childhood, all those little things that remind us of our innocence and how we can no longer afford it.

CHAPTER TWENTY-EIGHT

THANKSGIVING

T HE NEXT DAY I woke up giggling. The idea of Jesus with jugs somehow just plain tickled me. I was thinking of replacing my current Jesus expletive, "Sweet tap dancing Jesus!" with this new revelation when the bellboy came in with my morning Bloody Mary and the long awaited check from Mannly P. Tetmire, attorney at law. I was for a whopping 548.95, sweet Jesus with jugs! The rest of the five grand went for expenses and legal fees.

My agent, Mank, broke our agreement and actually called me at the hotel.

"Where's my story?"

He sounded angry and I had not had my wake-up drink yet.

"Mank?! I thought you weren't gonna' be calling me here, something about phone taps and…"

"Put a sock on it, hotshot. I want the story. My editor's crawling up my ass on this one."

"Hey, I've been in a state of nervous exhaustion…"

"Bullshit! I'm looking at your bar bill right now."

"I can explain that…"

"Yeah, well explain this."

He slammed the receiver down in my ear. Sweet Jesus with jugs! I thought a moment. There could only be one explanation for Mank's action. Things were not going well back in L.A. The paper was obviously becoming concerned that I really didn't know anything about the shallow graves and they had actually threatened to stop paying my hotel bill and sue me for what they'd already spent to date on airfare, clothes, etc., etc., etc. It had to happen sooner or later. Also, since they knew suing me would prove fruitless they had more than likely threatened to take the whole thing out of Mank's salary. I was tempted to call him back and relate my explanation but I didn't want to be accused of beating a dead horse, even if the horse lived in Hollywood and worked for a paper. Besides, I figured they wouldn't cut me off until after Thanksgiving.

I was wrong.

As Bubba and I, dressed in our "Sunday best", were heading through the hotel bar, on our way to Speedster's for turkey, the manager cornered us. He told us, in a particularly snotty manner, that, as of today, our credit was cut off. He wanted to know if we were spending the night this evening and how we intended to pay for it. I really didn't want to hold Bubba back, so I let him collar the manager and shake him up a bit before stepping in. By the time I had unsnapped Bubba's hands from the guy's expensive lapels he was much more cordial and assured us he would work something out. Bubba handed the guy his gold card then turned to me.

"My treat."

I had no idea the bodyguard business was so lucrative. As we got into the cab, I thanked Bubba but told him I really couldn't accept more than a night of his hospitality. Bubba just grinned.

"That's alright man, that card ain't no good. I just don't like nobody tryin' to make me look cheap. I shook his ass up pretty good, didn't I? He just ran that bill up on that card and handed it back to me without even callin' it in."

Bubba was a man after my own heart.

"Tonight we gonna party, on me. We doing the disco and everything. But tomorrow, I got to head back to L.A. Sorry man, you are one of the good guys but business is business."

We shook hands on it; it was one of the better deals of my life.

"Professaur! Come in, meet the gang. Who's this with you?"

"Speedster, meet Mister Bubba."

"How you doin' man? Come on in, join the party."

Speedster took our coats and walked us into the living room where a group of four distinguished but rebellious looking gentlemen were gathered around the fireplace drinking highballs and talking.

"Gentlemen, may I have your attention, please. Meet the Professaur and Mister Bubba."

Speedster's introduction made us sound a bit like a circus act. The men stopped talking and turned to us and started clapping. Good ole Speedster, he'd told everybody my secret. I'd have to remember not to get him a Christmas present. A tall man, big, with curly gray hair and a blue V-neck sweater, who looked like he'd misspent his youth wrestling grizzly bears and Indian women, stepped forward and took my hand.

"Joe Weller. It's a pleasure to meet you."

His handshake was warm, truly friendly.

"Nice suit, Professor. Armani isn't it?"

"A gift from the fourth estate."

"It must have pained you to slit the leg like that to make room for your cast?"

"No, actually, I enjoyed it."

"Bravo."

He turned and shook Bubba's hand.

"Mister Bubba, it's a pleasure."

Bubba shook his hand silently, he wasn't sure of what to make of these intellectuals. Speedster continued the introductions. A short, balding man with a maitre'd mustache, wearing a tweed vest with a gold watch chain came next.

"This is Charlie Sumner."

"I've heard a lot about you, Professor."

"And I was hoping to remain a secret."

"Put your mind at ease, Professaur, my friends are only here to help."

"Bill Kirkland."

A tall, thin man with glasses and long gray-black hair extended his hand.

"And this is Doctor Sam Kelly."

Sam was younger, late forties, with a jacket and turtleneck. He wore red-rimmed glasses and looked like a mature Buckaroo Banzai.

"So you're the young man with all the problems?"

"Problems?"

"Don't worry, Sam's an authority on the occult."

"A dangerous field to be an authority in."

"No, a dangerous field to be ignorant in."

"Come in the kitchen and meet the girls."

Speedster pulled us away from the group, through the dining room and into the kitchen.

The kitchen was long and large and smelled of heaven. Four young women, busy with mixing and mashing and boiling and baking, stopped for a breather and walked toward us, wiping their hands on cup towels and aprons.

"LuAnn will introduce you, I'll fix the drinks. Whatta' you boys having?"

"You have any tequila?"

"This is a dinner party, not a shoot out. Something civilized, Professaur."

"Jack Daniels, with a cube of ice."

"And a splash of water. Whatta' you have Mister Bubba?"

"Just a beer, any kind."

"One Jack and one beer, coming up."

LuAnn walked up, followed by her friends.

"Aren't you going to introduce me to your friend, Professor?"

"Oh, I'm sorry. LuAnn, this is Mister Bubba."

Bubba took her hand elegantly.

"Charmed."

He spoke in a voice like James Earl Jones. I was shocked. Bubba was a ladies man.

"Professor, Bubba, these are my friends. Patti Weller, Joe's wife..."

She was a shy brunette; impeccable is the only word to describe her.

"...Sarah Kelly, Sam's wife..."

Red haired, pleasantly chubby with sapphire eyes and a rosy-cheeked face, she wore a calico apron over her designer dress, obviously the baker in the group.

"...and Sharon Tosh..."

A sweet angel face, framed by lots of curly brown hair falling past her shoulders, there was something about her. She seemed both formidable and fragile at the same time, like a ballerina with a strong left hook. I caught myself smiling and staring again. James Earl Bubba moved in on her before I could catch my breath.

"Charmed."

Oh my God, he was kissing her hand like a damned Frenchman. This was not the Bubba I knew. Fortunately, Speedster returned with our drinks and ushered us back to the living room.

The dinner was nothing short of a feast. The long table was spread with a lace tablecloth, decked with bouquets in carnival glass vases and served with fine china, crystal and ornate silverware. There was a huge turkey with three kinds of dressing, two kinds of potatoes, sweet and mashed, steamed carrots, spinach, cranberry sauce, schooners of gravy, and sparkling decanters of wine. It was as sweet as a memory. I'd been seated across from Sharon and watched her secretly through the flowers. She was animated in conversation, reposed while listening and she took very small bites. She was like a child-girl acting very grown up and proper. Speedster kept steering the table talk to topics of my interest. We discussed the Knights Templar and I learned they had appeared and vanished with the Frankish kingdom of Jerusalem. During their prime they had been the most powerful society in the world, having had a hand in the composition of the Magna Charta and in forcing King John to sign it. In the Grail legends, they are the protectors of the Grail family and in history they are the ancestors of both the Freemasons and the Rosicrucians. Doctor Kelly was of the opinion that the use of the number thirteen by our Masonic founding fathers in the Great Seal of America, the one on the back of the dollar bill, indicated that thirteen separate branches of the Grail family were established here in this country to grow and flower under this "New Order of Things." The Grail family in Europe had become entangled with all the other royal bloodlines like a nest of serpents; the decadence was corrupting them. Here, protected by the Masons, who are the rebirth of the Knights Templar, the Grail families could grow and reach a new potential, unfettered by the pretensions of aristocracy. As to what made the Grail family so unique, according to legends, they are the descendants of Kings David and Solomon, to whom God promised a throne on the earth forever.

"In Washington D.C. there is a throne room built by the Masons, it is a complete duplication of the throne room of Solomon as described in the Bible. In my mind, it is sitting there waiting for the right member of the line to claim it, just like the Grail castle in the legends."

"But Doctor Kelly, I thought the Merovingian line of kings in France was the bloodline identified with the Grail."

"That's quite true, Professor, but you must remember the early Merovingians had harems of Biblical proportions. Their descendants could number in the millions by now and it has always been an obscure member of the line, as in the case of Jesus, that God had chosen to vindicate His promises."

It is also significant that all Jews, who call themselves Jews today, are of the tribes of Judah, Benjamin, or Levi, the two royal households and the priestly line. The other tribes rebelled and formed the kingdom of Israel. They were conquered and dispersed, leaving only the kingdom of Judah, for which Jew is the abbreviated form. Speedster here could be of the line of David."

"Thanks Joe. Another interesting fact of history is that the first European explorers considered the Native Americans to be those same Lost Tribes of Israel. Peter Styvenson, founder of New Amsterdam, refused to allow Jews in his colony because he believed the Lost Tribes theory and actually thought he saw Jews and Indians making secret hand signs to one another. The Tribe of Joseph, the Dreamer, was the other Royal House of Israel. Perhaps, the Masons, who founded this country, were trying to join Judah and Benjamin with Joseph and create the unconquerable kingdom of Israel prophesied by Ezekiel. The Professaur here could be of the line of Joseph, Joseph. Who wants more turkey?"

"I'll take a couple more slices."

"Alright, Bubba, pass me your plate."

After dinner, the gentlemen returned to the fire to sip brandy and smoke Havanas. I've always found this a lovely custom in spite of its increasing unpopularity. I believe it is good to separate the sexes from time to time by something besides a public bathroom door. Men and women placed together in close quarters for extended periods of time will either fuck or fight. Although some will argue the point, I find neither of those situations as desirable as a clean kitchen or a strong conversation. I also do not mean to imply by this that men and women cannot enter into an intelligent conversation together, perish the thought if this hasn't already perished by natural causes, but I will suggest that the custom I describe, and do honestly cherish, is better for the digestion. There are certain elements of social history that need not be tampered with to improve society.

We were having our brandy and cigars, making small talk by the fire. I believe Bubba was enjoying this Victorian convenience more than anyone. He stretched out in one of the overstuffed chairs and farted without shame or embarrassment. As I said, better for the digestion, at least Bubba's digestion; trying to put a lid on that one would have definitely given him cramps. I also believed such boisterous bodily functions were the reason behind smoking cigars, were it not for the sound, the smell could have gone unnoticed. The group did give Bubba a little "breathing" room, I noticed.

"So Professor, what is your opinion of these grisly murders?"

"I believe they were done to insure the success of certain movies, television series, and stars."

"Sacrifices, then?"

"Worse than that, standard industry practices."

"Come now Professor, you don't really believe the entire entertainment industry is involved in Satanism?"

"No? You don't really think they're all going to Sachi and Sachi. I mean think about it. Most of what's coming out of Hollywood today follows one of three unholy glories: the glory of violence, the glory of crime or the glory of pornography."

"What's wrong with sex?"

"I didn't say sex; I said pornography."

"What's the difference?"

"Pornography is stupid people who don't give a shit about each other having sex to arouse a third party who basically hates them both."

"Sounds like a description of my first marriage, right down to the mother-in-law."

"Why do you work in the industry then, it makes your big speech sound like sour grapes."

"Movies are the most powerful media we have—I thought I could make a difference. I grew up on movies, great movies, I was under the impression they still existed. I didn't find out how bad things were until they murdered a friend of mine. This isn't sour grapes; it's a cry for help. Sixty-five people got their hearts ripped out. I'm telling you it happens all the time. I'm telling this country's being brainwashed by people for whom evil is good, good box office that is. I believe our only hope is to tell the old stories, the ones from around those great ancestral fires still burning in our heart of hearts. The ones that tell about being human, not super, not demonic, not stupid. We are only as good as our stories, without our poets we're just a bunch of words in the mouth of a dictator. Hollywood is killing the poet in our soul."

The men looked at me then at their brandy. Sometimes it gets quiet after dinner, by the fire, with the women in the kitchen.

CHAPTER TWENTY-NINE

THE HEALING

THE QUIET CONTINUED for a long beat. I figured I'd just embarrassed myself by turning preachy. The men were too polite to comment but I was being given about the same amount of "breathing" room as Bubba after his faux pas. I was starting to get nervous when Speedster announced, "Ah the ladies!"

The women returned to grace the room and, in spite of my Victorian pretense, I was grateful. The conversation picked up. Angel face Sharon moved directly to my side and whispered.

"I thought what you said was wonderful."

"What I said?"

"About Hollywood."

"How did you...."

She put her finger to my lips to silence me. I looked into her smiling eyes and thought I saw admiration. She tugged my arm to lead me away from the group and into the dining room.

"Yes, we heard everything—the kitchen is not so far away."

"I thought I was a bit melodramatic."

"Not me. I'm disgusted by what I see on film these days, and television, forget it, even the commercials are becoming so, so..."

"Pornographic?"

"Everything is being pimped, instead of being advertised. It's terrifying, even children's toys."

"Yes, terrifying is the right word."

She looked up at me with that plucky smile of hers. She was shifting from fragile to formidable.

"What are you doing tonight?"

"You mean after this?"

"Yeah, after this."

"Well Bubba and I had planned to hit the disco."

"Mind if I join you?"

"I, ah, of course not. Sure."

She'd caught me with that left hook. I was dazed. I'd promised myself, no more romance, but here I was, falling again. I could get this young girl in a lot of trouble. People were after me; they were killing my friends. I had to say something. I had to back out, somehow.

"Who's ready for pie and coffee?"

It was LuAnn, passing by on her way to the kitchen. Cheers answered her suggestion from the living room.

"Sharon, can you give me a hand?"

"Sure."

I watched her walk away. It was a pretty sight, the way her legs moved and her body shifted. One night of dancing, maybe it was okay. I couldn't dance anyway with my broken leg and you can't talk in a disco, so she'd wind up being Bubba's date, really. I did like to watch her move. Yeah, it would be just fine.

Doctor Kelly offered us a ride to the disco; it was on his way home. As we got out of the car, he motioned me over to the driver's side window.

"You guys go ahead, I'll catch up."

Kelly rolled his window down and spoke softly.

"I believe you to be a brave young man but there are forces involved here that you don't understand, at least not yet. Doctor McDonald was a dear and trusted friend. I have one piece of information for you tonight. The Feast of the Beast is December twenty-third—you will not be safe until it passes. I may be able to help you. I'll be in touch."

He extended his hand and I took it.

"Be careful."

I stood there a moment, watching his car pull out of the lot and over the small bridge that connected the town to the small bit of island, which sheltered the harbor. It was a handsome bridge with old-fashioned streetlights, on both sides, illuminating the full length of its graceful curve. I walked slowly down the pier to the entrance of the nightclub, glancing back at the bridge as Kelly's red taillights disappeared into the darkness on the other side.

"I'd been right about the disco. It was too loud for conversation and Bubba was in a dancing mood. He was also in a buying mood. I downed three shots of tequila and four beers during my first half hour at the table. I was also right about enjoying the sight of Angel Face dancing. Her movements were both sensual and exuberant yet never overt—they celebrated the mystery of sexuality, not the act. Bubba's dancing was also a celebration—that of a nose tackle who'd recovered a fumble and ran for a touchdown. They cut quite a figure on the dance floor. Between dances they'd come back to the table and we'd scream at each other over the din. Every now and then they'd play a slow song and Angel face would drag me out onto the dance floor. We'd stand in one place and rock back and forth. It was nice to hold her in my arms. I felt the mortar loosening between the bricks in the wall I'd built around myself. I was glad we had no time to talk. I could repair my wall tomorrow and then, if I was lucky, avoid her until after Christmas. She was not like any girl I'd known in L.A., or Texas, for that matter. She confused me. Dazed me. This was not like the crush I'd had on T.Z., all fire and passion, the adolescent "hots." This was more akin to those feelings that cure the great heartbreak, the ones that renew us, patch us up, and give us courage. It was a very strange way to feel about this girl, a girl I hardly knew. But watching her was like watching the ocean. The sound and the motion of her tide lulled me into a trance, a rapture. I could feel its great power soothe the cracks and splinters left behind from living by the touch of something, if not eternal, ancient beyond our poor sense of time. This is how it was and why I had to stop it.

About three in the morning we put Angel face in a cab and walked to the hotel. We were feeling no pain as we staggered through the door and into the lobby. Suddenly there was the asshole manager. What the fuck was he doing here at three in the morning?

"I'm sorry gentlemen, **but your** credit card is no good and unless you have some other means **of paying** your bill I must ask you to leave."

Bubba doubled up his **fists.**

"I got the means right **here.**"

He lunged for the **manager** when out of nowhere two cops with nightsticks hit him from **both** sides. We'd been set up. He never had a chance. They beat him down to the floor then worked him over while the manager shouted encouragement. I'd moved to defend him and gotten knocked on my ass by a flick of the stick. They just kept beating his head. I tried to get over to him but it was too late. They stopped, cuffed us both and, with the help of a couple of burlys from the hotel bar, dragged us out to the car. We were taken around the corner to a police station and thrown into a cell. I crawled across the cold concrete floor and lifted his head into my lap. He did not look good. I tore the sleeves off my shirt and gently wiped the blood from his wounds. I could not stop myself from crying. Something was breaking apart inside of me. I'd only slipped once during this whole ordeal, that morning at the beach in Santa Monica. I'd gotten a grip on myself pretty quick then. But not tonight; I was exploding inside. I told myself that I was too drunk to stop the tears, but that wasn't it. That wasn't it at all. I was crying like the Magdalene, unstoppable tears, floods of tears; I was washing his wounds with my tears. I was shaking; I could not stop this time. I was overcome by feelings so strong, I could not contain, I could not control, could not say, "No, stop, I'm in charge here." My whole silly self-awareness was gone. I was lost, feeling with all of my heart for a friend who'd been beaten to death, or worse, because he wanted to do me a favor. All of the horror I had seen, all the misshapen monsters of malice man could conjure from the gates of hell, all the perversions and terror had not been able to break me as this one simple act of pettiness and brutality. This was not some ritual of witchcraft, these were not Satanic ministers out to twist their fate with magic, this was just a pompous clerk of a pretentious hotel and a couple of Joe Six-pack cops having a little fun with an uppity nigger. This was small town justice and that really tore it.

I held him close and prayed to God that he would not die in my arms. I had never prayed before, not really prayed. The cocoon around my soul shattered. I felt my hands glowing hot as I touched his ugly open sores, glowing hot, as if there was a force rushing through my body and out of my hands, like everything I was feeling was pouring out of my hands. Reeling in this strange ecstasy, emotions, compassion, pain sorrow, love, I was passing in and out of consciousness. I went black. I saw nothing but my hands then other hands, small hands, a child's hands, a boy, about thirteen, his face thin, kindly. He was holding the cup, handing it to me, the Grail, burning silver white light in my hands, in my hands, in my hands.

CHAPTER THIRTY

THE MEETING

I WAS AWAKENED BY THE GUARD, rattling my cage with his night-stick.

"Wake up! Wake up! Deadbeats! The judge wants to see ya!"

I had one of the worst hangovers of my life, but then, waking up in jail tends to make even a mild hangover unbearable. I squinted open my eyes. The world was fuzzy. I could barely remember last night and what I did remember I wanted to forget. I looked down at Bubba, who was still asleep in my lap. Something was wrong. Bubba's head should have looked like a busted watermelon. It didn't; in fact, he looked fine. I shook my throbbing head and tried to clear my eyes. Funny, he still looked fine. The guard, by this time, had stopped raking the bars and was threatening to throw a bucked of cold water on us. I pushed Bubba up. He woke with a start, flailing his arms, fighting off the nightmare of his beating. The guard had the pail of water cocked. I pulled myself out from under Bubba.

"Whoa! Wait a minute! We're getting up!"

Bubba was on all fours, shaking it off. He stood up and slowly stretched to full height. The guard got a funny look on his face when he noticed Bubba's head wasn't bashed in. He sat the bucket down and took a good, long look—he couldn't believe it.

"You guys make yourselves presentable..."

His face was puzzled, his words weak.

"You're due in court in fifteen minutes."

He backed away, staring at Bubba.

"I'll come get you when it's time."

"What the hell's the matter with him?"

"I don't know; I guess he was expecting to see you in worse shape. Actually, so was I. I could have sworn those cops really plowed your head."

Bubba felt his head; he didn't believe it either. He walked over to the sink, splashed some water in his face then stared at the dirty mirror.

"This is some real Twilight Zone shit here—there ain't a scratch on me."

Something funny was going on here. My bloody shirtsleeves were still in a pile on the floor. The front of my shirt looked like I'd caught a pizza.

"I don't know about you, Professor, but if I get out of this jail, I'm on the first plane back to L.A."

I washed my face. It didn't help. I put my jacked on and buttoned it over the bloodstains. Bubba was just getting into his sport coat when the guard came for us. He led us out of the cell and down the corridor, into the courtroom. When we walked in, I saw the snotty manager standing at one of the tables, talking to the D.A. and the two "arresting" officers. We were seated at the other table. The courtroom was almost empty. This had the look and feel of another setup. The judge entered, we all stood up. He was an older gentleman, white-haired, stern-faced. I was starting to become resigned to spending the holidays in jail when the courtroom door opened with a loud bang. It was Speedster. Nice entrance. I'd actually been expecting him; figuring last night's fracas at the hotel was big news in this small town. He strolled up to the bench and held a quiet conference with the judge. There was a lot of head nodding, then, Speedster came down and joined us at our table. He looked like he'd missed his morning coffee and just might be a little pissed at me.

"Just keep your mouths shut."

The judge pounded his gavel and called the court to order. The bailiff read the complaints against us. The D.A. stood up; he had a few bad things to say about Bubba and me. The cops and the manager kept whispering and nudging each other and pointing at Bubba. The D.A. sat down and Speedster stood up. The main point of his speech was that no real harm had been done and that, outside of the bill, there were no damages. The judge asked for the amount of the bill. The manager stood up.

"Well let me see—the room, breakfast, drinks—it all comes to $548.95"

The asshole had found my check. This was too much. I leaned over to Speedster and told him about the check. I also mentioned it was unfair to charge me for the room since I'd spent last night in jail, not in the hotel.

"The accused left a check for that amount in his hotel room, your honor."

The manager produced the check with a smile. The judge called the D.A. and Speedster up to the bench. There was another quiet conference. Speedster came back over to our table with the check.

"Sign it over to him and let's get out of here."

We walked out of the police station into bright, crisp, winter morning. The cold air felt good. It stunned my hangover.

"You guys alright?"

"I could use a drink."

"How you gonna' pay for it?"

"I don't know, my lawyer just gave away all my money."

"Who said I was a lawyer? I play poker with the judge on Thursday nights."

The hotel was a short walk. When we got there a cab was waiting out front.

"You the guys heading to the airport?"

The town was ready for us to leave. The cabbie even had our bags in the trunk.

"I am. Fuck this town and the horse's ass from which it fell. You coming?"

"Naw, tell Mank I disappeared of the face of the Earth."

Bubba grabbed me in a big bear hug.

"Professor, you are alright."

He pulled me back and squeezed a couple of twenties into my hand.

"But, you are one of those Rod Serling motherfuckers and I'll be glad to be puttin' some miles between us."

He walked over to Speedster and shook his hand.

"Thanks for helping."

"Anytime, Bubba."

The cab driver took my bags out of his trunk, got back in the cab and drove off with Bubba waving out the window.

"Get your bags, Professor, and follow me. There's someone I want you to meet."

"Do we have time for a drink first? My head is killing me."

Speedster was in a hurry so I tossed my bags in the trunk of his '55 Ford and we headed over the bridge to the island on the other side. I felt we were going to Doctor Kelly's, even though Speedster was making a big mystery out of our destination. He was acting differently this morning and it was not just because he had to get up early. We took a right at the blinking light; the sign said Shelter Island.

"Speedster?"

"What."

"Something strange happened last night."

"Professor, there is nothing strange about you getting thrown in the pokey on a D&D charge."

"In that cell last night, Bubba was beat up bad, I wanted to help him. I was holding his head, crying, and this kid came out of nowhere...."

"Kid?"

Something strange flashed across Speedster's face.

"What kid?"

"I don't know. It's all pretty jumbled. It was like a vision."

Speedster looked at me and cocked one eyebrow.

"Were you drinking Mescal last night?"

"All I know is that Bubba's head was whipped into hamburger last night, by those two cops, and this morning there ain't a scratch on him."

"And you're sure about this?"

I opened my jacket and exposed my bloodstained shirtfront.

"You wanna' try some Tide on my shirt?"

Speedster looked down at my shirt then back up to my face.

"Professor, your nose is still bleeding a little; it may be broken."

I felt my face. It was still numb and my nose did feel a little larger than I'd remembered, but it did not feel broken. Speedster was hiding something from me. I felt he knew all about last night. I also knew I would not find out what he knew until he was damn good and ready to tell me, but I did feel that he would tell me soon. That thought sent chills up my spine.

The ferry was big enough to hold about fifteen cars. It wasn't very crowded this morning so we got out of the car and stood near the edge. So far, this was the best ten minutes of the day—a view of the fog, fading on the ocean's face, with the white sun sparkling of the breakers. The salt, so thick in the air I could taste as well as smell it. I wanted to drown in this momentary intoxication of my battered senses. I wanted to high-jack this ferry and sail down to Mexico, spend months on the sea, dodging the coast guard, then land in some small port and sell cars to drug runners. I was almost there, curled up in a hammock under a palm tree, drunk on tequila.

The roads on Shelter Island are steep and winding. The landscape looks like Sleepy Hollow. We pulled off the main road, down into the woods, until we came to the driveway of an old cottage.

"Who lives here, the three little pigs?"

Speedster ignored my joke; he was being uncharacteristically serious. We parked and went up to the door. He did some kind of signal knock then stepped back, leaving me standing there.

"I'll see you inside."

The door opened. A tall man in a butler's outfit ushered me in.

"Good morning, sir. You are to wait in the library."

He opened the door to his left. I walked in. A semi-circle of seven high backed, ornately carved, mahogany chairs had been arranged in the middle of the room with a small stool in the center of them. The room was dark and very old feeling, with a low ceiling, bookcases on all of the walls and a Franklin stove in the North corner, for heat. The butler motioned me to the stool. I sat down.

"The Masters will be with you shortly," he said as he closed the door.

CHAPTER THIRTY-ONE

THE MASTERS

I SAT THERE FEELING SILLY, wondering what kind of gag Speedster was pulling on me. The lack of sleep and breakfast, coupled with that bad hangover, had me contemplating curling up on the floor in front of the Franklin stove, when the door opened again. Seven men in dark, hooded robes, with some kind of symbols embroidered down the sides, entered and took their seats. One by one they pulled back their hoods and opened their robes, all but the man in the center chair. I was relieved to see Speedster and his friends, Joe, Doctor Kelly, Kirkland, Sumner and the butler, under those spooky robes. They were wearing the regular clothes with the addition of the little Masonic mini skirt I'd seen in that old engraving, back in L.A. The man in the center remained concealed, the rest of them were looking at me, smiling. I smiled back.

"I hope this is not one of those fraternity initiations with the leather paddles and all that stuff, 'cause if it is..."

The hooded figure in the center chair raised his hand. I instinctively shut up.

"What is your name?"

"I don't have one, not a real one anyway. I've been going by aliases since the day I was born."

For some reason, the group found my answer amusing, I didn't. I found it depressing. The man in the center chair slowly slid back his hood and opened his robe. His face was familiar, aristocratic, with a fine roman nose. He wore a heavy gold chain around his neck with a grand medallion hanging from it. He smiled and shook his head from side to side as if saying "no."

"No, my son, your name is David. David La Rocca de Sion. The Rock of Sion of the line of Plant Ard."

The name was greeted by polite applause from the other men.

"And, I should know, I gave it to you. I am your father."

At this point, he stood up and opened his arms wide. I didn't know whether to shit or go blind. It was all happening too fast. I stood up, trembling, a hurricane of emotions roaring through my weakened body, and something in my blood, in my heart, saying "yes this is true, this is true." I stepped forward. He embraced me with such tenderness and longing that I ached from the feeling. His tears told me again, "yes, this is true." I was shaking so hard; I had to sit down.

"Now, you have seen your name in the stone. You know who you are, but you do not know what you are."

He held my hand a long moment, then smiled, and returned to his chair.

"Why did you leave me?"

The fierce rage of my childhood was, at last, being released.

"After Mom died, I was only four, but I could feel lost and I could feel lied to. "

He looked at me, his eyes full of pain.

"I know, my son. I was never far from you. But, that is the way with the men of our line. Someday you may have to do the same. We are kings, awaiting a throne, a throne that has been usurped. There are many forces, which seek us out, to find us and kill us. The males of our line are most vulnerable; they constitute a threat to other royal lines. Our women are sought as prizes to be married, so that the blood of the usurpers may mingle with the blood of our line. For the males, our heritage must remain a secret. If you take a wife, she is never to know. If she finds out, you must leave her. It is the only way to protect our children."

"You could have left me something, a letter. Instead I had to hear that bullshit half-true story of my life when I was twenty-one. I've been so lonely; I always thought there was something wrong with me."

He stood again and came over to me and hugged me. This time I cried, clutching him, burying my head in his chest.

"My son, no father ever loved his child more. No father ever bore such pain. All my life I've waited for this moment, to hold you, to hug you, to show you how much I love you, and, to tell you the story I must now relate."

He pulled back just a bit, but held onto my shoulders. He looked into my eyes.

"What I must tell you will be hard for you to believe at first, but you must. Your very life depends on your belief."

I looked into his face. He seemed to almost glow. I nodded. Yes.

"I understand."

He returned to his chair.

"First, I should explain why I've waited so long to make myself know to you. I had to wait until the vertu, the secret power of your blood, became activated by the fire of an act of supreme compassion. That happened last night when you healed your friend."

"I healed Bubba?"

"Healing by the laying of hands is part of the natural power of the blood you possess."

"But, I couldn't have healed him; I was out of my mind, alone, in that cell...."

"My son, you are never alone. You are never out of my sight. It has taken a long time for you to stop feeling sorry for yourself. I have watched you with great sadness as you squandered your substance, drinking, carousing, toying with women, working for scoundrels."

He paused a moment to gauge my reaction. I hung my head, he was right—my life was a series of wasted days and wasted nights.

He smiled.

"Like the prodigal Son in the Bible, but I also noticed something else, very early on. There was this love in you, this seed of compassion. Those who you came in contact with grew to love you. I was watching the dawning of your light. The power to inspire love by loving was not lacking in you. It is a rare gift. The mark of a true king is that he makes those around him feel like kings."

There was truth in what he said. I thought of the rabbit.

"You're thinking of your friend who has become your guide."

How did he know?

"Yes, I can read your mind and more, I can read your soul."

At that moment my soul would not have come under the heading of light reading—my soul was confused, troubled. I didn't know what was expected of me. I didn't understand how I was capable of healing anybody when I was so full of pain myself.

"Father, forgive me, but I'm just a drunken soldier in this war of dark and light. I don't have any idea what is going on or how a guy like me can be of any service in some grand design to preserve an ancient bloodline."

"Do you know what bloodline is involved here?"

"Some French kings from the fourth century, maybe connected to King David."

"And if I were to tell you it was more sacred than that?"

"Sacred?"

"I told you before that what I had to tell you would be hard to believe. It is the blood of Jesus Christ that runs in your veins."

He waited again to see my reaction. The words he was saying sent shivers through me.

"The Sangrael which Magdalene brought into France was the girl child of Christ. Jesus was of the house of David; Mary Magdalene was of the house of Saul. Israel had two royal families, two royal tribes, Judah and Benjamin. David had married Saul's daughter, but they had no children together. The marriage of Jesus and Mary had healed an ancient breach in the kings of Israel. You see. Jesus was truly King of the Jews, a serious threat to both Herod and Rome. As Son of man, He had come to fulfill the promises God made to David of a line of kings lasting until the end of the age. As Son of God, He had come as a priest for atonement, at-one-ment between God and man. He fulfilled both of His purposes, both king and priest. The purpose to which you have been called from your birth is to continue with honor this sacred line. That is why there is great power in your blood and why the evil one seeks it for his own."

This was not something a man with a bad hangover is ready to hear. The story burned through my brain like a red-hot sledgehammer. The idea of great- grandpa Jesus brought a lifetime of accepted realities crashing down around my already sputtering consciousness. I was going into flashes, pieces of life fluttering like lightening bugs through the blinding darkness of knowing absolutely nothing for sure. I saw all of the madness of the past weeks, all the faces, all the moments of death and pleasure, soft hands and claws all jumbled together, and the shadow, the shadow I'd seen in the good doctor's kitchen, the shadow I now called my father, swirling among them like smoke. I felt I'd stopped breathing, like my heartbeat was gone when the vision of Magdalene and her cup stirred out of the smoldering ruins of my mind and sent the room spinning. I felt off the stool into velvet black, blessed night, I felt so at peace in her arms.

CHAPTER THIRTY-TWO

AWAKENING

I DIDN'T WANT TO WAKE UP. I didn't want to know where I was. I wanted to remain where everything was black and there was no such thing as thought. If I thought at all, I wanted to think that none of this was real. If I woke up, I wanted to wake up and not go to Paps' funeral. If I smelled sausage cooking, I wanted it to be…Sausage cooking? Why did I smell sausage cooking? There was a temptation to open my eyes that originated in my stomach. I fought it as long as I could, which was not long. I was so hungry. I opened my eyes and saw I was in an old four-poster bed in a small but comfortable bedroom. The low ceiling and the "George Washington slept here" décor told me I had not left the "little pig's" cottage on Shelter Island. Somebody was making breakfast. I really didn't want to believe what I'd been told. It was too crazy. It was crazier than all the other things that had gone down. To be victim, an object of someone's obsessive madness, this I could stand, it required nothing of me but to use my instinct for survival to stay out of their way. I was still me, maybe scared, maybe hurt, but still me. What they wanted me to be was much more, they wanted me to be someone else, to scrap everything and start again. And who they wanted me to be was God. I could not handle the part, no way. I was not cut out to play God. Even my speech about the evil of Hollywood had flopped. Morality was not my strong suit. But they knew the damn sausages would get to me. They knew, no matter what, I'd wake up hungry. They knew I was just a man. I threw the covers back and started to drag my cast over the side of the bed. Only there was no cast. My leg felt fine. It looked dirty gray from spending almost two weeks without a bath, but it had healed. I didn't like it one bit. I was just getting used to the constant pain. It gave me a good excuse to drink. There was a soft, terrycloth robe draped over the foot of the bed. I put it on and paced around, looking occasionally at the door that must lead to the kitchen. Well, it was the only door in the room; sooner or later I'd have to use it. I would tell them, thank you very much but I believe you've made a mistake. I am not the guy you're looking for. Maybe I'd better not start an argument right away. I should just walk in and say, hey what's for breakfast. I walked to the door and opened it.

"Hey, what's for breakfast?"

Nobody answered. I walked out into the long country-style kitchen—charming place. A long row of diamond pane windows ran down the wall opposite my door. The sink, preparation counter, and old-fashioned gas range were on the same wall under the windows. At the end of the room, to my left, were French doors leading out into a screened mudroom. On the same wall as my door were the refrigerator and cabinets. To my right were a small fireplace and a door leading into the dining room. The kitchen table and chairs were in the center of the room. On the table sat a small bouquet of flowers in an earthen vase, a pot of coffee with cups, cream and sugar, a pitcher of orange juice and a small plate of delicious sausages. I sat down at the table and poured myself a cup of coffee. I was just about to dig into the sausages when I heard the French doors open.

"Ah-ha! So you're finally up!"

I turned around and there was Sharon Tosh, wearing a red and white checked apron over her gray sweat suit, walking into the kitchen with an arm load of kindling wood.

"Don't eat that yet."

She walked straight across the room and dumped the kindling into the fireplace.

"I beg your pardon?"

"You got your choice, pancakes or eggs."

"I'm sorry, but what are you doing here?"

"I live here. I got the guest apartment over the garage. Speedster stopped by this morning with Doctor Kelly. They told me you'd be staying here a few days. Kelly removed your old cast; he's coming back tomorrow to see about giving you a new one."

She moved to the stove, turned on a burner and slapped a skillet on the fire. She was different than I'd remembered, coarser, she talked differently.

"In the meantime, I was asked to feed ya' an' give ya' a bath, scrub all that dead skin off your leg. Then, I put ya' to bed. Satisfied?"

"More than satisfied, I'm overwhelmed."

"Don't get cute; just tell me, eggs or pancakes?"

"Oh, ah, pancakes."

"Good choice—I don't trust eggs these days."

She went to the fridge and pulled out a bowl of batter.

"How many?"

"How many...."

She gave me an irritated look.

"Pancakes."

"Oh, ah, three...no two."

She walked back over to the hot skillet and flapped a dab butter in it.

"Two? No wonder you're so skinny."

She was amazing to watch, a true adept in the kitchen. Every move was smooth and flowing. The way she swirled the butter around in the skillet. The way she poured the batter. Not one jot of wasted energy, every movement flowed into the next like a dance.

"It's truly beautiful, the way you do that."

"Knock it of, pal. I'm only doing this until you get your new cast. Then, you're on your own. I got plenty of nieces and nephews if I want to spoil somebody."

She flipped the pancake with the ease of a short order cook.

"I'm sorry but you seem like a completely different person from the girl I met last night."

Suddenly her whole manner changed, her face lit up with a glorious dimpled smile.

"I do, you mean it?"

She'd caught me again with that sizzling left hook. I sat there, looking stupid.

"Well, yes, I mean it."

"Great! It's working; I've got that one down."

"What one?"

"Betty, the waitress. She's a character in a play I'll try out for in the spring."

She pulled a chair up and sat down across from me.

"That's what I do out here all winter. I perfect my characters. I find out what they'll be casting for in New York in the Spring and Summer stock in Provincetown and other places. I sublet my apartment to N.Y.U. students and make enough to pay the rent here plus a little left over to live on. That way I can concentrate on my art. So, was I convincing?"

"Ah, very."

I was still confused and stunned stupid by her rapid transition from person to person.

She hopped back up, flipped the pancake onto my plate and started another. She was Betty again.

"If you're thinking about brandy for your coffee or tequila for your orange juice, forget it. No alcohol, doctor's orders."

I could only hope it would be Sharon not "Betty" who gave me my bath later. Unfortunately, it was neither; it was "Clarissa," the neurotic English nanny, complete with Cockney accent. She scrubbed my leg painfully pink then dropped it back in the tub so sharply that I arched out of the water in pain.

" 'Ere now! Yowl be washin' 'at thing dere, yourself."

Later that night, "Meagan," the teenage teaser, put me to bed. I was exhausted. I'd been awake only five hours and four different women had fed me, bathed me, teased me and tucked me in. I really wanted a nightcap. I needed something to calm me down. I was developing a fetish for girls with multiple personalities. Everything she did turned me on. I was not easily dazzled but she had done that to me, and much, much more. I'd forgotten everything else. My life started with the sausages. I had just been born; I had no past, just an all-consuming desire to be with this girl again. It was then that I heard it, her voice, distant and clear through the cold air. She was practicing a song. A strange song without words, just notes pure as crystal, a lullaby, hushed by the night and nowhere of Shelter Island.

CHAPTER THIRTY-THREE

THE KINGDOM

"**H**OW ARE YOU FEELING this morning?"
I recognized the voice. It was Speedster. I opened my eyes. He and Doctor Kelly were standing over my bed like a couple of vultures. I sat up stiffly. They could tell I was wary of them.

"I just wanted to look at your leg."

He pulled the covers back and examined my leg.

"It looks just fine, but stay off of it for another couple of days. I'll be back to check on you then."

He covered my leg back up then he and Speedster turned to go.

"Wait a minute, that's it?"

"There was something else?"

"Was there something else? How about that little scene yesterday with the robes and the weird stories? You guys want to tell me what the hell's going on!"

Speedster came over to the bed quickly with an expression on his face so intense I got an involuntary shudder.

"Keep your voice down. You wanna' know what happened yesterday, your body was too weak and your blood too polluted with alcohol for us to complete the psychic transfer of the genetic knowledge necessary to save your life. Now you eat, you rest, and you lay off the sauce until we say you're ready then, God help you, pray we're in time."

He turned on his heel and stalked out of the room. Doctor Kelly smiled.

"We'll see you in a few days."

What'd I do? I just asked a simple question. Maybe that was it; maybe the question wasn't as simple as I thought. I could no longer play with the pieces of this puzzle. I'd never see the complete picture. I'd been falling in and out of consciousness so often the past three days the line between those two states of being was blurred to the point where it no longer served as a useful frame of reference. Of course, I'd spent the week prior in my hometown of Blottosville, so my frame of reference was pretty well bent before I'd become the Son of God. And what did he mean by polluted with alcohol? Alcohol is a purifier. I know it may put a strain on the liver if consumed in large psychoactive size doses and if the dosage is maintained over a long period of time one might addle one's own brain, but at least it won't rot the skin right of your body like prolonged doses of good ole healthy sunshine. Or turn your lungs into toilet paper like the "Fat Lady" of L.A. Or grow golf ball sized tumors all the way up your spine and into your head like the good ole ground water in the plum groves in Oregon. No sirree! As the Son of God I should be entitled to a drink if I wanted one. After all, Great-great-great-great-grandpappy had turned water into wine.

On the other hand, my mind still echoed with imps and serpents and all consuming hellmouths, things that seemed held back by the powers under whose protection I now rested.

I was a pawn, being moved to the back row where the chess master would change him into a knight. I was at the mercy of powerful forces who understood the strategy and timing of this game. My whole vain effort to understand, to know what was going on, was just another part of the master's plan. Nothing had been left to chance. Speedster's call, those many weeks ago, was no fluke, no accident. His advice was not just friendly, not just helpful. Some how they could see into the future and they know how to tip the scales. A moment here, lost, another moment there, put back—and all of a sudden the whole future's different. There were no choices for me to make, I was the chosen, and therefore I was without choice. But, for the moment, I was safe. I was in a different world than the one to which I was bound.

"Can I come in?"

It was Sharon.

"Of course, please."

She walked in all herself this morning, shy and precious as a baby doe.

"The doctor says you need a few more days of rest. I promised I'd nurse you along."

For the next few days I was her perfect playmate. She taught me to act, to assume other personalities. I was being introduced to childhood all over again. My own childhood had been distanced from play with other children by my secrets. I didn't want to slip and let someone in close enough to find out my "cousin" was actually my mother and that my father had disappeared. Plus, as the detective had pointed out, I did not look Mex. I had a hard time fitting in the Mexican world, and in Texas, the white world was also out of reach.

But Sharon was erasing all of that with ease. She could imitate anyone. One day while we were out shopping, she stood next to this old lady picking through the vegetables, and boom, she became an old lady picking through the vegetables. Watching her metamorphosis was delightful. But, she wouldn't let me just watch; I had to join in.

She coaxed and connived and soon I was loving it. I could be anyone; it was absolute freedom. We'd go into stores posing as English tourists and get away with it. It was unbelievable. As a writer, I had always been one step to the side and two steps back from my life, recording it in my mind. Most of my conversations were with myself about what just happened, so my responses to the outside world were always brief and just a shade late. But, now I was learning to be right there. I was moving so fast in the present tense at times I totally lost sight of myself. It was exhilarating. One moment followed the next like jewels in a necklace or pearls on a long strand that stretched into tomorrow.

I was quite adept at playing royalty by the time Doctor Kelly returned with Speedster to look at my leg. I couldn't stop acting the part. I could hear Sharon giggling from the kitchen as I tried my new accent and attitudes out on them. To my surprise they seemed to enjoy it; Speedster smiled, so did Doctor Kelly. They even played along.

"Your leg looks much improved, your grace."

"Do you think you'll be ready to assume your duties soon, your highness?"

"Indubitably."

"I think he'll be ready by Saturday, don't you Doctor? It seems he's learned our first secret."

"Secret?"

"Yes, your grace. The kingdom is reserved for children."

CHAPTER THIRTY-FOUR

THE KNOWLEDGE

I HAD NEVER ENJOYED a chaste relationship with a woman more in my life. In fact, I enjoyed this relationship much more than others I had which had not been so chaste. I admired everything about this person, her self-discipline, the love she had for her art, and with her it was truly an art, a form of magic. When she assumed a character, all of the features of that character became second nature to her. She did not have to guess what a character would do in certain circumstances; it was already there, at her fingertips.

She was patient in her instruction. When I'd lose what she called my center in a character, she would nudge me back to it, without ridicule or unkindness. She insisted I play nobility, which came to me with great ease. She warned me about being lazy, never allowing me to play a shallow aristocrat.

"Nobility was not an affectation," she would tell me, "acting is not mere mimicry, it is the assumption of life."

We progressed from the silly to the sublime. She was expanding my ability to feel, to enjoy the sensation of great emotion coursing through my heart.

I never tired of her for she was endless. Through her, perhaps for the first time, I began to understand that being alive meant more than just waking up the next day feeling bad.

Saturday morning they came for me. The butler woke me up.

"What's your name anyway?"

"Harrison, your grace."

"Harrison, are you psychic?"

"What do you mean, sire?"

"I mean do you know things about people that aren't apparent or things that maybe they don't know about themselves or maybe that they do know but won't admit...."

"I don't follow you, sire."

"My father said that I healed Bubba."

"And so you did."

"But I was real drunk and beat up and...."

"Sire, is it not possible for a beat up drunk to feel compassion, to care for someone else?"

"To tell you the truth, I've seen more compassion and caring going on among the beat up drunks of this world than among the rest of the members of our so-called polite society."

"Compassion is not the best career move for the upwardly mobile, is that what you're saying?"

"Something like that, but in that cell that night I thought I saw a young boy, about thirteen, holding the Grail, handing it to me."

"Perhaps it was your spirit."

"My soul?"

"Oh my lord no, your soul grows, it ages, in a sense, it mirrors your body, or to be more precise, it holds the matter of the body together in shape observable to the senses. The spirit is another creature entirely, all potential, forever young, forever creative. Do you understand?"

"Not really."

"It is time for you to dress, sire."

"One more question, Sharon's part of all this, isn't she?"

"Sharon is an actress who rents the space over the garage. She has nothing to do with our purpose nor is she aware of it. We decided her talents would be useful in preparing you for the challenge you must face—nothing more, nothing less. She is a fine, sensitive girl; otherwise we would not have rented to her. But, I suggest you learn from her what she has to show you and impart to her none of the matters that concern only us."

I took my time getting dressed. I still was not sure I was in the right place. It had all been too perfect here. I was more at home with danger, with the edge; this was not my cup of meat. And this was what I'd secretly longed for all my life. I was a kid in my father's house. I could play all day and there would still be food on the table at night. I had a servant to wait on me. I had a girl to entertain me. What the hell was I bitchin' about? Things were bound to get ugly again. They always do. I'm sure this challenge Harrison referred to would not be hitting a glass of beer with a quarter on the first bounce. No, something much darker lay down the road for me, something that would make the events of Los Angeles look like a tough round of trivial pursuit.

"It's time, your grace."

I finished dressing and walked out to the kitchen, through the dining room and into the library to sit and wait for the masters.

They entered wearing the long hooded robes and sat down as before. My father stood up and approached me.

"It is good to see you again, my son."

I stood up and embraced him.

"It is good to see you, Father."

"I'm sorry we put you through such a test last time, but it was important to make the initial contact while your blood was still charged with power."

As usual, a lot of what he said went flying over my head. I just nodded, knowing he knew I didn't know.

"You will do just fine. Please, relax your mind."

I smiled; he was always ahead of me, even my own thoughts could not move fast enough. He returned to his chair and we both sat down.

"Open your mind and your heart to me now, my son. Put all concerns far away."

I relaxed and let myself gaze blankly into his eyes.

"Very good, shall we begin?"

The other men turned their attention to me as well, and within minutes I became very aware of a subtle buzzing in the back of my head.

"Just relax now and close your eyes."

When I did I could feel that strange rocking sensation that sometimes comes right before sleep. Slowly, the darkness behind my eyelids faded into a deep blue. Then came clouds, followed by vistas of time and history. On an ancient boat facing a strange shore, I saw a new Magdalene. She was different. She was Mary of Bethany with her brother Lazarus, whom she called "Beloved John". I felt I was inside of her, feeling with her heart, seeing with her eyes, thinking with her mind. Then my vision faded and I saw the courts of medieval kings, their harems of a hundred wives, all of them beautiful, many pregnant, or with babes at the breast, young ones on their laps. I saw wars and battles, Jerusalem aflame and re-conquered. I watched a strange ceremony, Templars surrounding a man crucified; his body was being taken down from the cross and laid in a shroud. The Templars knelt around the covered body and prayed for a miracle. I saw the birthing of America and France reborn. It was as if my soul touched the souls of those in my visions, as if their experiences were mine. I felt I'd been living for two thousand years—I felt strangely at home in eternal time.

When I came to myself again and opened my eyes, my father was slumped in his chair. I turned to Harrison.

"Is my father all right?"

Harrison smiled and stood up.

"He rests."

He walked over to my father and gently reached under his robe and removed the gold chain and medallion. He walked over to me holding it out in his hands.

"Bow thy head humbly, Sicambrian, revere what thou hast burned and burn what thou hast revered."

With that he placed the chain around my neck. There was polite applause then I was asked to stand. Harrison led me out of the room. He paused in the dining room.

"Tomorrow your enemies are throwing a party. I shall take you myself and introduce you to the great East Hampton Society. What you sought to avoid in Hollywood is here, older, more established. So, do not be surprised to see some of your old acquaintances there, paying respects. Hold yourself as a man. Today you became the end of a long and prestigious line."

He turned and went back to the library.

CHAPTER THIRTY-FIVE

THE POWER

THAT NIGHT SHE CAME TO ME, Sharon, herself, dressed in gossamer, holding a candelabra.

"So, you're a prince now."

I couldn't say anything; I could only watch her glide toward my bedside like some sweet dream thing.

"The pixies told me."

"The pixies?"

"I've seen them since I was a child; they're the main reason I choose to live out here."

"There are pixies out here?"

"They don't like it in the cities."

She spun around in a circle, a dear pirouette, as if dancing with her unseen friends.

"Those old men of yours think they're so clever but I have my friends, too."

She paused to curtsy at the edge of my bed.

"And they tell me things, not everything. They say if I knew everything about you, I'd never see you again."

"And what did they say about tonight?"

"They said to lie with you and keep you warm."

She sat her candelabra on the night stand and climbed into my bed. I reached out to touch her; she took my hand, softly kissing my fingertips. She shimmered like a vision, as she placed my hand back over my heart. Sitting, she pulled her nightgown up over her head, and revealed her nakedness with a childlike coo. Her breasts glowed in the candlelight, smooth, plump and firm. She shivered as she dropped her nightgown to the floor then leaned over to kiss my forehead. Her hand soothed my cheek. She whispered in a misty voice.

"I've come to seduce you, my foundling Prince. You must not move; do not lift a finger or else you'll break the pixies' spell. Loving a woman is something you know nothing about. Only this spell can teach you. So, be still my dove, my darling one."

She tickled my lips with little fairy kisses then pulled the covers down past my feet. She ran her hands lightly over my body, touching me more with her soul than her fingertips, making me tremble.

"Learn the first touch of love, let feeling touch feeling."

She was indeed weaving a spell, coaxing my spirit up just past the edge of my skin and caressing it. She looked down, into my eyes.

"The touch of the lips is a sacred touch, part body, part breath."

Her kisses were slow yet delicate, leaving my face, my lips, my chest and belly, arms and legs, to tingle and ache with the passion she'd inflamed in both body and soul. I longed for her—to grab her, to take her, embrace her—but the spell held me still, shaking with desire. She laid next to me now, her lips to my ear.

"When the feast is prepared then come to the touch of the tongue and the teeth, the touch of hunger."

She lick-nibbled my ear, my neck, then pulled herself up and tasted my mouth. I was near frenzy. I moved to her; she pulled away. I held myself back. She returned and touched me all over with hunger and moaning.

"The feast had been tasted; the last touch is the touch of the belly, the touch of communion."

She mounted me softly, slowly pulling me deep inside her then holding me there, quiet and still for a time. I felt tears on my shoulder.

"We are one now, let us travel together."

I put my arms around her, held her tight, kissing her, loving her, moving inside of her. She had been right; I'd known nothing of love till tonight.

I learned and relearned her lessons of love till the candles burned out and the birds sang for dawn. I remember her leaving. I was almost asleep when I heard the door close. She was crying.

"Wake up, your grace. Wake up, you're late."

I rolled over. It was Harrison.

"Late for what?"

"For the party, of course, you do remember."

"Oh, yeah, the party."

I sat up and rubbed my eyes.

"What time is it?"

"It's after seven in the evening."

"That late."

"I suggest you get up, take a bath and get dressed. I'll prepare your, ah, breakfast."

"Oh, while you're at it, would you see if Sharon wants to go with."

Harrison handed me my robe.

"Sharon doesn't want to see you for awhile."

That hurt. I pulled my robe on and got out of bed.

"Whatta' you mean?"

Sir, this may come as a surprise to you but not everyone is as shallow as you are. Apparently you two were intimate last night. For her, joining the flesh also joins the spirit. She was not only aware of your spirit but she was also painfully aware that your spirit was totally unaware of hers."

"Plain English, Harrison."

"Sir, you have the soul of a bimbo...oh and try to stay close to me tonight; I will attempt to shield this chink in your armor from the enemy's second sight."

He turned and walked out. I stormed after him.

"Me! I have the soul of a bimbo!"

"Unfortunately, yes. A dangerous trait for someone in your position."

"Well, that's just your opinion!"

We were arguing in the kitchen now.

"And what is your opinion?"

"Well, I think I have the soul of a...a...."

"A poet?"

"Yeah, a poet."

"Poets, sir, are not afraid of their feeling, they exalt in them."

He slammed a skillet on the burner, turned and brushed me aside on his way to the fridge.

"Well, if I'm such a wash out maybe I shouldn't go to this damn party tonight."

"Good, don't...."

He brushed past me again, his hands full of eggs, butter and bacon.

"If you don't go you'll die like a pig and two thousand years of history will go up in smoke."

He turned on the burner and slapped the bacon into the skillet. Just then the back door opened. It was Sharon. She looked shaky, a little nervous. She must have caught the tail end of our argument.

"I'm sorry to disturb you, I'll come back later."

"No, don't go."

I moved to her and put my arms around her. She looked up at me and smiled, weak and brave at the same time. She pulled gently out of my arms.

"I just wanted to tell you, I'll be going home for Christmas, down to Baltimore. I'm leaving tomorrow."

"But Christmas is still weeks off."

She looked down at the floor. I looked away.

"I want to visit my family."

I turned back to her. She looked up at me.

"I just wanted to tell you, in case I didn't see you, you might not be up...."

"I see...I'll miss you."

"Yeah, me too."

She tiptoed up and kissed my cheek.

"Merry Christmas."

She smiled again then quickly turned and disappeared out the French door, into the night. I looked back at Harrison, expecting to see him gloating. He wasn't; his face showed remarkable sympathy.

"One egg or two, sir?"

"Fix whatever, I'm not really hungry. I think I'll take my bath now and get dressed."

The ride down to the ferry was quiet. When we pulled the car out of the garage, I caught a glimpse of Sharon packing, through her window. It was to cold to get out of the car on the ferry ride so we just sat inside, not saying anything till I couldn't stand it anymore.

"Harrison."

"Yes, sir."

"Can you really keep these people from finding out I'm a bimbo?"

He turned to me and smiled.

"I'll do my best sir."

I nodded. It got quiet again.

"Harrison."

"Yes, sir."

"You know everything about what's been going on, don't you?"

"Yes, sir."

I fondled the ancient medallion hanging from the chain around my neck.

"Do you think I've got a chance in hell of coming out of this thing alive?"

"There's always that possibility."

"My father's a very powerful man, isn't he?"

"Right now, sir, you're all the power he has."

CHAPTER THIRTY-SIX

THE PARTY

W HEN WE GOT TO East Hampton we pulled off the main drag, down a dark side street, into the world of the obscenely rich. We had gone but a short distance when Harrison pulled over to give me some last minute instructions.

"We are going into the den of the beast. I must warn you, how you present yourself is of the utmost importance. Remember, you are a Prince, speak not familiarly to anyone, even those whom you may have met before. Give to all the impression that they have true cause to fear you, as indeed they have; you are destined for the fall of many. Stay close to me, do not drink and do not linger, we are here for a purpose and we will not stay long. Open the glove box, and you will find a few more props for your role."

I opened the glove box and found several small boxes. Inside were rings of gold and diamond and a Rolex watch that looked like it had once belonged to Elvis.

"Who am I supposed to be anyway, Liberace?"

"I know it's all gaudy but it will silence your petty detractors for whom ostentation is intimidation. And by the way, you are the titular Prince of Jerusalem, which though only a title and no longer a kingdom, is still a position of honor and dignity. The medallion you wear was struck in the fourth century, the oldest in existence of the Merovingian crest. Your possession of it proves your claim to the title. Wear it over your suit jacket. Are you ready?"

I could have said no, but Harrison had gone to so much trouble for my coming out party I didn't have the heart. The thought of disappearing with enough "ostentation" on my person to live comfortably for the rest of my life did cross my mind but it only made me realize more acutely that I really did have the soul of a bimbo.

We pulled down a long driveway with the trees on both sides all done up in Christmas lights. The mansion at the end of the drive looked like a four star hotel. It was huge and ornate in the style of a grand villa of the summer palace of Louis XIV. It too was bedazzled with strings of colored lights. There were lines of limos and chauffeurs and blond teenage boys in red jackets to park the cars of those crude enough to drive themselves. Harrison's classic 1933 silver Cadillac made a fine impression on the carhops.

A security guard checked our invitation as we walked up the steps to the church-like front door. There were uniformed butlers and maids in the traditional French black and white, short skirts, petticoats, aprons and caps. The butlers took our coats and the maids offered us champagne. We were shown to the great hall, which looked like the ghost of Christmas Past had decorated it.

It was huge, with four three-tiered chandeliers hanging from a ceiling, which must have been imported from an old castle in France. On the wall opposite the entrance stairs, fifteen-foot high windows stretched from ceiling to floor with only small columns between them, providing the dancers with a nearly uninterrupted view of the ocean. The windows were wide, with round dormer tops. The one in the middle was actually an atrium door, so similar in design, that its function was invisible. Garlands of evergreen, tied with red ribbons and hung with candy canes, ornaments and berries, were strung like bunting around the windows and along the carved moldings, which capped the tall walls. In the left hand corner was a giant Christmas tree, as brilliant as the ones on the five-dollar Hallmark cards. Next to it was the refreshments bar and buffet, what was called in the careering business "a sumptuous feast," more decorative than digestible. In the center of the wall, behind the buffet, was a monstrous walk-in fireplace with a half a tropical rain forest burning on its hearth.

At the opposite end of the room was a chamber orchestra, strings and piano, playing merry old English aires. Between the band and the bar, a sea of dancers, all dressed in their holiday best, rose and swelled and swirled at the edges. I recognized a few of the players—L.A. people whose parties I had attended, though never by invitation. Also there were many of the characters in my recent drama in attendance: Chris Boone, B.B., Producer Ed, even Old Dad. It was all very strange to see them there, dancing in this picture from Dickens.

The rich always, it seems, always decorate from Dickens—it must remind them of when they had things their way. The middle class decorate from the major department stores—it reminds them of how much they spent shopping. The poor decorate from last year, to remind them there's always next year.

The Mexicans, at least where I grew up, decorated for Christmas with skulls from Halloween and firecrackers from the Fourth of July— any feast that celebrated God was wild and scary. God was to be feared if He was to be loved properly. I'd always felt they were right. Most Americans were a little too cocksure of God. They treated God as if He were an employee. As if he wouldn't dare toast their buns because, after all, they were "Christian". The Christ on their crucifixes looked like He was taking a nap, not suffering from a multitude of wounds. Those little drops of blood all arranged like beauty marks. Barrio crucifixes were scary; the wounds were bloody and real. Yes, these jackals should fear me. I knew something about God they could not face—He was perfectly capable of revenge.

"His Royal Highness, David de Sion, titular Prince of Jerusalem."

An old guy, in an English lord's outfit, pounded a silver topped staff on the floor and announced the entrance of each guest. My entrance caused a slight pause in the dancing and a ripple of whispers. Harrison and I walked down the stairs into the grand ballroom. As we reached the bottom of the stairs, the ladies curtsied and the men bowed. It was a ridiculous feeling to see people who used to have me thrown out of their parties behaving like this, but I went with it, waving my jeweled fingers like Liberace. As we ambled toward the bar, B.B. caught up with us. She started to hug me; I backed off. She blushed and curtsied.

"Professor, I didn't know...I mean I had no idea you were so, so...."

Harrison stepped in.

"Pardon me madam, but you must address the Prince as, Your Royal Highness, and, unless you have something intelligible to say, please do not detain us."

B.B. stood there with her mouth hanging open; I waved my diamonds at her and walked on. Harrison walked ahead, brushing the "riff-raff" aside. He turned to me and whispered as we approached the buffet.

"If at all possible, your grace, please talk to no one unless I encourage it."

We stood at the buffet table; Harrison was selecting tidbits for me on a small plate when I heard, from behind me, a low murmur closing in like impending doom. I turned and saw an elderly man in a wheelchair being rolled towards me by two heavies. His eyes were evil black dots in his white, hatchet face. He smiled as he approached.

"Ah, Harrison, you did not let me down. So, this is the young Prince."

Harrison stepped forward and took the old man's hand cordially. He looked back and motioned me to come closer.

"Yes, yes. May I present His Royal Highness, David de Sion. The right honorable Mister Horace Sinclair, master of this grand estate and our host."

The old man bowed his wicked head then caught Harrison's arm and pulled him close for a confidential whisper.

"Most certainly, sir. Your Grace, kindly permit Mister Sinclair to observe your medallion more closely."

I bowed at the waist and leaned the medallion over into his face. He produced an eyepiece from his vest pocket and studied the medallion for a moment with the eye of a jeweler. Then he looked up at me and smiled triumphantly.

"The genuine article. It is a pleasure to meet the last American Merovingian, the thirteenth son of the thirteenth son."

I straightened up and stood there a moment, unsure of what to say or do. Harrison leaned over and patted the old man's shoulder.

"Perhaps there is someplace private where matters of import can be discussed."

The old man cackled in a truly unwholesome manner.

"How right you are, Harrison. Shall we move on...Oh, I have a lovely surprise for the young Prince."

He snapped his finger; one of the two bodyguards leaned over and he whispered instructions. The goon smiled and walked away briskly. The old man waited a beat, staring at me with those evil black peepholes, and then snapped his fingers again.

"George, to the elevator. Follow me gentlemen, Your Grace."

George wheeled the chair around and we followed them to the elevator, near the orchestra in the far corner of the room. There was a great deal of whispering and nudging among the guests as we filed past them and into the small lift. We were taken to a room on the third floor that appeared to be a study. It was a dark room with inlaid wood panels on the walls and a bookcase behind the large, carved mahogany desk. He was wheeled to the business side of the desk; we were offered two overstuffed brown leather chairs on the opposite side. As we sat down there was a knock at the door. George opened it. The other goon entered, followed by five waiters, each carrying a large silver tray with a round silver cover n it. The waiters sat the trays down on the desk and left. The old man cackled that disturbing cackle of his again.

"Let's see what special treats the chef has prepared for us."

He lifted the lid of the first tray. There sat the head of Doctor "Lovedeath," the L.A. Medical Examiner, so freshly severed the mouth was still moving.

"Surprise! Lovely, isn't it, the head of the man who tried to kill you."

The guards lifted the other lids simultaneously, one in each hand.

"And the heads of the other leaders of this same coven that sought your life."

Harrison stood up abruptly; I followed.

"Really sir! This is an outrage! Do you not think we have the men and the means to exterminate these vermin ourselves? Cover them up quickly before His Highness becomes enraged. You have deprived him of his greatest pleasure, cutting the hearts from his enemies himself!"

The trays were instantly covered and removed by the guards.

"I apologize to your Majesty; I did this as a gesture of goodwill, you must believe me. These vermin made an attempt on your life as part of a petty game of power with a rival cult. They had no idea who you were; they only knew you were of value to their rivals. I wanted it to be clear and understood that we had no part in their undertaking and that such untoward initiatives were dealt with swiftness and severity. Please sit down, please, Your Grace."

I motioned to Harrison; he nodded. We sat down again. The old man beamed.

"I wanted to offer Your Grace the throne of honor at our celebration of the feast. We would consider it an honor, a great honor indeed. We know it is prophecy that one of your line will be the last king of the end times—the beast incarnate. Ours is the most powerful cult in the Americas; your presence would place us in a position to rival the ancient cults of Europe. Join with us Your Grace and the world shall be yours to rule."

I feigned boredom and turned to Harrison; he nodded.

"Our line, Mister Sinclair, is the purest and oldest in the world today, as the medallion attests. Europe has made us a similar offer, forsaking their own claimant."

The old man's eyes narrowed, a wily grin drew his thin lips back across his teeth.

"We have kidnapped the other claimant; he is to be our sacrifice."

Harrison arched his eyebrows in a gesture of pleased surprise.

"In that case we will consider your offer. I'll be in touch."

With that, we stood up again. The guards came back in and escorted us down the hall and into the elevator.

A group of well-wishers were waiting for us when we reappeared in the grand ballroom. I wanted more than anything to get the hell out of this place. Harrison politely shooed them away and led me back towards the stairs. Old Dad waved at me from the dance floor, then smiled and drew his finger across his throat, wiggling his eyebrows and completing his grim gesture with a "Buckwheat O'Tay" sign. We made it up the stairs without appearing too anxious to leave and waited in the entrance hall for our coats.

"Your Grace, may I have a word with you?"

It was Chris Boone; my evening was now complete.

"We have only a moment, Your Grace, please be brief."

I couldn't believe Harrison was turning me over to Boone. I walked with Chris to the front door for privacy.

"It was I who first learned of your true identity and informed Mister Sinclair. Remember me at the feast."

"Chris, I've been wondering, did you kill your brother?"

I don't know what possessed me to ask him that. He related with great pride, how he'd accomplished the "sacrifice." How he had first demoralized his brother with broken promises, then destroyed his marriage with clandestine phone calls to Goat's wife, and finally turned their parents against him with stories of drug abuse. Goat had come to his brother in a shattered state after all that and was easily led into the coven meeting where Chris tore his heart out.

"It was my first step towards becoming the Prince of my own coven. The great and terrible act of Cain."

"Time to go, sir," Harrison interrupted.

"Remember me at the feast."

The Nazi youth carhop opened my door then held his hand out for a tip. Harrison put a bill in the kid's hand and closed the door. Harrison would have a lot of explaining to do on the way home, but for now, I was quiet. I was just glad to be leaving the den of the beast in one piece.

CHAPTER THIRTY-SEVEN

THE SECRET

"Harrison."

"Yes, Your Grace."

"Can I ask a question?"

"Certainly, sir."

"WHAT THE FUCK IS GOING ON!!"

We were traveling down the smooth bit of highway that runs between Sag Harbor and East Hampton through the still December night when my shouted question rattled the windows of the old '33 Caddy.

"SWEET JESUS WITH JUGS! THERE WERE FIVE DEAD HEADS ON PLATES BACK THERE AND YOU WERE SUCKING UP TO THAT OLD BASTARD LIKE HE HELD THE MORTGAGE ON GRANDMA'S FARM! AND WHERE DO YOU GET OFF PROMISING HIM I'M GONNA' HIGHPREIST THEIR DEVIL CHURCH?!"

Harrison remained unflappable.

"To answer your questions in order sir: Number one: Doctor Zachary McDonald is, at long, last, avenged. Number two: I was not "sucking up," as you so colorfully put it, to Mister Sinclair. I have had to deal with him before and courtesy is part of my nature. Number three: I promised him nothing."

"You said you'd be in touch."

"And I will."

"Yeah, with a ten foot pole, as far as I'm concerned."

"Sir, there are matters a stake here of which you are totally unaware."

"So, enlighten me. What'd he mean by the thirteenth son of the thirteenth son and what's all this about a Merovingian Anti-Christ?"

"All in due time, sir, at this point I can only tell you there is both frankincense and sulfur in the perfume of the Magdalene."

The car continued down the smooth dark road into the night and the moonlight. I turned on the radio to ease the tension that was rapidly building between Harrison and I. After a bit of channel changing I found Willie Nelson singing "All of Me." I sang along partly just to irritate Harrison, but mostly because of the state of mind I always got from country music. There is a confidence in the hillbilly sound that is unshakable, that no amount of heartbreak, liquor, bad luck or lost brawls can ever remotely disturb. I believe this accounts for its popularity in these times when sane men are sucking gun barrels rather than face another day of this crap. The confidence that says, "Hey, the worst is true but piss on it, you can't make me crawl," flowing from the sweet-sour strings of a pedal steel guitar had definitely kept a bullet out of my brain pan on more than on dark night of the soul.

Slowly, I became aware of a dull thumping coming from the front tire on my side of the car.

"Slow down chief, I think you've got a flat," I said in my best Tex-Mex drawl.

Harrison eased the car over to the shoulder and coasted gently to a stop. We were now parked at the bleakest part of that bleak stretch of highway; no houses for at least two miles in either direction, just a long dead punkin' field on our side of the road and thick woods on the other. Harrison and I both got out. The tire was about half flat and fading.

"Looks like you got a slow leak to me."

"I can see that, Your Grace, but it doesn't make sense, the tires are brand new."

"Maybe the guy saw you coming and stuck you with some retreads."

Harrison took offense at my suggestion he'd been had by the tire man. He got a hurt look on his face and walked slowly past me towards the rear of the car. I caught his arm as he went by.

"Better let me handle this; I'm an old pro at changing flats."

I took the keys from his hands and walked whistling to the trunk. I put the key in the button and turned it to the unlock position then tossed the keys back to Harrison.

"Here you go, Hoss, get back in start the motor, turn that radio up nice and loud and get that heater cooking. I'll have us back on the road in a flash."

I stood there grinning as Harrison sniffed a bit then walked back around and got in. I waited till he looked real comfortable, and then popped the trunk. A tire iron flashed out. I missed getting clipped but what I saw crawl out rocked me back about three feet. The body of Lovedeath, topped by an ugly stump of neck, out of which, peeped the hissing slit out his exposed vocal chords. They bore a remarkable resemblance to Susan Dey's upper lip. After the initial jolt, the sight of this thing proved paralyzing. I stood still and stared as it moved towards me tossing the tire iron from one hand to the other. The trunk lid was still up, which meant that Harrison could see none of this. He'd also switched the channels and now Mozart was blasting from the car radio. I imagined Harrison safe and warm inside the car conducting his symphony while this brute beat me to death. I summoned up the fighting skills of years of T.V. wrestling and attempted to dropkick the bastard into next week. I bounced off his chest and landed sprawling on the blacktop. I was not Hulk Hogan. The tire iron came whizzing through the darkness and chipped up a piece of asphalt an inch or so from my ear. I rolled away before it slammed down again. I caught a glancing blow on my shoulder as I spun down the gravel gutter and scrambled to my feet. Just then a shot rang out. The zombie's chest exploded; behind him I saw Harrison standing poised like an eighteenth century duelist with a .45 in his fist. The bullet did little more than distract my attacker as he turned around and lumbered towards Harrison.

"Get in the car, Your Grace. I'll hold it off!"

Harrison shot the tire iron out of the beast's hand. I sprinted around the backside of the Caddy, slamming the trunk lid on my way to the driver's side. The sound of Mozart, gunshots and that horrible hissing coming from Susan Dey's lips, lodged in that monster's neck, rang out in the black night.

I was backing up as Harrison jumped in and the zombie's mangled hand slapped against the passenger window. I had the bastard in my headlights. I slammed the Caddy into gear and charged. He lurched forward as I hit him. He slid up the hood, spattering against the windshield. He grabbed the edges of the hood and smeared his bloody stump around and around across the glass. I was doing sixty with zero visibility. I slammed on the brakes. The car went spinning dizzy doughnuts off the road. Our friend lost his grip and went slipping down the hood slight seconds before we hit a tree. His body cushioned the crash, leaving him pinned between the bumper and the tree. I jammed the car into reverse and scooted backwards up the embankment to the highway. The zombie folded in the middle as if taking a bow.

"You've severed his spinal column; good show, Your Grace."

Good show. The words walked back and forth in my mind as I hit the blacktop and made tracks for town. Good show. The English stayed about as remote from the reality in front of them as one could and still have any part in it at all. Good show. Good show. Thank God there wasn't an encore.

Sharon's lights were out when we pulled into the garage. I looked up at her window—I missed her already. She was something tranquil, something hopeful, in the middle of this churning chaos. Harrison and I walked the short distance back to the cottage in silence; we went in through the French doors, into the kitchen.

"Shall I make you some coffee, sir?"

"Why, are we gonna' sit up and talk about Lovedeath?"

"I'm afraid not, sir, I must meet with your father and discuss the events of the evening."

"Did I kill him?"

"You stopped him, sir, he was already dead."

"And what about the rest of them?"

"Sir, it is possible they are undead but not likely. In either event, they would have no power here. This is our oldest home in the land of

America and the repository of our ancestral treasures, believe me, it is well guarded."

"It doesn't look well guarded."

"Oh, but it is. You are safe here, forget Lovedeath."

I rubbed my eyes; fatigue was setting in.

"Where is my father?"

"There is a large house on the hill above here. Good night."

He paused at the door, then left.

I sat at the table and waited for the car to start. It did. He was gone. I thought about what he'd said, about the incense and sulfur in the perfume of the Magdalene. It was as if these people could use either good or evil to accomplish their purposes and in ways so subtle. It was obvious to me that my appearance at the party had caused the demise of Doctor Lovedeath and his warrior cult and that act had avenged the murder of Doctor Zak. The zombie proved that someone was still after me. I was slow, but I was starting to understand the power of the Merovingian kings who "ruled but did not govern." The simple fact of my existence was power—to be was power. Harrison was a perfect "Mayor of the palace": he governed. He spoke to the heads of other states and implemented all actions that my existence necessitated. I was not being told of their plans because I did not need to know, in fact, that very knowledge could be dangerous to me. I might attempt to govern, to make plans or change them, or by knowing about them, change my own attitudes and actions. If I had known I would be served five heads on a plate and chased by an undead, my being at the party would have been altered greatly. I wouldn't have gone. Everything I did or felt had enormous meaning and consequence. According to my father, the mantle of this empire had shadowed me since the day I was born. I thought of my life and the meaning of the things I'd done, the things I'd been allowed to see, the things I'd been protected from.

I was a child of the Sixties, one of those kids you see in the pictures with the hippy mommies painting flowers on their faces. I'd been exposed, at a tender age, to the cult of the promise and the idea of universal love.

By the time I was eighteen, the war was almost over. As the only son of a poor father, attending a second rate university on scholarship, I was protected—I was a solid 2S, the much sought after student deferment. I thought about that. I was being exposed to the knowledge of the casual destruction of our physical and spiritual environment while being shielded from participation in a maniacal war. A war which, as I had learned from Doctor Zak, was contrived and fostered by the Satanic elements in our government.

I had lived through an era of violence where the thought of blowing up power plants and production lines, in order to stop the war machine, made sense to young college kids all across the nation. Actually putting that thought into action, however, was a different story. Unfortunately, before the pros and cons of radical action got sorted out for the youth of that period, the contrived oil shortages put and end to cheap living, destroyed the family unit and turned society into a mega corporation. It was almost impossible to live off the company dole; both parents had to work while their children learned jobs. Money replaced truth and freedom as the most sought after commodity, but hey, you got to earn a living, right?" You have to provide for the future. Home became an employees' lounge, a rest pit between shifts. But, in the end, all that was really provided for future generations was a desert to live in and sewerage to drink, with the promise of poverty, famine and disease on a scale unknown since the Dark Ages.

My tenure at Atlas, with the Common Poets, had given me a great love and respect for the working man, even though I felt he had swallowed the party line and would, no doubt, choke on it. Hollywood lifted my cynicism to new levels. I could not fight the system, I could not convince it to mend its ways but I also could not work for it in any capacity. Hollywood was one of the last refuges for my kind. If you got lucky, you could sit by your pool and write sarcastic obituaries for the world you'd grown up in, the world you'd almost come to love.

So, they'd taken this kid with a mish-mosh of feelings about life and reality and dropped him into a lurid microcosm where adults killed babies and fed children excrement, just like the real world was doing covertly to those who drink tap water. They'd opposed this great darkness by a mysterious force of light whose secret was hidden in the power of the words "To be."

Tonight as I sat alone in the kitchen, I felt that power unfolding to me, their secret revealing itself, opening to me like a lotus on a lily pond, in the first rays of dawn.

CHAPTER THIRTY-EIGHT

THE NEWS

HARRISON CAME BY THE NEXT DAY around eleven; I was having coffee. We sat and talked for a while. He'd been given permission to explain to me a little more about my family tree and the meaning of the phrase, "the thirteenth son of the thirteenth son," that Sinclair had used. He'd also discovered that it was the Molochians who had reanimated Lovedeath's body and sent it after me.

"Why, I thought they wanted me alive?"

"They have put forth their own claimant to the position of Highpriest. It is important, for the moment, that they believe they have succeeded in disabling you."

"Who are they pushing?"

"Chris Boone."

He refused to talk further on the matter but instead drifted into a lengthy disposition on my family heritage.

"The Merovingians had two lines of succession, one priestly and the other kingly. The kingly line was passed on according to the royal tradition to first born sons, the priestly line, however, was passed on in the Davidic tradition to the younger sons.

"King David, as the Bible records, was the youngest son of his family. Solomon, David's chosen successor, was his youngest son. David's eldest son, Absalom, sought to take his father's kingdom away by force, and he almost succeeded. When Solomon became king, it was over the dead bodies of his half brothers.

"Hence, the Merovingians separated the youngest sons and gave them a life of meditation and the pursuit of the arcane sciences. They were almost married exclusively within the bloodline to preserve its utmost purity. No royal alliances with other ruling houses were needed to secure their metaphysical office. So, as the kingly line became more entangled with the blood of corrupt rulers, the priestly line became purer and purer since the wives of the Highpriest were chosen for qualities of character rather than for their families' fortune.

"In 496 A.D. Clovis, the first Merovingian king to unite all of France and parts of Germany, made a pact with the bishop of Rome. Clovis agreed to adopt the Catholic faith and recognize the bishop of Rome as Pope, spiritual leader of the Christian faith. In exchange, he was given the title of "Novus Constantinus" or "New Constantine" Emperor of the Holy Roman Empire; a title that the Church guaranteed would belong to his bloodline forever. The old mystical religion, which Jesus had handed down to His inner circle and family, would now have to be practiced in secret by the younger sons of the priestly line while the kingly line paid lip service to the Church of Rome. The phrase, 'Bow thy head humbly, Sicambrian...' which I spoke when I placed the medallion around your neck, was first uttered by Saint Remy, at the baptism of Clovis.

"On December 23, 679 A.D., Dagobert II last of the powerful Merovingian kings, was assassinated by Pepin the Fat with the help of the Roman Church. The church gave the crown over to Pepin's son and thus began the Carolingian line of rulers. The Merovingians never forgot or forgave the Church of Rome for its betrayal, and the Roman Church never ceased trying to destroy the Merovingian line.

"The priestly line had already been in seclusion for almost two hundred years, so it had no problem escaping the wrath of the Church. However, through the course of time, it had adopted many rituals aimed at mocking the Church of Rome. The Church learned of the ancient religion and its rituals after Godfroi de Bouillon, a member of the priestly line, conquered Jerusalem and set up the Knights Templar. Their secret mystical practices were drawn from the old religion, as was the red cross pattee of Rose Croix, which became the emblem of the order."

"Is this the Order of Melchizedek?"

Harrison arched his eyebrows, as if irritated at my interruption. He rubbed his eyes. "Ah, the Order of Melchizedek. You are referring to Doctor Zak's pet theory, are you not?"

"Yea, I want to know about the nine Magdalenes."

"There was only one Magdalene. In the bible she is also known as Mary of Bethany, the sister of Lazarus and Martha.

"But the painting my father did of Magdalene looks like an Indian."

Harrison smiled. "Well I guess it is time to tell you the true story of your origins. That painting was a portrait of your mother's spirit. Your mother grew up on what was soon to be called Cancer Alley. At the age of twelve she was diagnosed with an inoperable tumor in her brain, near her pituitary gland, and given six months to live. Your grandmother sought the help of the Gris-Gris Family as a last resort. At the time, your father was staying with that family, studying the ancient versions of the Psalms of David, which are the source of Gris-Gris medicine power. Your father healed your mother, and in doing so, touched her spirit. He saw clearly she was to be his thirteenth wife. With the tumor gone and puberty arriving, your mother developed quickly into maturity. They fell deeply in love. He called her his Ancient One. The Gris-Gris Priest married them secretly. Your grandmother approved because of the healing; your grandfather was unaware. When your mother became pregnant the rumors around the town of a witch child in her forced them apart, and your mother was sent to Dallas for her protection. Your mother's death was a tragedy. In the bitter, cold winter she developed pneumonia. The doctors gave her penicillin, not realizing she was allergic to it."

"And nobody did nothin'? I thought my father could heal."

"Your father was not there. Your aunt and uncle became your surrogate mother and father. They did the best they could."

I felt great sorrow welling up inside of me. Harrison put his hand on my shoulder and, without showing any emotion, he said, "I'm sorry but I must continue with the story of your lineage.

"With the discovery of the New World, the Freemasons of England and the Knights of Christ in Portugal devised a great plan to transplant the priestly line to the new land. By the Eighteenth century, the Masonic Lodges here in America, created a new nation under the traditions of Masonic justice; the priestly line had been established here for over one hundred and fifty years. Since that time, the wars, the plagues and assassinations sponsored by powers abroad, have decimated the priestly line in America, leaving only your father and yourself.

"'The thirteenth son of the thirteenth son' refers to the number of generations or 'sons' between the great scions of the family line: thirteen between Jesus and Clovis, thirteen between Clovis and Godfroi, thirteen between Godfroi and the heirs sent to America and thirteen between those heirs and your father. You are your father's thirteenth son by almost as many wives, the last son, the child of his old age."

After relating this tale over several cups of coffee, he took me into the library.

"Here are the treasures of your house, books on the mystic teachings of your ancestors. Read them, they will open your heart. The heart is the only true guide for a priest of your order."

He made his usual grand exit promising to return soon and warning me to stay inside since the cult was now aware of my presence.

After he left, I tried to read the old books but arcane rituals are not exactly fun reading. Besides, there was something spooky about the history lesson I'd just received. I couldn't put my finger on it but I felt I was being misled, that something was being hidden or disguised here. Sinclair had mentioned an Anti-Christ of Merovingian descent and any heir to the title of Emperor of the Roman Empire, holy or otherwise, would be a natural for Sinclair's title as well. He also seemed to think that I'd be happy to join his feast. Could it be that his cult had its origins in the Templars? Did Harrison disguise the black and white magic here under the pretext of the priestly and kingly lines?

I also remembered the spear of Parsival, the sacred totem, which in his hands, destroyed evil and healed the Grail king. I'd researched such a spear once for Chris Boone. He was writing a screenplay called The Godspear, about the spear that pierced the side of Christ. It was said that whoever held the spear, held the destiny of the world in his hands, as the centurion did when he prevented the executioners from breaking Christ's legs by stabbing His heart.

I found a copy of Eschenbach's Parsival among the books in the library and read it again slowly, carefully. Doctor Zak had left me the book as a guide. I'd found the Sangrael but I needed the spear.

I had learned from my earlier research that the spear, unlike the Grail, was an extant historical object. It still existed and was supposedly on display in Vienna. It had been held as a talisman of power by such notable hands as Constantine's, Charlemagne's, and Fredrick Barbarrossa's. All of these names figured into the story Harrison had told me. It was also coveted and actually held by Adolf Hitler, who seemed obsessed with the Grail romances and the magic therein. My researches into the spear had brought me to the fanciful conclusion that it had been stolen by Harry Houdini prior to World War I and been replaced by an exacting duplicate. My reasoning was that although Germany held the spear it did not hold the true destiny of the world in its hands during either war, America did. Germany held a convincing but ultimately fraudulent destiny. Houdini certainly had the expertise to steal anything held under lock and key. He had the opportunity, as he was touring Europe at the time as it greatest sensation. He was a fanciful collector of antiquities and magic. He was also skilled in creating convincing fakes. He did not return to America until she had entered the war on the side of the Allies. When he did return, he legally changed his name to Harry Houdini, adopting April sixth, the day the U.S. declared war on Germany, as the new birth date on his new birth certificate. He also hated the German government and went to great lengths to embarrass them, including filing a lawsuit against them and winning the only public apology ever given by the imperial government to a Jew. Chris Boone was unusually pleased with my research and theory, though he didn't express his pleasure with a large check. The movie, in fact, never even made it to development.

Thinking about all this made me feel like I was spinning around in circles again. I'd spent months chasing the Grail, only to discover the forces involved had me chasing my own tail. I was the Grail; it was the spear they were after. The Carolingian usurpers had held the spear until the Germanic Princes stole both the spear and the title of Holy Roman Emperor. Had I not read in Parsival, those many weeks ago at T.Z.'s, that it was the spear the young knight had been sent to recover? If the Merovingians were anything like the Grail family of Parsival, the spear was necessary to heal them and make them rulers again. And, Sinclair had said that if I joined them I could rule the world, which had to mean either, he had the spear or he knew where he could lay his hand on it. Chris Boone had said he was the one who first learned of my true identity. Could I have somehow guessed at the true disposition of the spear and my knowledge of its theft implicated me as being a member of the Merovingian line? Could that wild guess be responsible for not only the coven's interest in me but the Merovingians' interest in me as well? What if this elder priest-king was not my father and all this was just an elaborate hoax to secure the spear or discover its true location? My feelings would deny this as even being in the realm of possibility; my father and his friends were truly kind to me, though they were, I felt, hiding something from me. Yet, it was just as obviously true that the spear and my knowledge of its theft had played a major part in all this, and that somehow this news had taken a long time to reach me.

CHAPTER THIRTY-NINE

THE VISITOR

I ALWAYS FELT BETTER when I didn't trust anybody. It made me feel like I had both feet on the ground. I'd slept little the past couple of nights. The sight of Doctor Lovedeath, without a head, still trying to talk, had disquieted my subconscious. I'd gone almost without sleep the night it happened. Harrison's pep talk the next day and my subsequent ponderings had done little to soothe my churning psyche. There was also the feeling of being held captive. As if I'd been given a comfortable cell, a last meal and was waiting on the parson to walk me down home. Everybody was hiding something from me. Although I'd attempted to resign myself to the obvious fact that I might never know exactly what that something was, the absence of a female within walking distance had started me thinking again. Thinking was always dangerous, that's why most people want somebody else to do it for them. My morning thoughts were interrupted by the sudden appearance of Harrison.

"Back so soon...."

"Something's gone wrong."

"Something always goes wrong."

"No, I'm serious."

"So am I."

"There's a young man in town asking questions about you. Our prescience tells us that he might foul everything up if he stays long enough and talks to the wrong people."

"Your prescience?"

"Precisely. You must come with me into town right away, confront this young man and send him on his way. There's not a moment to lose."

Harrison seemed genuinely unnerved. I dressed quickly and we drove to the ferry. At least I was being let out of my cell. I'd decided to sit in the back and let Harrison play chauffeur. On the boat ride to the mainland I asked Harrison for a description of this nosey young man.

"He's young, dark hair, appears to be wealthy but his clothes are all wrinkled."

Mank. Nobody else fit that description. The paper must have sent him. They didn't want to waste the money they'd invested in me.

We pulled into Sag Harbor; I spotted him right away. He was coming out of the American Hotel, a newspaper under his arm, looking up and down the street. I had Harrison pull over and rolled down my window.

"Hey Mank! Over Here!"

He came right over.

"Nice wheels."

"Get in."

I opened the back door; Mank piled in.

"Just drive around, Harrison., someplace scenic."

We took off up Main Street.

"So, what'd you do, sell our story to the Enquirer, Professor?"

"Not yet, waiting on a better offer. What are you doing here, paper send you?"

"The paper's so pissed about you they almost fired me. But no, they didn't send me. I got family in the city. I come home every Christmas. I just thought I'd pop up and see what happened to you. Bubba said something about you jumping off the face of the Earth."

"Yeah, well, I found the edge; I'm just waiting for the right time to jump."

"So what's with the chic wheels and chauffeur?"

"I'm visiting my family, too. They belong to my dad."

"Which one, Hugues or Pepe Lopez."

"Pepe. He made a lot of money posing for that tequila bottle label."

"You seen Chris Boone, he's in town you know."

"Everybody's in town. They had a big party a couple of nights ago."

"You went? The Sinclair's, right? Jeez, you're still the best party crasher in the business. That was a gilt-edged invitation-only affair, always is."

"You've been?'

"Once, when I was a kid. My Dad never liked Sinclair, besides we generally stayed in the city for the holidays—more Park Avenue that East Hampton."

"Rich is Rich."

"Rich is boring."

"Right, I should be so bored."

Harrison took us around the park with its pond. The ducks and swans were chasing crumbs on the banks thrown by kids in brightly colored balloon coats, under the winter trees and the gray sky.

"So, what'd you want to see me about?"

Mank shuffled a little, his gypsy prince eyes trying to catch a glimpse of my soul.

"You're in with a bad crowd."

"Three's a bad crowd these days. What else?"

"Still playing the lone rider, huh, Professor? You see this morning's paper?"

"I only read the tabloids."

"Maybe you should read this."

He folded his paper and pointed to an item on one of the back pages. The headline read, JEWISH MUSEUM ROBBED.

"This looks like a job for the Anti-defamation league."

"Read on."

"Upper west side…blah…blah…Rabbi so-and-so…blah…blah…."

The next sentence caused me to pause.

"Among the items taken was an old Greco-Roman spearhead, a gift to the museum from Harry Houdini. The spearhead was not especially unique or valuable according to the Rabbi curator and, in fact, it had never been on public display. Its value was symbolic, as it was part of a large donation made by the famed magician toward the end of his life."

"Remember the piece of work you did for Chris Boone? Bingo."

"This can't be the reason you came all the way out here from the city. You didn't even know about this until this morning."

"I came to warn you. Sources say you're a marked man. This just confirmed my suspicions. You're in over your head, Professor. Get out and stay out. Find that edge of the Earth you were talking about and jump off. These people are sick and they're serious."

"What's that supposed to be, a news bulletin? In L.A. you told me I had nothing to worry about then I damn near get killed and all you wanted to do was exploit my misfortune. Now you come up here and tell me to get out of town. Why?"

"Because, deep down, I care about you."

"Please Mank, you wanna' do me a favor? You get out of town and don't say a word about me to any one."

Mank looked a little hurt, but not that much. He grinned his Gypsy grin.

"Okay. If that's what you want. To the hotel, James.

Harrison wheeled down a side street then cut back over to the main drag. We dropped Mank off and headed out to the ferry.

"Do you think he'll really leave?"

"I dunno', Harrison. I gave it my best shot."

I didn't say anything about the spear to Harrison—chances were he already knew. Chris Boone, the Molochian claimant, now possessed the spear and I was on my way from Highpriest to victim. I was safe when they thought Lovedeath had mangled me. Maybe they thought I'd get to the spear before them if they didn't get me out of the way. But now, they had it.

CHAPTER FORTY

REFLECTIONS

DECEMBER TWENTY-THIRD HAD COME with amazing speed. I had been in virtual hibernation since Mank had left, as if my body needed to store all the strength it possibly could before the great confrontation. My dreams had been of pure black, without sights or sounds—a state on non-being. During the few hours I was awake, my mind restlessly sought answers, turning the events of the past over and over, checking both sides for clues that might lead me out of the maze. I'd wandered my cottage cell, actually going upstairs for the first time since I'd been here. There were two rooms upstairs: an attic, full of dust and useless, broken things, and a small gallery, with paintings on the walls and a small writing desk from the 1700's. The paintings were all enigmatic, strange portraits of my ancestors. One of the strangest was of a guy with long hair and a beard, wearing Roman style armor and a crown of thorns. He was standing over a naked, vanquished foe while an angel offers him a crown and a palm frond. The others had similar themes but this one held special interest for me; the man looked familiar. I would study the painting for a while each afternoon as the warm light came in the round window over the desk. Then be drawn downstairs to my bed by some special force that said, "Rest."

"Wake up, Your Grace."

It was Harrison. I rolled over and opened one eye warily.

"It is time to prepare you for the Feast."

There was a low rumble of distant thunder.

"There's a great storm brewing out over the ocean; we must hurry and make ready, the ferry will not be running much longer."

I sat up and stretched. As I looked around I noticed candles lit all over the room.

"Is the power down?"

"No, Your Grace. Tonight is an ancient night; it is the custom of the ritual that only fire may be use to illuminate the darkness."

"I'll get dressed."

"No, you must come with me naked; the masters will clothe you with power and light."

This was not at all comforting to hear. I could assume Harrison had agreed to Sinclair's request and that tonight I would preside over the great Feast of the Beast. My father and his friends had some sort of protective magic spell to put over me. This spell and a little luck would be all I'd have against a coven of God knows how many homicidal maniacs. I did not like the odds. The distant thunder rumbled again.

"Please hurry, Your Grace."

I got out of bed and followed him, naked, to the library where the chairs had been arranged as before. This room, too, was lit by a host of small candles placed all around, on the shelves, the stove and in circles on the floor. On each of the chairs was a head fashioned of a different metal—silver, gold, copper, steel, lead, tin, and pewter. The faces were strange, allegorical, some male, some female, one both, all with magical symbols and markings, all with a finger sized hole in the top. There was no stool for me to sit on this time so I stood in the center of the semi-circle and waited. The Masters came in dressed as before in their long hooded capes. Each went to his chair and picked up a head and sat down. My father looked at me kindly and spoke.

"Tonight you will enter into the beast and fulfill the destiny for which you were born. Remember how great is the power of God. We, as your masters, have each brought a gift, preserved through the centuries by the power of God. Remember how great is the power of God.

With that they all began chanting in Latin. Then, Speedster stood up and approached me, holding a copper head.

"I am Ulysses."

The voice was almost grotesque, it seemed to be coming from the head as well as from Speedster. He dipped his finger into the hole at the top of the head, and with the oil he found there, drew symbols on my forehead as he continued to speak.

"I am cunning, wily; I know where the enemy is weak and where I am strong. I know his trap before he springs it. I can use his own pride to deceive him."

He returned to his seat and they all began chanting again. Then Joe stood up with the head of steel.

"I am Hercules."

The voice echoed and boomed. Joe took the oil from the head and anointed my arms.

"I am strength, agility. My enemy trembles at the sight of me, for he knows, in me, there lives no defeat."

Again they chanted; again another of their company rose. Doctor Kelly came forward with the silver head of a maiden.

"I am Magdalene. I am the heart."

He anointed my chest. The voice rang out like a glass bell.

"I am love, which casteth out fear. I am the conquering clarion call, the sight of the Lord, Who arose with the dawn."

Sumner was next with the head of lead, both male and female.

"I am Orpheus."

This head was double-voiced, with the throat of a pipe organ. An angelic octave.

"I am song, the heartbreak of the king of the dead."

He wrote on my belly strange symbols in oil.

"I am harmony, the sound of the spheres."

I was shivering; now, I could feel spirit hands moving inside me. The chanting seemed louder; the words pumped through my heart and ran in my blood. I closed my eyes and heard Kirkland's voice, mixed with the wind in the voice of the head of tin.

"I am Lazarus, called from the grave."

He touched my legs and my feet.

"Stand in my place and come out of your tomb to the voice of your Lord. Enter the upper room, rest your head on His breast, you are called His beloved, alone stands the test."

I had the sensation of floating, of being lifted up, not by a force outside of me but by a power from within. Harrison brought forth oil from the head of pewter and anointed my back, between my shoulder blades.

"I am Benjamin, the youngest son of Israel."

His finger moved slowly down my spine.

"The beloved of the Lord dwells securely between my shoulders. This is the blessing of Moses, the prophet. Israel, my father, called me the wolf—in the morning I devour my prey, in the evening I divide my spoil."

My father stood up last, with the head of gold. He lifted it high and poured the oil over my head.

"I am David, the lion of Judah. This scepter shall never depart from my hand."

He returned to his chair.

"Ye have been clothed from on high with the power and the light. Remember how great is the power of God."

Harrison stood up and led me back to my bedroom. Laid out on my bed was a Centurion's armor, all of gold. A breastplate and backplate, greaves and wide wrist cuffs, all of gold. Leather sandals and the skirt of leather strips, all tipped and studded with gold. He helped me dress, and then led me back to the library where the masters still chanted. My father stood up and turned to his right. Speedster brought out a helmet of gold, shaped like a roaring lion and put it on my head.

"Remember, my son, the great power of God. He has seen Himself in the mirror of man and we are all His reflections."

CHAPTER FORTY-ONE

The Feast of the Beast

"YOU TWO GUYS GOIN' to a costume party? You're lucky to-night, boys, ya'll just made it! I hope you plan to spend the night in town; there won't be any more ferries till tomorrow, maybe not till late tomorrow. Big storm coming."

The boat ride over was choppy. I was still shaking from the magic. To ward off the night's chill, Harrison had given me a long, red, wool cape, which attached to my breastplate at the shoulders. It wasn't much help as I looked out my window over the dark water, rising in white caps, at the far horizon where the great thunderhead crackled its lightening. If there ever was a night made to order for the devil's doings, it was this night in dark December with the storm coming in off the water.

We drove slowly; we were no longer in a hurry. There was a time to show up for the devil's big party and that time was late. We dawdled, looking at Christmas lights. I'd gotten my first kiss under a tall outdoor Christmas tree in Dallas. I could still remember the taste of her pink lipstick, the candy of her mouth. They say before you die your whole life flashes before your eyes. All I could really see was that first kiss. My life was all downhill from there anyhow. Maybe the magic wasn't working. I didn't feel like Ulysses or Hercules, but then, maybe I did; maybe they felt just like this before every battle. Maybe the life flashing past their eyes, like mine, got stuck on love's first kiss, every time.

"This is as far as I go, Your Grace. You must walk the rest of the way."

He'd stopped about ten feet from the entrance to the long driveway that led to Sinclair's place.

"Are we early?"

"You still have a little time. Is there anything I can do for you, Your Grace?"

"You wanna' trade lives?"

"You will not fail, sir, it is your destiny."

"Yes, but it's also my ass."

I opened the door and got out.

"Where do I meet you when this is all over?"

"Right here, sir; I'll be right here the whole time."

He smiled at me and nodded. I nodded back, then turned and walked through the entrance with the wind whipping my cape.

As I approached, the mansion was dark, the driveway deserted. Maybe I'd missed the party. I walked up the steps to the cathedral-like front doors and knocked. The peephole opened and through its ornate bars, the tired, evil eyes of the butler peered out.

"You're late."

He opened the huge door with a groaning and creaking straight out of a horror flick.

"Master had given up on you." He chose a replacement, Mister Boone."

"Mister Boone is a coward, totally unworthy. Tell him I said so."

Inside the great house, only candles and torches illuminated the darkness and cast dancing shadows on its pillars and walls. The butler just sniffed at my remark. He tried to take my cape, but I wouldn't let him. It was then I noticed something different about his uniform, his privates were exposed and a short cat-o'-nine-tails hung from his waist. The maids approached. Their costumes had been drastically altered—they were nude. Around their slender necks, wrists and ankles, heavy manacles clattered against dangling chains. They still held the silver trays with those cut crystal glasses, but instead of champagne, they now contained what could only be blood and urine. Each girl bore fresh strips from the butler's whip. I avoided their eyes and their offered libations and proceeded through the glowing darkness to the top of the stairs. The old guy at the head of the stairs had also added an exposed groin and whip to his English lord's outfit, and the top of his staff was the head of a goat with an upside-down pentagram burned into his forehead. He looked shocked to see me, but then a creepy smile curled his lips. He took a long step to the head of the stairs and pounded his staff on the hard wood floor.

"His Royal Highness, David de Sion, titular Prince of Jerusalem."

The great ballroom was dark. Again, only candles and torches and the great fire of its hearth pushed against the darkness, twinkling off the unlit chandeliers. Against the walls, grotesque standards stood each in its place, each an upright shaft with three or four crossbars from which hung the trophies that identified each cult. The Molochian standard, with the skins of flayed infants, stood a little higher than the rest and held the place of honor, leaning against the grand center window, which was also a door. The standard of the other leading cults—the warriors, the slavers, the animalists, the poisoners, the spoilers—each occupied one of the big windows that faced the sea and the approaching storm, each hung with the grim reminders that these people meant business. Thunder and lightening from far out over the deep accompanied the announcement of my name. In the hush that followed, I slowly descended the stairs, taking it all in.

The crowd was smaller than the last party, about one hundred and fifty people, all dressed in long, hooded robes, pulled open in the middle to reveal their nakedness and a belt around the waist, which held a sheathed dagger. Some of the members wore their hoods back, exposing their faces to the flickering light. Ugh, mostly people I didn't want to see from L.A.

The room was still hung with the evergreen bunting from the last party. The Christmas tree was still in the corner; it was not lit up. The buffet table was where it was before, only this time there were trays of roasted babies, excrement and body parts. The punch bowls were filled with the same repellent libations I was offered upon arrival. The servers were naked, manacled and chained, as the maids were upstairs. It seemed to me that great care had been taken to include all races and age groups as if symbolic of the whole world enslaved. Body parts hung over the blazing hearth, filling the room with the stench of burning flesh. To my left, where the bandstand had been, there was a young man, crucified upside down. Going down those stairs was like descent into hell. The only sounds now in the room were my footsteps on the stair's hollow wood, the snapping of the flames and my medallion striking my breastplate, the ringing of gold on gold. The silence was broken by a shout behind me.

"YOU LYING BASTARD!"

I turned and froze. It was Chris Boone, dressed as a centurion, charging down the stairs toward me with the spear in his hand. I felt paralyzed by his rage, his twisted face, his ember-fire eyes. Half way down he hurled the spear with all his might. I was ready to die, but before I knew what was happening, my left hand jerked up. I caught the spear and spun, striking Chris in the back of the head with the butt of the lance as he lunged for me, sending him crashing down to the floor below. I paused a moment, unsure of what I had done. The magic was working. I felt suddenly powerful as I stood there, spear in hand, staring with utter disgust at my shocked audience.

From the back of the hall came the sound of one man clapping. It was Sinclair. He was being wheeled to the foot of the stairs. The others joined him, till the applause sounded like hail. Then, the force of the storm shook the hall with its thunder and the wind from the sea blew the door open, toppling the Molochian banner and snuffing out the candles in the far side of the room. It was silent again as the slaves pushed the door closed. One of them moved to retrieve the fallen standard.

"Leave that where it lies," Sinclair shouted.

The slave dropped it and moved away. The old man looked up at me, rubbing his hands, his eyes gleaming.

"I knew it; I knew you were the one."

I walked down, a step at a time. Chris was coming around, moaning on the floor at Sinclair's feet.

"Strip him, bind him, and hand me his dagger!"

By the time I reached the bottom of the stairs, Chris was naked, his hands tied behind his back, on his knees before Sinclair. One bodyguard held him in place as the other, George, wheeled the old man up. He extended Chris's dagger to me.

"I will not rob Your Grace of his pleasure a second time. Here, take his blade and cut his heart out."

I took the knife from his hands, smiled and tucked it into my sword belt.

"It's late. I will deal with him after the sacrifice."

The old man cackled.

"Bravo! Bravo. I knew it; I knew you were truly the one."

He clapped his hands; a golden Sudan chair was brought forward on the shoulders of four slaves.

"Mount up, Your Grace; the throne is yours. Let the sacrifice begin!"

I mounted the throne and was lifted above the heads of the crowd. As slaves gathered the standards from around the room, a path was cleared between the door and me. Chris Boone was yanked to his feet by his hair as George lifted Sinclair from his wheelchair.

"Where's my Baby Squirrel? Where is she?"

The old man was calling out for someone, a scrawny girl of about twelve, wearing a coven cape and hood, pushed her way through the crowd.

"Here I am Grandpa-pa!"

Her voice was the timbre of fingernails on a chalkboard; she came up to George and wrapped herself around his leg. Old Sinclair's hand reached down and petted her head.

"There's my baby. You be a good girl and bring Grandpa-pa's chair."

She looked up at him and smiled unwholesomely, then turned to me and stuck her tongue out. Her eyes were the devil's and her mouth belonged on a horse; outside of the Imps, she was truly the most frightening creature I'd ever seen.

"We're ready now! On to the beach, where the beast rises out of the sea!"

The crucified man was lifted off the bandstand and carried to the door by slave girls. The procession began. The cross first, followed by torchbearers, then George carrying Sinclair and the young girl with the wheelchair, then myself on the throne, followed by the standards and torchbearers, cult by cult, then lastly Chris Boone, shoved along by the bodyguard.

We marched out to the beach where they set the cross up, facing the sea. My throne they sat down between the cross and the waves. Sinclair's chair was wheeled to the side of the cross, close. George placed him in it and slowly stepped back. The old man waited till the cults were assembled then he shouted to me over the howling wind and surf.

"Abbadon, the Destroyer! Come down from your throne and open the Grail with the tip of your spear that your servants may drink of the Blood of the Lamb, and the Beast, being pleased, will rise out of the Deep!"

I stepped down, spear in hand, and stood poised at the cross. I looked down at my kinsmen. He was covered with wounds; the blood ran from the nail in his feet, down his legs. He writhed and moaned, but not in an agony of pain. He was in some sort of sexual ecstasy, foaming at the mouth, spitting obscenities and grinding his hips like a two-dollar whore.

"It's the aphrodisiac."

Sinclair's voice was hoarse with lust.

"A delicious mockery...."

I turned my head slowly and looked at him. I felt a loathing so intense, so deep inside; it was as if a serpent, thick with centuries of accumulated bile, was twisting around in my guts.

"I see it pleases you, STRIKE!!"

As he shouted, a bolt of lightening struck the sea so violently it exploded, the ground shook. I drove my spear into Sinclair's belly, ripping up and out with such force that I staggered. He screamed above all the mad poundings of nature.

"ABBADON!!"

Then he pointed at me and smiled.

"I knew you were the one; I knew it."

He slumped in his chair as the first heavy raindrops beat down. George made a move; I braced with my weapon but he just wanted room to fall to his knees.

"ABBADON!!" He shouted, "ABBADON THE DESTROYER!"

I turned and the whole congregation followed him to their knees.

"ABBADON THE DESTROYER!"

They shouted and shouted as the hard rain fell and I walked through their midst. The storm came in raging and knocked down their damn cross. As I mounted the steps that lead back to the hall, Chris Boone broke away from his keeper, ran, and knelt down before me.

"Abbadon the destroyer! Name the Prince of the Covens!"

The big man caught up to him just as he finished and pushed his face forward, down into the sand.

"Release him!" I ordered.

The big man obeyed. He pulled Chris to his feet and took his bindings away. I drew Chris's dagger from my belt. I threw it; it stuck in the sand at his feet.

"Pick it up."

And he did so, his mind in confusion.

"Now show me the thing that I taught you tonight."

In a flash he had buried his knife in his captor and bloodied his blade to the sound of his laughter.

"I say this to all, be they chieftain or slave, man, woman or child. The Prince of the Covens is the one who survives!"

I heard the sound of their daggers unsheathing. I turned. I heard screams, the roar of the storm. I walked into the grand ballroom without looking back and closed the door behind me. I stood there a moment looking around the room, listening to the battle outside. The sight of the buffet and the human barbecue on the hearth filled me with rage. I grabbed the torch near the door and put it to the dry evergreen boughs hanging down the walls. They went up like flash paper. I began torching the rest of the room—the chairs, the drapes, the tables. The flames drove me wild, kicking over the buffet table, the torches and candelabras. I stood in the middle of the room. I swung the torch over my head lofting it into the Christmas tree. I looked at the conflagration I'd created and felt good. I turned and headed for the stairs when I heard someone laughing.

"Good job, Professor."

Out of the shadows, near the base of the stairs, a large brooding figure lumbered towards me. I braced with the spear and waited for him to move into the light. Christ, it was Bubba, dressed in a bizarre military uniform.

"Hey, Bubba. Jesus, you scared me. What are you doing here? Never mind, let's get the hell out of here, this place is going up fast."

He stood before me, his arms folded across his chest.

"Give me the spear and I let you go."

Bubba wasn't kidding. I stepped back.

"Bubba, what's wrong with you?"

"My name is Bhudal, not Bubba. Nothing is wrong with me. My commander has need of that spear. With it we will unify Africa, then conquer the world."

"Gee Bubba, that sounds like a long range plan...."

He was moving towards me; I was fencing at him with the spear.

"The white man is the devil."

"Yeah, right. Listen, stay back, I'm warning you."

I lunged at him with the spear. He grabbed my arm and held me while he punched my face three times, hard and fast, letting go on the last punch, which sent me flying across the floor. I landed semi-conscious, in a heap. My nose was broken, a few teeth were loose and my lips were bigger than Bubba's but I still held the spear.

"Give it up man he'll break you in two."

It was Mank's voice; I looked to the stairs and saw him standing about midway down, in a wet, wrinkled trench coat. Bubba was moving in on me. I tried to scramble backwards but he stepped on my leg, pinning it to the floor.

"Just hand me the spear."

"Better do as he says, Professor; he used to be head of the secret police in Uganda a few years back."

He extended his hand. He was crushing my leg. I gave in. Slowly I moved the spear up; he reached for it. As he snatched it, he stomped my leg and laughed. I was in real pain, physical and spiritual, watching him walk away with this treasure. I struggled to my feet and stood there. I still had my sword. Bubba broke into this wild warrior's dance, stamping his feet and stabbing the air with the spear. Mank looked at me, grinning.

"Cute, huh. Bubba's also descended from the Zulu tribe. Okay, Bubba, you can celebrate later; let's go pick up my ten mill."

"My name is Bhudal."

Bubba had reached the stairs. He smiled up at Mank. He put one big hand on Mank's wrinkled shoulder, and the spear to Mank's throat.

"I got you and I got the spear. So, tell me Mank, how come I got to pay you anything?"

I limped toward them, quietly drawing my sword. As I got close, I heard a soft click then an explosion. Bubba's ass was blown apart and a shard of metal smashed into my shoulder, spinning me around but not knocking me down. Mank must have had a sawed-off loaded with explosive, dum-dum shells tucked under that trench coat. The damage to Bubba was massive; he'd dropped the spear and was hanging onto the banister with both hands. The recoil had sat Mank down on the steps; the hole in his trench coat was burning.

"Now what's to keep me from selling the spear to the Aryan Brotherhood in South Africa for twenty mill in diamonds and platinum?"

Bubba screamed and flung himself on top of Mank, choking him crazily with his last bit of strength. The shotgun roared again, tearing a hole in Bubba's back. He arched up, twisting his hands with all his might. There was a snapping sound as Mank's head was turned back, away from his body. Then, Bubba collapsed on top of his foe and things got real still and quiet. I picked up the spear; I did not feel like crying but I did.

The whole ballroom was burning as I staggered up the stairs, wondering how sane I would be after all this. I stopped at the top and looked down. My friend, my protector, just bodies on the floor. Parts of the ceiling fell, flaming like comets. It was time to go. The Feast was over—the Beast had come and devoured his followers.

CHAPTER FORTY-TWO

THE TRUE PRIEST

T HE RAIN WAS COMING down in sheets as I stumbled out the front door and down into the long driveway. I was feeling dizzy from the loss of blood but the adrenalin kept pushing me on. I arrived at the car, out of breath, leaning on my spear.

"Harrison! Wake up! Help me!"

He opened the car door and stepped out.

"Come on, open the back door; help me in and let's get the hell out of here."

It was then that I noticed he had a gun in his hand.

"Aw, Shit! Harrison, not you, too! Aw, Fuck!"

"I'm afraid so, sir; please hand me the spear."

I shook my head 'no'. I had trouble standing. I was losing my grip on the spear, sliding down the length of it as I doubled over. Harrison moved closer, which was what I wanted him to do. Using my position and leverage, and his belief that I was fainting, I lured him in further then snapped the lance end up between his legs, landing a hard unexpected blow to his "heuvos." His eyes bugged out; he went down like a sack. I picked up the gun and kicked him as hard as I could in the butt with my good foot.

"Goddamn it, Harrison, why'd you have to be an asshole?"

I snatched the keys from the ignition, walked around and opened the trunk.

"Come on, get in, we're going for a ride."

Harrison was in pain when he pulled himself up by the bumper and tipped himself into the trunk. I drove through East Hampton, then out past Sag Harbor, down the road that led to the ferry. Before I got to the end I pulled over and turned down an abandoned driveway. I stopped the car and got out. I unlocked the trunk, then stepped back and used the butt of my spear to push the release button. I was taking no chances on being surprised.

"Okay, Harrison, get out. Now if you don't take me to my father right now, I'm gonna' tie you up, take your money, the car, the spear and all the gold and disappear. You got that?"

"Sir, the storm—the ferry won't run until tomorrow."

"You keep jerking me off and I'm gonna' shoot you. My family's been on that island for two hundred and fifty years. Now I know the value of a moat but I also know my family, and a moat with a tunnel under it is even more valuable. So, how do I convince you?"

I cocked the gun and aimed it at his sore balls.

"Very well, sir, there is a tunnel but it's very dangerous to use it during a storm like this; it's over one hundred years old."

"Get in the car and drive."

We turned around and headed back up the road to town. It was not long before we came to an old stone arch; the entrance to an abandoned estate. He unlocked the chain across it and drove down the driveway, past the crumbling remains of an old mansion. Down the drive, a short piece past the mansion, the road led to an old covered bridge. The far end of it appeared to have collapsed and landed half way down on the stream bank. It was actually the entrance to the tunnel. We drove onto the bridge and down into the tunnel.

As we moved down the tunnel, I could see the old walls shake with the violence of the currents stirred up by the storm. Harrison went slow, afraid that the weight and motion of the car would cause enough extra stress to collapse the stone walls. Water leaked from the sides and the ceiling as the whole tunnel echoed with the groans of the strain.

"I warned you, it's much too dangerous now."

I heard something crack; far back behind us I saw in the red glare of the tail lights a bad leak. The water spurted out in a small stream that seemed to grow larger just as I lost sight of it in the dark.

"Harrison, I got a funny feeling you better step on it."

"I told you, sir, that would be dangerous."

"Not as dangerous as the water coming up on our tail."

He sped up a bit, as he did we could feel the whole tunnel shake. Out the rear window I could see the water coming.

"This is no time for chickenshit, Harrison. Step on it!"

He looked in the rear view mirror.

"Oh my God!"

Harrison floored it. The old Caddy went sailing through the rattling tunnel, sending cracks up the wall. The water was pouring in behind us; up ahead, large blocks of stone were shaking loose. Soon we were rocketing through a salt-water car wash, the end of the road still a ways away.

"We're not going to make it, sir."

"That's the spirit, Harrison, defeat. Just what we need."

The water was roaring down the tunnel after us, we were doing fifty and just staying in front of it.

"Punch it, Harrison, all the way!"

The faster we went the wetter we got. Up ahead the roof was sagging and leaking. Just as we went past, it came crashing down, bringing the ocean in with it. The water came in with a rush, smashing into our backside, shooting us through the tube of the tunnel like an air bubble in a water hose. We came squirting out the other end of the tunnel and landed in a streambed down the hill from the cottage with the motor drowned and steam billowing up from the hood.

"Well, I hope you're satisfied."

"Well, I'm not. I still want to see my father. Now!"

We walked up the hill in the rain to the big house above the cottage, which glowed eerie blue-white in the flashes of lightening.

"Harrison, thank God you're all right. Have you got the spear?"

As my father opened the door and spoke, I rammed Harrison into him and sent them both sprawling to the floor. I walked in holding the gun in one hand and the spear in the other. I kicked the door closed behind me.

"All right! Where is he?!"

They both looked up at me, shocked and astonished. I cocked the gun.

"I said, where is he?"

"Who? What are you talking about?"

"The real David de Sion, your real son."

They looked at each other, then back at me.

"Don't play stupid. Harrison wouldn't threaten your real heir with a pistol. Besides, you said the prince was the child of my father's old age; I'm over thirty, I'm not the child of anybody's 'old age'."

"Put that gun down, you're not really gonna' shoot anybody anyway."

The voice was childlike, almost cartoon, a little nasal with an accent that changed "R's" to "W's", as in "weally". It came from the other side of the room. I looked up and saw a frail looking young boy, about twelve or thirteen, with thick glasses and tousled yellow hair. The same boy I'd seen in the jail cell with Bubba that sad Thanksgiving night. He was leaning in the doorway, looking at me with these gray-blue eyes that were so deep and compassionate, yet funny, with an elfin twinkle.

"Come on, put it down."

He moved his hands in an odd circular gesture, bent at the wrists, the fingers extended. He stood up straight and moved across the room to me, a gangly walk with child-clumsy feet, that almost but not quite, kept getting in his way.

"Do I have to come over there and take it away from you?"

He made me laugh. When I did all the pain I was in came rushing back into my brain, making me woozy. He took the gun, then my hand and led me to the sofa. Harrison and the man I now knew was not my father, got up and helped out. They removed my armor and laid me down on the couch. The young boy moved his hands softly over my face and down to my shoulder.

"They hurt you, didn't they?"

He moved his hands slowly, down to my belly.

"Uh-oh, this looks really bad, I'll have to start here."

His fingers were slender, long and graceful. They mesmerized me, so small yet agile. Suddenly he pushed them right through my skin and into my stomach; I could feel them moving around inside of me.

"Got it."

As he drew them out, I felt a burning sensation like the scalding of acid. He had the head of a snake in his hands.

"Easy now, just relax."

As he pulled it out, the burning increased to unbearable. Christ! A thick black serpent several feet long was being hauled out through my navel. I screamed with the pain, which made the snake writhe and hiss, turning its powerful coils around and around in the flesh hole of my stomach. The boy child yanked hard and the wet tail came out, slapping and stinging my chest and belly.

"Sorry, I know it hurts but I got him out. Now all I have to do is crush his little weeba head."

The snake was most hideous, yet the boy was totally unafraid. He wiggled it like it was a toy puppet, singing to it.

"A-dum-dum-dum-dum-weeba head-a-dum-dum-dum-dum-weeba head…."

He wiggled the serpent down to the floor then BAM, stomped its head flat.

"Harrison, get rid of this please, and wipe up the floor. Pop, you go to bed now, I'll take care of our friend."

"Goodnight, Professor."

The elder smiled, kissed his son and went off to bed.

"Goodnight, is that it?"

"The priests of our line become absolute rulers when they reach the age of thirteen…hold still…there was nothing else for him to tell you… easy, now…If you need to know anything else, I'll tell you."

The boy was working on my shoulder. He stuck in his finger and pulled out the metal shard; I felt no pain, no pain at all. He then healed the wound with a touch and sealed it by blowing on it. He moved gently, his warm hands to my face, setting my broken nose with a click, and then touching, smoothing and healing my tattered flesh. His hands felt so warm, so gentle.

"I can't replace your lost blood. You're going to have to get some rest. You can sleep in my room tonight and I'll watch over you."

He helped me to my feet just as Harrison returned with the soapy water and some towels to clean up the mess of the snake.

"I'm taking him to my room."

"Yes, Your Grace. Is there anything else?"

"No, after you clean up, you can go to bed, too."

"Yes, Your Grace."

The young prince led me by the hand up a broad spiral staircase to a large room on the second floor. He laid me down on a large canopy bed. The room was a strange mix of past, present and future. There were ancient icons and old armor next to posters of Marilyn Monroe and Mae West and strange blinking things that looked like they fell out of a U.F.O. There was a set of bunk beds against one of the walls. I was trying so hard to notice more of the room, to get my bearings, but I was fading fast into a tired, deep sleep on the bed of the true priest.

CHAPTER FORTY-THREE

LEAVING

OPENING YOUR EYES after a night like I had is a slow, guarded task, which I was not really up to. I could hear the young prince singing softly off to my right. There was a peace in the sound of his voice that waylaid all my fears of returning to consciousness and cut them to ribbons. Still, I never did like waking up, ever, even under the best of circumstances, because life is just a series of good things going wrong, but sleep, ahhh... that was really living.

"I know you're awake; I can feel you complaining."

"I wasn't complaining; I'm not awake enough to complain."

"Yes you are."

Normally I disliked "know-it-all" kids but that was because they really didn't know it all. This kid was different—he really did now it all.

"How come you know everything?"

"Because priests of our order are like Dali Lamas of the West. We are born with great knowledge, which we spend a lifetime unlearning. I'm wise because I'm still young, by the time I'm your age I'll be as dumb as you are."

I sat up, I had to; I wanted to watch this kid talk.

"You're a Dali Lama?"

"No, I'm like a Dali Lama; I am the same spirit as the true priests before me."

"You mean your father?"

"No, I mean Jesus."

He hopped off the top bunk and bowed.

"Ta-dah! You're looking at me, you're looking at Jesus."

He made me smile.

"So what's Jesus doing with a poster of Marilyn Monroe?"

"I like her. She was a great comedienne. Did you ever see that movie where she sang, 'My Heart Belongs to Daddy'? She was great."

I had to admit that was a great number.

"So, tell me, Mister Know-it-all, what am I going to do now?"

"You're going to leave, and it will make me sad 'cause I really like you, you're funny. But you won't stay, even when I ask you."

He hopped up on the bed with me and looked into my eyes with those tender gray-blue eyes of his.

"I'm really going to miss you."

"But we just met."

"You just met me, but I've been watching you for a long time."

"Really?"

"Sure, in my crystal ball."

"Aw, come on."

"The first Merovingians were contemporaries of Merlin, true adepts in a time of magic. The crystal I use was discovered in 1653 when they opened the tomb of Childeric I, father of Clovis. There were other crystals in the tomb along with a golden bull's head, amulets, sacred stones and three hundred gold bees that Napoleon had sewn onto his coronation robes. I still have a few of the bees but the crystal is one of my greatest treasures. You wanna' see?"

He gave me a white tunic with a red cross over the heart to put on. I dressed, and then followed him through the upstairs to a small door at the end of the hall. It led to another spiral staircase. This one was tiny and looked like it had been built by Saint Joseph. It was the kind you see in old Spanish missions of the Great Southwest, no nails or dowels of any kind, just thick planks of wood, cut and fit perfectly together. They last for three hundred years and occupy a space so small that it is impossible to figure out how they were built. They usually led to a choir loft. This one led to a pyramid shaped room all covered with gold, the walls, the floor, all covered in gold. In the center of the room was a small platform with two low, three-legged stools and a small table on it. On the table was a large crystal ball, made from a stone that had clear streaks of purple and flecks of silver.

"Come on up and have a seat."

We sat there a while with him concentrating, staring into the crystal. The feeling of the room is hard to describe, it had the same smell as the air after a high voltage discharge of electricity, very rarified, almost making the skin tingle.

"Oh, someone is down at the cottage, looking for you. A girl. Oh, it's just Sharon."

"Sharon's looking for me?"

"Merry Christmas."

"Should I go down and see her?"

"In a minute, some things are troubling you that I have to clear up."

"Like what?"

He looked at me.

"A couple of things. You want to know what happened last night with the covens and if they're still chasing you. Chris Boone and those people are all dead. He and Baby Squirrel were the last to go. She'd jumped on his back, choking him with her belt. He kept trying to stab her but she'd move out of the way and he'd stab himself. He finally got her down and slit her throat but it was too late, he'd already lost too much blood. You also wanted to know about the spear. It doesn't mean anything to me. Harrison and my dad are into all this totem stuff because they've forgotten the real magic comes from the heart.

"Harrison jumped you last night because they thought you'd be possessed at the Feast of the Beast and come back here and kill me. But I knew that even with the serpent in your guts, you didn't take yourself seriously enough to be fooled by pride. You also feel bad about killing Sinclair, you shouldn't. You think he was the first man you ever killed. But actually, he died about a hundred years ago. He was a priest of our line that got lost and forgot to turn his body off. You released him from a dreadful possession and, believe me, he's very grateful. Oh, the guy on the cross was a fake, a coven member, so don't worry about him either. Now, you want to know who your real father was. He was a young sailor who died in a knife fight in a New Orleans bar called 'Las Casas del la Marinenez' a few weeks after conceiving you. My dad is your Godfather. It is a tradition among us to adopt the 'Son of the Widow'; in fact, that is a secret name for Jesus in our family religion. My father loves you dearly. I know you feel betrayed by my father, please understand, he was only protecting me. He would never have harmed you. You are the Holy Fool, our Parsival. Without you, our kingdom could not have been healed. Let's see, was there anything else, oh, sorry about Mank. I know you were his friend, and he did care for you at one time. But, the siren call of unlimited wealth and power caught his soul. Like Chris Boone, he guessed your position by your understanding of the hiding place of the sacred spear. He tried to play two ends against the middle and lost. He's the one who told T.Z. to give you books on Parsival. Yes, T.Z. was his accomplice, and would have shared in his ill-gotten gain. Your friend the Rabbit also likes to play two ends against the middle, that's why he had you set up to fall in love with T.Z. By the way, the Rabbit's gone on now, into the light—one more soul you've saved. Steaks got married, same guy...."

"Will I become rich if I stay?"

"You are rich already, but you won't stay."

"Why?"

"You are the son of a sailor; your home is the sea. You can not stay in one port for too long." He looked at me with those kind, wise eyes then said with a twinkle, "Don't worry Nine Wives, you'll get your answer."

I walked down the path from the hill to the cottage, trying hard not to think. I knew if I did, I'd just get confused. The air was clean and cold, the sky bright blue. The storm had been a cleansing one.

Sharon was just leaving the cottage when I came up. She ran to me and hugged me and gave me kisses and tears and love, the only things I value in a relationship. She led me back inside and sat me down. We talked while she fixed breakfast. She had come back early because she had a dream that I was in danger. She said I should feel very special for she'd never placed being with anyone above her family before. I thanked her and ate like an orphan. She had to fix another breakfast.

After that we went back to my bedroom and we didn't come out till the next day. She made breakfast again then went back to her place to get dressed for the Christmas day celebration at the big house that she knew about but I didn't.

We walked up the path to the big house. She held my hand and spoke of happiness. Inside the Masters and their wives welcomed us with hot buttered rums and hearty hugs of goodwill. We sang the old songs. The prince passed out presents, and then we feasted on turkey and bright conversation. It was Christmas the way I had read it should be, full of warmth and good spirits, laughter and toasts and old men with full bellies, smiling by the fire from their armchairs. I thought about Texas and my mother and all those years with the short skinny trees and the baked chicken and in the midst of all this plenty I grew lonely and hungry for home. The prince truly did know it all—within the week I was gone.

CHAPTER FORTY-FOUR

THE ROAD

I WAS SITTING IN A SMALL BAR on Highway One with a bunch of farmers and truckers, watching the wrestler Hacksaw Jim Duggan, on T.V., salute the American flag. His eyes were crossed and his tongue sticking out. He had just defeated a Russian wrestler and the shot on the screen was a beauty, Hacksaw's face and the American flag in a heart warming double exposure, one of the purest representations of our society today I'd seen since Jim Nabors, a.k.a. Gomer Pyle, sang the Star Spangled Banner.

I was drinking again, and as a result, I was having the first clear thoughts I had in a month since Speedster pulled me off the sauce. The story rattling around in my brain was hard to believe, even harder to relate. I had done things stone cold sober that would shame the meanest drunk, seen things that would curl the hair on a drunkard's nightmare. And, for all of these bizarre activities, I had no excuse, or actually only a lame one—I hadn't been drinking. No drunk in his right mind would have fallen for the machinations I'd let myself be led through. I'd been fooled into believing I had a father and was a member of a royal family. I'd been talked into facing off against one hundred and fifty killers to retrieve a worthless totem. I'd been beaten, battered, jailed, leg broken, heart stopped, run off the road, damn near killed, exploited, betrayed, and generally run through the mill, by a family whose members had been preparing me from my birth for just this insane series of events. They were rich beyond my power to imagine and yet never once in my long life had they ever done any thing to ease the poverty of my mother or myself for fear it would betray their plan. I ordered another drink.

I'd been teased with love, Angelface Sharon, with whom I could not stay, no, not yet. I needed to put a few bottles and a few hundred miles between what had been and what will be, before I could face what might have been or what could yet be, with her.

At first, I'd felt like a whore, taking the young prince's money and Harrison's silver Caddy, but I'd made peace with myself on that score once I'd hit the road and felt the wind. Whatever had happened, and I still wasn't sure, I'd earned a car and enough money to spend a good year chasing the dream dogs my life was going to. I ordered another drink.

I liked the young prince, in a way, I was happy to have been part of a strategy that had saved his life. I still had no idea what the outcome of all this would be; would he run for public office? I doubted it; by the time he was old enough to run, he would be, by his own admission, too dumb to do much good. The battle for the soul of the nation, which Washington had foreseen, was raging. The citizens were being bribed to turn a blind eye to the abuses of power. Every form of pollution was being justified by economic concerns. The middle class was being squeezed down into the lower income bracket, pushing the poor right out of the system and onto the streets. "Cover Thine Own Ass" was replacing "In God We Trust". "Where will it all end?" was the questioned being asked, in hushed tones, around the dinner tables of the heartland. Drugs and hormones fed into our beef and poultry were popping out in our bodies, growing hair on the faces of our women and sending our children to the hospital. Our vegetables were hybrids; they looked like pictures and tasted like paper. Liquor was one of the last pure things. I ordered another drink.

It was midnight; the drunks in the bar were singing.

"Should old acquaintance be forgot and never brought to mind...."

I joined in. It was nice to be facing oblivion with these people, people of the earth. They knew, as only the people of the land can know, that next year would be better. Not in any way you could really put your finger on but just better. There would be days with blue skies, new crops to plant, more loads to haul, and a few more warm nights to spend in the arms of a lover. And should the end come, they'd embrace it as they would a newborn child. As for me, I had something they didn't have, I had time. And somewhere out in the dark, starry night, time stood still on the road and waited for me.

ACKNOWLEDGMENTS

THE REVEREND GOAT CARSON gratefully acknowledges the help and support of his editor, Alexis Stahl, publishers, Georgia Dent and Paul Cohen, agent, James Fitzgerald and friends, Kinky Friedman, Dr. John, Levon Helm, Mike Pillot, Paul Antonelle, the Jaffe family, Joe Heller, Jimmie Vinyard, Michael O'Donoghue, Tom Baker and Speed Vogel.

the United States
'00003B/57/A

9 780978 942724